Praise for Robyn Carr, bestselling author of the hit Netflix series *Virgin River*!

"This story blends painful realities with healing love in a strong, uplifting tale that will lure both women's fiction and romance fans."
—*Library Journal*, starred review, on *The View from Alameda Island*

"This novel of sisters and secrets...will please fans of Carr's Virgin River series. Themes of responsibility, forgiveness, and the agony and ecstasy of female relatives will appeal to readers of Debbie Macomber and Susan Wiggs."
—*Booklist* on *The Summer That Made Us*

"A satisfying reinvention story that handles painful issues with a light and uplifting touch." —*Kirkus Reviews* on *The Life She Wants*

"Classic women's fiction, illuminating the power of women's friendships, is still alive and well." —*Booklist* on *Four Friends*

"A heart-grabber that won't let readers go until the very end.... A rewarding (happy) story that will appeal across the board and might require a hanky or two."
—*Library Journal*, starred review, on *What We Find*

"Robyn Carr has done it again.... A romance that truly inspires readers as life hits them the hardest."
—*San Francisco Review Journal* on *What We Find*

Also by Robyn Carr

Sullivan's Crossing

THE COUNTRY GUESTHOUSE
THE BEST OF US
THE FAMILY GATHERING
ANY DAY NOW
WHAT WE FIND

Thunder Point

WILDEST DREAMS
A NEW HOPE
ONE WISH
THE HOMECOMING
THE PROMISE
THE CHANCE
THE HERO
THE NEWCOMER
THE WANDERER

Virgin River

RETURN TO VIRGIN RIVER
MY KIND OF CHRISTMAS
SUNRISE POINT
REDWOOD BEND
HIDDEN SUMMIT
BRING ME HOME FOR CHRISTMAS
HARVEST MOON
WILD MAN CREEK
PROMISE CANYON
MOONLIGHT ROAD
ANGEL'S PEAK
FORBIDDEN FALLS
PARADISE VALLEY
TEMPTATION RIDGE
SECOND CHANCE PASS
A VIRGIN RIVER CHRISTMAS
WHISPERING ROCK
SHELTER MOUNTAIN
VIRGIN RIVER

Grace Valley

DEEP IN THE VALLEY
JUST OVER THE MOUNTAIN
DOWN BY THE RIVER

Novels

A FAMILY AFFAIR
SUNRISE ON HALF MOON BAY
THE VIEW FROM ALAMEDA ISLAND
THE SUMMER THAT MADE US
THE LIFE SHE WANTS
FOUR FRIENDS
A SUMMER IN SONOMA
NEVER TOO LATE
SWEPT AWAY (formerly titled
   RUNAWAY MISTRESS)
BLUE SKIES
THE WEDDING PARTY
THE HOUSE ON OLIVE STREET

Look for Robyn Carr's next novel
available soon from MIRA.

ROBYN CARR

The
Friendship
Club

mira

Recycling programs
for this product may
not exist in your area.

ISBN-13: 978-0-7783-0788-4

The Friendship Club

Mira
22 Adelaide St. West, 41st Floor
Toronto, Ontario M5H 4E3, Canada
BookClubbish.com

Printed in U.S.A.

The
Friendship
Club

ONE

"And that's a wrap," the director said. "I think I have everything I need. I'll do some editing and you can review it."

"Thanks, Kevin," Marni said. "My sister and my daughter are coming by for a glass of wine. Would you like to join us for a drink to celebrate finishing another season?"

"Thanks, no. I'm on the timer. New baby on the way," he said.

"Of course! How's Sonja feeling?"

"Huge," he said with a laugh. "But the baby's still cooking. The midwife says she has a few more weeks. Sonja cried for an hour after hearing that."

"I remember that feeling," Marni said. "Like it was yesterday. You better stay close to her. Thanks for everything this season. I think we got some good stuff." Then Marni turned to her intern, Sophia Garner. "But you'll stay, right?"

"I wouldn't miss it," she said. "It's going to be an intervention, I think."

"Oh, fabulous, I love those," Marni said with a hint of panic. "If you and Ellen clean up, I'll put out some hors d'oeuvres."

Of course she was prepared; just a little fixing up and presentation required. Marni Jean McGuire worked every day and took very few breaks from cooking, writing, studying, traveling and experimenting with new recipes but they only filmed the segments of her show sixty days a year. But filming was intense. Twice a year they'd film for thirty days over six weeks—enough for two seasons. She hosted one of the most popular cooking shows on a cable network. Today marked the last day of filming and they always celebrated.

Marni's kitchen was essentially a set; all their filming was done in her home as opposed to a studio. She smiled as she watched her producer, Ellen, who was busy cleaning up with Sophia. Ellen was a bona fide chef but she had no interest being in front of the camera. Sophia loved the camera and the camera loved her; after being caught on camera accidentally a few times, she had become beloved by the viewers for her quick wit and delicious accent.

Marni Cooks was very popular but hosting a TV show had never been her lifelong goal. Far from it. It fell into her lap like a glorious miracle. When she was a young widowed mother, she did whatever she could to make a dollar and raise her little Bella. She took a job handing out food samples for a chain of grocery stores. With her baby in a carrier on her back, she turned out to be a hit. She sold out her product day after day, probably because Bella was so funny and flirtatious and Marni, despite the fact that life hadn't been easy, was personable and approachable. Almost immediately after she began, shoppers came looking for her, engaging her in conversation. They gave her good reviews and told store managers how much they liked her.

Once she filled in for a product demonstrator for the same grocery chain, showing interested patrons how to slice, dice, shred, spiral and chop vegetables. Again, Bella rode along; childcare was impossibly expensive. Her sense of humor and ease with being in front of a small audience charmed people—including the producer from a television station. Marni was hired to demonstrate a couple recipes every week on a local morning show. Along with that she did cooking demonstrations at fairs or exhibits, published a couple of small cookbooks, helped out at catering services, began writing a short cooking column for the newspaper and filled in when other chefs were unavailable as a guest on various cooking shows. Then she landed a full-time job as the on-air chef for a cable cooking show. She had been thirty-two. Her viewing audience grew quickly and soon after she hired Ellen, who was an expert in her own right. Marni was syndicated to a handful of affiliates and her popularity continued to grow. She knew she owed as much of her success to Ellen as to her own hard work. Ellen had a knack for delectable creation but she was such an introvert she would never agree to join Marni in front of the camera.

But in Ellen's hands the food became a living, breathing wonder and she had become the associate producer over time, thanks to Marni. She knew what a gift she had in Ellen and took very good care of her. And Ellen knew what a great opportunity she had with Marni; no one else in the business would let her just cook without taking on any management responsibilities and yet pay her so well. But every time Marni's fortunes improved, Ellen benefited as well.

A little over twenty years ago Marni had met Jeff, a news anchor for the local affiliate. Since she lost her young husband when Bella was only nine months old, she hadn't been optimistic she'd ever find another forever man but fate shocked her by delivering up Jeff. It was a great love, filled with promise and passion. They were a team from the start, both of them being in TV and very visible in the community. They worked together, shoring each other up and urging each other on. Jeff was a fantastic stepfather for Bella and proudly walked her down the aisle six years ago.

Shortly after that something changed. Marni was concerned that a woman Jeff worked with had ulterior motives. She'd been stalking him for years, texting him, asking his advice, professing to be his friend and protégé and constant supporter. Marni had warned Jeff many times that he needed to be careful not to encourage this woman and he always said he could handle things. But his behavior changed and Marni grew suspicious. She caught them making out in Jeff's car in the parking lot of a local park that sat in the shadow of the beautiful Sierras.

When she realized what she was witnessing, she drove very slowly up close to Jeff's car and laid on the horn. They jumped apart like two heart attacks. It was divine.

She knew in that moment that her marriage, which she had enjoyed a great deal, was over. Clearly Jeff had been lying and leading a double life for years. The pain of that was excruciating. She also instinctively knew that Jeff and the woman had both gotten what they deserved—each other. Neither was honest nor faithful. In an instant she knew, she would not go a second further with a man who could look her in the eye and deceive her. She told him to leave. He didn't argue or try to save their marriage, but he did hire a good lawyer and fought for a healthy settlement. At that time they both had solid careers, but Marni was edging ahead. Jeff went after a big slice of that success; indeed, he took credit, as he'd given her so much wonderful advice. At least that was his perspective.

At Marni's insistence, they settled and divorced quickly. Marni had asked herself if she should pause and think it over, maybe try marriage counseling, but a gut instinct said end it fast. When he asked for a percentage of her future earnings, she knew she'd been right. It had to be over as swiftly as possible. She gave him half, though he hadn't earned half. Since there were no minor children or businesses involved, he couldn't possibly do better. She cut him a big check, waved goodbye and ran for her life. She learned you can still sprint pretty well with a broken heart.

After a couple of years of hating him, things settled down. Marni had handed over more money than seemed fair to her, certainly more than Jeff deserved, and that angered her but the relationship was over in her heart. And Karma being a vicious soul, Jeff was demoted in his job while Marni's popularity soared.

Jeff had used his settlement to open a restaurant, hoping to capitalize on Marni's notoriety as a television chef. But Gretchen, the other woman, was his business partner and Marni refused to endorse the restaurant. While he was busy trying to cash in on her success, Marni just put her head down, worked hard and became even more popular.

Then there was a sea change. Jeff had not married Gretchen, but he had spent a lot of money on her, found her cheating, and she unceremoniously dumped him, leaving Jeff a broken, much poorer man…with a struggling restaurant. Of course he brought his tons of regret to Marni, begging her forgiveness. Telling her that letting her go was the biggest mistake of his life!

"No doubt about it," Ellen had said.

"Too little, too late," Bella said. Bella was, if possible, angrier than Marni about Jeff's betrayal.

"Men are so stupid," said Sophia when she heard the story.

Marni had long since stopped complaining to her friends. To Jeff she said, "You broke my heart and tore my family to pieces. Don't expect any sympathy from me."

"You don't understand, Marni," he said. "I think she used me and turned me against you, the only woman who truly loved me."

"Oh, I believe I understand completely," she had said. The story was as old as time. He'd succumbed to flattery and been thinking with his dick. No amount of his regret would change the fact that she'd be an idiot to ever trust him again. She was no idiot.

But she did soften her anger slightly and they were now cordial. Every now and then Jeff would call her or text her or stop by, though the locks on the house had long since been changed. Over the past couple of years he had suggested a few times that they go out for dinner and she always declined. He clumsily proposed she might cook something for him. "One of your favorite new recipes… I would love that."

"Not in your wildest dreams," she had replied.

Marni heard the dishwasher start and snapped out of her thoughts of the past. She pulled her pesto canapés from the oven, took the artichoke dip from the refrigerator and heard Kevin depart.

The door opened again. "Mama?" Bella called.

"Right in here," Marni said. "How is The Bump?" Bella was five months pregnant and cute as a button. It was a pregnancy hard won through wildly expensive in vitro fertilization.

"A little feisty," she said with a very proud smile.

The door opened again and Marni's sister, Nettie, came in from the garage.

Marni put down her hors d'oeuvres and transferred the centerpiece from the kitchen island to the long rectangular coffee table in the great room just as Ellen was bringing in a tray of wineglasses. Sophia followed with a large oval-shaped bucket filled with ice and two opened bottles of white wine. She went back for a chilled bottle of sparkling cider in an ice bucket on a tripod stand for Bella since she was off alcohol.

Marni loved watching them enter the room, her colleagues and loved ones. Ellen came into a room with shy demeanor, standing nearly six feet tall, lithe and graceful. She wore her once blond and now white-gray hair in a simple pageboy. She always bent her head slightly and Marni wasn't sure if her height made her uncomfortable or if it was her shy nature.

Nettie, ten years younger than Marni and the mother of two sons, was an English professor at the university in Reno.

Marni brought out a couple more plates of hors d'oeuvres, Sophia placed napkins all around, Ellen pushed over an ottoman for Bella to rest her feet upon, and they settled in. First was a toast. "A very good season, I think," Marni said. "One of our best. I'm sleeping in tomorrow."

Glasses were clinked in agreement, small plates were filled, napkins unfolded. And Marni looked around with a feeling of warm satisfaction. This was her happy place. This great room with her closest friends and family. And outside, through the patio doors, reflected in the backyard infinity pool was the sight of the Sierra Nevada mountains, still covered with snow, though it was May. They all lived in Breckenridge, Nevada, a picturesque little town nestled into the base of the mountain range just south of Reno and Lake Tahoe. There was a winding road, not exactly a secret but little known, that went switchback up over the mountains and then down into Lake Tahoe. People who grew up in Breckenridge knew it well.

This was an agricultural and ski town, with the mountains so close, and it was beautiful with its million-dollar views of nature at her best. To Marni, it looked similar to Austria.

Marni had overseen every aspect of the construction of this house, the kitchen being the focal point. She and Jeff were married at the time and while he helped by sharing advice and supervising construction, it was *her* house. She approved the plans and made it part of her business. And she loved it. Knowing it would be caught on camera, it was beautifully decorated in beiges, browns, pinks and mauves. It was redecorated almost annually for the same reason—updating for the viewers. But the most important thing to Marni was that the house felt like a hug to her, making her feel safe and protected.

When Jeff moved out, she filled the empty space he left in no time at all. Filling the empty space in her heart had taken longer. Even though she had stopped loving him and stopped hating him, there was still a hole there. A black cold hole. It frequently reminded her that she had no talent for love.

"So we were talking, Nettie and Sophia and me..." Bella said.

Marni immediately thought nothing good could come of that.

"You've been alone long enough," Bella continued. "You should start dating."

"I'm sure you mean well, but I have no interest in getting married again," Marni said.

"Who said anything about getting married?" Bella shot

back. "It's not like you're planning to start a family. But wouldn't it be nice to have a boyfriend? A companion? You should at least have a look around. You're only fifty-seven. You have years of fun ahead! Don't you want to have someone to enjoy it with?"

"Bella, the thought never crossed my mind," she said. And she said it rather tiredly. "I've been married twice but spent a lot of my adult life alone. Maybe I'm not meant to have a partner."

"But you're meant to be a successful businesswoman," Ellen said, her voice quiet but earnest. She sipped her wine. "And to have wonderful friends."

"I'm pretty happy with my life," Marni said.

"You haven't been married that much," Bella said. "My father for what? Two years? And Jeff for fifteen? Or so? Maybe it's time to look at other types of relationships. You don't have to get married. But wouldn't it be nice to have someone anxious to see you for dinner? Or to travel with sometimes? Or just to talk to?"

"I have plenty of people to talk to," Marni said.

"Or to get laid?" Sophia threw in.

They all laughed. "That hasn't even crossed my mind," Marni said. But it was a lie. It was about the only thing that crossed her mind where a man was concerned, but it seemed the trade-offs were just too big. There would be all the juggling of emotions and deciding if it was worth the risk. Once one crossed that line, so much introspection followed, deciding if you liked him quite enough to worry about little things like tidiness. Or big things like fidelity. Or what about the possibility of learning that he liked your money more than you? And ultimately was your heart strong enough to withstand learning he'd found someone he liked better. It would be someone younger, prettier, more clever. Someone who had the power to pull him away, use him for a while, then take his money, which was your money, and then dump him. As Gretchen had done with Jeff.

Or worry that he might get very angry and...hit her?

"Mom, aren't you lonely?"

"I'm much too busy to be lonely," she said. But of *course* she was lonely! It would be so lovely to have someone who was just there. If he loved you, respected you. Someone close who could actually be trusted, depended upon. There in case you needed him. Or how about someone who actually liked you as you were, someone who thought it was cute the way you slept with your mouth open and let out the occasional sound that was something like a chain saw...

"It wouldn't hurt to check it out," Nettie said.

"Well, Mom?" Bella asked. "What do you say?"

She laughed lightly. "I wouldn't know where to start!"

"Aha, but you have me! And I've worked up a profile for you! I think we should check out some dating sites!"

"We?" she asked.

"I could help," Bella said. "I'm objective."

"Oh, God," Marni moaned.

"Okay, I'll get us started."

"No to dating sites..."

"I'll just kind of ask around. Friends of friends. I'll keep my eyes open. We're just interested in a companion. I promise not to set up a date until you've had time to look everything over, but it's time to at least open that door a crack and see if there isn't a nice man who wants to spend time with you. Someone to hang out with. Right?"

"I'm really not interested. I have my family—you and Aunt

Nettie and The Bump. And close friends. Nice coworkers. A demanding job."

"You didn't mention Jason," Bella said. "Your son-in-law."

"I didn't mean to omit him," Marni said. "But of course, Jason, the best son-in-law a woman could ask for."

"I think you might be overcompensating, but I'll let it go since he hasn't been all that great lately. He's grumpy and a pain in the ass. I'll post your profile and we'll see what a fishing expedition brings in. Good. Done."

"Nettie?" Marni said. "Do you go along with this?"

"It wasn't my idea," she said. "But I admit, I wouldn't mind seeing you in a happy relationship. And I have a lot of friends who found their match on internet dating sites."

"Here's the thing," Marni said. "Sometimes they start happy and don't last. Sometimes it's happier to be independent, to have the love and loyalty of good friends and family rather than take a chance on some man living up to his promises. I'm not unhappy!"

"I'm not suggesting you need a man to find happiness," Nettie said. "That would be stupid. But I will say this—you work so hard and you have for years. Luckily it has paid off. But I'd like to hear you laugh more. And I wish your eyes sparkled like they used to. Back when you felt you had something to look forward to besides more work."

"I love my work!"

"All work and no play..."

Makes Jane a dull girl, Marni finished in her head.

The name Marni wasn't short for anything; it was her given name. She was named for a maternal grandmother she barely knew. Her grandmother had been described as feisty, smart, funny and daring. She was taken from them early when she stepped in the path of a streetcar in San Francisco, leaving three grown daughters and a grandchild behind. Nettie, a second granddaughter, was born seven years after her death. Marni had been three and did not remember her grandmother, but she grew up on tales of her.

Marni was raised in a simple house in Reno with her mom, Celeste, and dad, Ernie. Eventually two aunts joined them, Ruth and Dahlia. Ruth had been married and divorced twice while Dahlia had been married though childless when her husband of seventeen years dropped dead. Celeste had been the youngest and had had the longest marriage. It was a house of women and her father, Ernie, had very little to say. The women, on the other hand, hardly ever shut up. Ernie passed away at the age of fifty-seven, a fact that crossed Marni's mind from time to time, since she was that age now. The family doctor said it was heart failure but Aunt Ruth said it was probably desperation. Because of that, Marni had recently had a full cardiac workup and was pronounced healthy and strong.

Marni and Nettie, short for Annette, got plenty of attention, but they didn't have much in the way of a male role model. Ernie was pretty much it. He was an auto mechanic and had worked in the same garage for years and had permanent black oil and dirt under his short nails no matter how much he washed his hands. He wore the same navy blue pants and light blue work shirt with his name on an embroidered patch over the left breast pocket every day.

He was a good man. He was kind. He worried about people with problems. He sometimes did mechanical favors for free, something that scorched Celeste's temper. Marni might have learned good will from Ernie but he hadn't taught anyone much about how to have a successful marital relationship.

Thus, her short and unhappy relationship with her high

school boyfriend, Rick. It was something she really didn't think Bella could benefit from knowing the truth about. And the truth was, she was dead in love with him from the age of seventeen and he became abusive. The good news was he enlisted in the army at eighteen and from that time on he was away a lot. The bad news—he came home a lot. They married when she was nineteen and he was twenty-one; she thought about leaving him at twenty but she discovered she was pregnant. Soon after Bella was born, Rick was killed in a car accident. Rick had been drinking and by the grace of God had hit a tree and not another car. No one knew he had been abusive. In fact Marni herself wasn't really clear on that until long after he was gone. Marni carried the shame of that secret just as so many battered women did. She moved back into her mother's house with Celeste and Nettie and Aunt Ruth and Aunt Dahlia. People often remarked on how strong Marni was, moving forward with such optimism and hopefulness.

Of course she was optimistic. There were days she even missed him, wondering if things might have improved over time, though her deepest instincts told her that was a pipe dream. But she was happy for the most part. The danger was gone. And she was devoted to Bella.

As the years passed Marni confided about her husband to a couple of very close friends. Even though she knew the abuse wasn't her fault, there was a small part of her that feared being judged. Such was the secret shame of an abused wife. She said her reason for not getting involved with a man was her growing career and her daughter—she was too busy. And she didn't want to risk Bella's stability or her own career growth.

After chatting for a little while longer and once again toasting another good season, Bella got ready to leave. "It's my night to cook. And I really miss wine so I'm going to leave before you open more! After this baby comes, I'll probably drink it straight from the bottle."

"Oh that should be attractive," Nettie said. "I have to leave, too. It's Marvin's night to cook," she added with a laugh because it was almost always Marvin's night to cook. "I'll walk you out."

Sophia picked up glasses and plates, heading for the kitchen, where Ellen intercepted her, taking the glasses. "I've got this, Sophia. You can call it a day."

"You sure? Because my car is making unhappy sounds and I thought I might call my friend who likes to play with engines."

"By all means, that's a priority," Marni said. "And if you need help or a ride or anything…"

"Thank you, if I need help, my papa will be on his way home very soon and he knows about the sounds. I can call him if I need him and it will be no trouble."

Marni cleared the rest of the dishes while Ellen resumed the washing up. "Would you like a cup of tea?" Marni asked when it was down to just the two of them.

"That would be so nice," Ellen said. "It was a long day and good to be finished." And while she was setting up the plates to drip-dry, she said, "I've been having wonderful dreams of gourmet meat entrées like stuffed pork loin and beef braciola."

"Of course you have," Marni said with a laugh, putting out cups and tea bags. When the kettle whistled, she poured for them. "Let's go sit on the sofa. Let's not talk about recipes yet. I know you'll have a list of suggestions when I'm ready."

"A very nice list," Ellen said.

"What do you think of this idea of Bella's? This dating idea?" Marni asked.

"Better you than me. But it doesn't matter what I think,"

she said. "That doesn't interest me. Nor do I think your eyes lack sparkle or that you don't smile enough."

"Be honest, do I seem unhappy?" Marni asked.

"Not in the least. I don't think you have to be dancing a jig every minute to demonstrate you're happy. Sometimes all the proof you need is that you sleep well and have a decent appetite."

"I wouldn't mind having a man in my life," Marni said. "I just keep wondering if it's worth the trouble."

"And there's the question. You know where I stand on that."

Ellen had spent the majority of her adult life caring for a severely disabled husband. She didn't marry until she was thirty-eight, wed a man ten years her senior and within two years of their marriage he suffered and survived a severe aneurism that left him crippled and mentally challenged. He spent seventeen years confined to a wheelchair, many of those years in a nursing home. Ellen never said so but Marni imagined she met his death with something close to relief, if not for herself, certainly for him.

Ellen had family; there were a couple of sisters, some nieces and nephews who were grown now and producing their own families. She wasn't completely alone.

"Do you ever get lonely?" Marni asked.

"Never," Ellen said. "I have never minded being alone. There's only one thing I feel slightly cheated of. Grandchildren. Children would have been incredibly difficult, balancing them with Ralph's disabilities. Grandchildren would have been nice. But there are the nieces and nephews..."

"You've never mentioned, were there romances in your youth? You know about me—in love in high school, much to my mother's panic."

Ellen gave a short laugh and sipped her tea. "I went through much of my life feeling utterly invisible. I was so tall and gangly and never could do my hair. My mother forbid me to wear makeup but my secret was I didn't want to. As long as I didn't draw attention to myself, I was happier."

"I had a friend in high school… I guess she's still a friend, though we don't have a relationship. She was…is…beautiful and very vain. She said if every head didn't turn when she walked into a room, she would wonder what she'd done wrong," Marni said.

Ellen laughed loudly. "If even one head turned when I walked into a room, I'd look to see if I was dragging a length of toilet paper stuck to my shoe!" Ellen sipped her tea. "What was it like being hopelessly in love at seventeen?"

"Not as fun as you might think. It was a little like food poisoning. I was so young and stupid that I was widowed for at least a few years before I realized I'd lost my identity while I was with Rick. Rick was controlling and made all our decisions. We argued a lot. It wouldn't have lasted. Or at least it shouldn't have."

"I never knew," Ellen said.

"Well, he's dead. I gain nothing by speaking badly of him. And I know this is probably silly, but I wouldn't want to disappoint Bella."

"You've never said anything…"

"It was so long ago and I'm afraid I let people think I was a tragic young bride who had lost the love of her life. It sounds so romantic and I didn't own up to the young idiot I really was. Someday I'll tell you all about it."

"That's why you hovered over Bella so," Ellen said. "You watched her like a hawk, especially around the young men!"

"I tried. I think we did all right with Jason. Now I have

to worry how determined she is with this idea that I should be dating."

"Hmm," Ellen said, sipping. "I've known Bella for a long time and I've rarely seen a gleam in her eye so fierce."

"It was frightening," Marni agreed.

"I have a feeling this notion has taken hold," Ellen said. "I know you're doing fine just as you are, but you're a people person. You might just open your mind to the idea there might be a special someone out there, right for you, with similar expectations. Just to see what happens."

"Would you?"

"Don't be ridiculous," Ellen said. "I don't want anyone else in my space. I don't want any advice from a presumptuous man. There's nothing a man can offer me that I don't already have plenty of. But you..."

Marni's mind did a spin. She wouldn't be opposed to feeling the flesh or fur of a man's chest against her, provided it was a good man who wasn't going to break her heart. She really missed having someone to laugh with. Not that she didn't laugh with her sister, daughter and friends; they laughed hysterically at times. But that late night crazy laughter in the dark had been so briefly hers and so long ago. She thought it might be somewhat wonderful to have a man interested in what she was doing. *Passionate* about what she was doing. As Ina Garten had in the husband who dropped into her show regularly to gasp in awe over her stellar culinary skills. She wouldn't mind someone romantic to travel with, someone who wanted to do the same things she wanted to do, like visit farms, vineyards, distilleries, mysterious hideaway kitchens, hole in the wall restaurants.

There was no such person, she quickly reminded herself.

"You'll have to shave your legs regularly," Ellen said.

"I've been very happy by myself," Marni said. "And wearing long pants or leggings."

"As I see it, you've been perfectly fine on your own, but you'll never know for sure unless you open your heart and mind to the idea of a special someone. As long as you're closed off...? You know."

"You think a person can just chant 'okay, I'm open to the idea' and the universe steps up?"

"Yeah," Ellen said, sipping her tea. "Pretty much."

TWO

The sun was still making its lazy decent when Ellen finished her tea and left. The May days were getting longer and stretching out to greet summer. In little mountain towns like Breckenridge, it was still chilly in the evening. Marni turned on the gas firepit in the backyard, left the sliding glass doors wide open and went back to the kitchen. She wasn't hungry, not even slightly, but she pulled out fresh onion and garlic and began slicing and chopping at her kitchen island. She poured a little chicken stock in a pan, brought it to a quick boil and added some linguini. She knew from what she had in her fist it was the right amount of pasta. She washed mushrooms and spinach leaves.

She thought about Bella's suggestion and their conversation. The prospect of dating. It sounded, frankly, awful.

She threw some chicken breasts in the oven and while they cooked, she sliced the mushrooms. She was making her twist on chicken Florentine. By the time she was ready to drain the pasta, saving the stock, the chicken was almost ready to be shredded. She let it cool and then, using two forks, she pulled it apart. She added the mushrooms and spinach to the garlic and onion, mixed in the pasta, chicken and stock, thickened with a bit of flour, half a brick of cream cheese and some black pepper. The aroma and texture, so creamy and smooth, caused her to relax. Some women might pour a glass of wine to relax after a long day but Marni prepared food, even when she wasn't hungry.

She did spoon a small portion onto a plate and tasted it. Then she added sliced black olives.

Marni had trained herself to be a taster rather than a big eater. There was a real danger in spending your life in the kitchen and falling in love with each creation. While most women mindful of their figures might give themselves a five-pound leeway, Marni sometimes went ten or fifteen pounds over, at which point she had to calculate calories and bites diligently. If she weren't on television, she might never have bothered.

The doorbell rang, startling her. She glanced at her watch. It was nine fifteen. Anyone who knew her knew she'd most often be in her bedroom by eight thirty. That is, if she was at home rather than traveling. There were times she had to go out—a business meeting, dinner, fundraiser, community affair. Being a local television personality did require a lot of appearances outside of her day job.

She tapped on the phone app that brought up her security cameras and there, standing outside the front door she could see her ex-husband, Jeff. He was holding champagne and flowers. She took a calming breath. She'd been putting him off lately, dodging his calls, avoiding his request to visit. Clearly, he was determined to see her for some reason.

What she also gleaned in that split second of recognition was his attractiveness. Yes, he was most definitely handsome. He had what they called the "cosmetics for television." He was also charming and sexy and—her Achilles' heel—funny. He could make her laugh even when they were in the middle of a battle.

She opened the door, resentful of his attributes. "I guess I'm about to find out what you want."

"I want to congratulate you," he said, handing over the flowers. "Didn't you just finish shooting your season?"

"And if we hadn't finished?" she asked, but she took the flowers.

"That was doubtful, knowing you. But if you hadn't, this would be even more necessary," he said, holding up the champagne. He sniffed the air. "It must have been a good shoot. It smells amazing in here."

"That's the garlic."

"What did you wrap around it?" he asked hopefully.

"Chicken Florentine. Sort of."

"I'm not starving, but I could give it a taste and let you know what I think. I know it will be brilliant, but just in case..."

"Fine. Come in. I'll give you some. It's not from our shoot. That went into the freezer." She turned and let him follow her.

"The house looks great," he said. "You did some redecorating."

"I always give it a refresher before a shoot. The kitchen might be the focal point but the viewers enjoy brief trips into the house and garden and they notice the improvements. We hear from them all the time. And the social media people post all the new pictures on Instagram and such. People frequently ask for recommendations."

She pushed a plate of her pasta toward him.

"That's another source of income," he said, smiling smugly. "Including items and products on the set that people then buy. Incredible advertising opportunities."

"I know," she said, but didn't elaborate. She'd been doing this for years, but subtly. A floral arrangement provided for her set, a piece of furniture, a decorator item, a kitchen accessory. She didn't perform a free commercial but if the item appeared and viewers asked, the brand name and store was provided. She might occasionally go so far as to say, "This is a handy tool," and leave it at that. For that privilege, retailers paid.

"You've called several times," she said. "What's going on?"

He chewed, savored with eyes closed, swallowed. "This is amazing. Of course. I just wanted to see how you're doing. And how's Bella?"

"I've never seen her happier or healthier. And I'm doing just fine."

"The show ratings are high," he said. "Better all the time."

"The pandemic didn't hurt. I was in the right place at the right time. People were forced to stay home, searching for anything to watch on TV. We were syndicated and had so many earlier shows to run that filled in the gaps. Add to that, people were phoning in their grocery lists and eating at home."

"It didn't go so well for me," he said. "Your meat was my poison."

Don't ask, she told herself sternly.

Gretchen had talked Jeff into retiring early from the television station and opening a small boutique restaurant specializing in some Basque cuisine along with other things, so not only did he lose much of the fortune he'd gotten in the divorce, Gretchen was still half owner of the restaurant. Then came the pandemic. No one suffered as much as restaurateurs. She had heard from distant mutual friends that Jeff and Gretchen, while still in conflict, were back and forth in their relationship. Marni wished continued misery for them.

"Timing," she said, feeling absolutely no sympathy for him. "Even a marketing genius couldn't weather that storm." She silently and begrudgingly admitted Jeff was a gifted marketing strategist. But still, no sympathy. "Is it starting to come back?" Damn, she thought. I asked!

"Barely," he said. "I'm way behind. But I'm relieved that you're doing so well. And Bella is at least talking to me again. Also barely. But I didn't think we'd ever reconcile."

"I'm staying out of that," Marni said. "I'm sorry if the two of you are having problems in your relationship, but..."

"Don't say any more," he said. "It was entirely my fault. And she's gentler lately. I think it's pregnancy. She's softer. More amenable."

And on cue, that made Marni want to be kind. "Maybe you are, too."

He laughed lightly, chagrined. "I'd like being a grandfather," he said. "If she'll let me."

"That's very sweet," she said. Then without quite realizing what she was doing, she began gathering food again. He sat at the island with his plate of chicken Florentine while opposite him she gathered fruit. Apples, kiwi, pears, bananas, tangerines, walnuts, raisins and cherries. She began washing and slicing and chopping. She hadn't planned for a fruit salad but handling and combining flavors and scents just plain made her feel stronger. She'd whip up a Waldorf salad while they chatted. The way she skinned and sliced with a large extremely sharp knife was like ballet. Or more like a bartender who flipped bottles through the air.

"Let's have a toast to your year," he said, wrestling with the champagne cork. "The knife is nerve-wracking."

She brought out two glasses and put them on the island. When they were poured, he lifted his glass. "To an even better next season."

"Thanks," she said, taking a sip.

They made a little small talk while Marni cut up her salad ingredients and Jeff ate his pasta. He asked her how things were going at the station and she gave her usual answer; she didn't spend that much time at the station, just meetings now and then and scheduling or production issues. She asked him when he'd last spoken with Bella and he said he made it a point to call her at least twice a month and had had lunch with her just a week ago. Jeff and Marni talked about a few of their mutual friends; Brad Thomas had taken a job with the chamber of commerce and Gloria Neiman had been promoted to morning anchor. Elizabeth Reynolds had been offered a prime-time anchor position in San Francisco.

"I never liked her," Marni said.

"No one did," Jeff replied. "You would almost think that's a prerequisite for getting a big-time slot."

By the time she was finishing the Waldorf salad and he was rinsing off his plate, the real reason for his sudden visit came out.

"Listen, things have been a little more shaky than I let on," he said. "The restaurant isn't making it. I'm underwater here."

She bolstered herself. "I'm sorry to hear that, Jeff. In ordinary times it would have been successful."

"I've been everywhere, looking for help, looking for financial aid or loans or even a buyout. I'm out of ideas."

She didn't say anything for a moment. After a long pause she said, "Have you talked to your mother?"

"Of course," he said. "There's not as much there as I thought. And my sister will be the executor and she's unwilling to let me borrow against the estate because my mother needs care and there's no way of knowing how long that will last. She could last two years or ten."

"But she's comfortable and happy for the moment?" Marni asked.

"Yes. I saw her just a few days ago. She was playing bridge with some ladies at her new residence. She seems happy. Jasmine is closely guarding her care."

Jeff's mother was an heiress of sorts. Her husband's death a few years ago brought not only a handsome insurance policy but a tidy net worth to her portfolio, both in trust and protected from greedy children or their spouses. But there was the reality that if Jeff's mother lived for ten years in an expensive residential care facility, there would be very little left to quibble about.

"As she should..."

"Agreed. In the meantime, I'm losing the restaurant. Just when we're so close to turning it around."

"We?"

"Well, Gretchen," he said. "But more important, we, the staff and I. Several people depend on that place. Gretchen just looks at the books sometimes, by court order, to be sure she's not being swindled out of her half, for which she doesn't lift a finger. I want to save the place because of the people who have invested their lives there. The chef, his wife, his daughter and son, various family members. They're all Basque; their work ethic is enviable. When the restaurant goes, so do they."

"Have you thought of selling it?" she asked.

"Of course, but I'm so far in the hole it would be a steal and I don't think I'd ever clear the debt. My best course of action is to find a loan. I'm a bad risk, but that's the best I can do."

"And this has to do with me how?" she asked, though she feared she knew.

"If you could see your way clear…"

"What are we talking here? And what's your collateral?"

"A few hundred thousand would make a difference…"

"A few *hundred thousand*?" she shouted. "I gave you five million in the divorce!"

"I contributed to that net worth, you know I did. And I'd sign over my share of the restaurant…"

"Oh, God, why didn't I get a prenup! That five million still smarts! More to the point, why didn't *you* get a contract with Gretchen before partnering with her? I told you that woman had ulterior motives! She was in it for the money! And a great deal of money that turned out to be. The only thing I can think of that's worse than you defaulting on the loan is me ending up partnered with Gretchen!"

"Don't you think I have regrets that I let myself get played? I thought… Never mind what I thought! I guess the answer is no…"

"Only a fool would allow that kind of insanity to happen twice! In just a few years!"

"I'm sorry I asked," he said. "I wouldn't have but you were seriously a last resort, the only possibility I could think of. Um, listen, the knife…"

Marni had pulled a few celery stalks, an onion and some mushrooms out of the refrigerator and was absently chopping them into tiny pieces. She stopped, a little shocked by her actions. "Oh, Jeff, what have you gotten yourself into?"

"There have been plenty of long hours of blaming myself," he said. "I'm not an experienced restaurateur, but I did put in the work. I lived at the place. But the pandemic buried me and Gretchen didn't just leave me, she bailed without putting in her share. She managed to get more money out than I ever will."

"You didn't get yourself a limited liability partnership?" she asked.

"No," he said. "But she did."

Marni whistled. "She took you for a ride," Marni said.

"A ride with a dead end."

She shook her head. "I don't feel sorry for you," she said. "But I don't want to fight with you anymore. I'm just plain tired of being angry! I can't give you a loan that size. In fact, I can't give you a loan at all; it would be so foolish. I know the law; I know that no matter what you might have done to hurt me, it's a community-property state and also a no-fault state, so you got your half and never had to say you're sorry. I gave you half and it was a fortune."

"I did say I was sorry," he said. "And I have tons of regret."

"Too bad you don't also have tons of amends," she said.

"I don't know how I could possibly make it up to you," he said.

"Frankly, I'm tired of all the divorce business. I want to be done with that. I'm sorry I can't help you. But I'm not a monster—I'll never let you starve. If you find you can't feed yourself, let me know. I'll see you have food and I can help you find a way to cover your head. You won't ever be barefoot and homeless. Even though the thought holds some appeal..."

"I'm not in straits that dire," he said. "But thank you."

"Don't thank me," she said. "Your regret doesn't bring me nearly the pleasure I thought it would."

They said an uncomfortable goodbye just a few minutes later and after cleaning up the kitchen, Marni went to bed. Her heart was heavy. There was a time she had loved and trusted Jeff and believed he loved and trusted her. The separation had been five years ago now; the divorce almost as long ago. She had no explanation for why it would still hurt. Karma had done her work and he'd been shafted by the woman he'd chosen. Shouldn't that feel like closure?

Betrayal, she thought, *must be a mighty sword that left deep scars.*

Of course she didn't sleep well, Jeff taking up space in her head. She spent what seemed like hours screaming at him about all the things she hadn't thought of at the time. She awoke groggy and stiff. And early. The sun hadn't been up long.

After coffee, still in her pajamas, she went barefoot into the garden. While the Barefoot Contessa might have posted beautiful professional photos of her luscious gardens, Marni's was purely functional. She relished growing some of the food she prepared. She was relaxed by the long even lines of plants and the smell of dirt. It was an organic garden and she struggled with vermin and insects. She sprayed the borders of her garden with a repellent against bunnies and, less often, deer. She fought the aphids with dish soap and water. And it helped to burn off her anger with Jeff when she tugged out the weeds. She dug around the roots with her handheld cultivator and aerator. In no time at all there were muddy patches on her knees and dirt under her nails. The doorbell rang and she was not nearly finished mentally berating Jeff. Nor did she feel in any condition to answer the door.

But she went, using the camera on her cell phone to see

who was visiting at such an early… On second look it wasn't all that early. She'd been in the garden for over two hours and it was now a respectable hour to ring the bell. It was Sophia's father, Sam. He was holding a large wooden box.

She had forgotten about her attire, and its condition. At least until she opened the door and Sam looked her up and down slowly, smiling faintly.

"My timing isn't usually perfect, but I can see this time it is," he said.

At that Marni looked from her toes to muddy knees and dirty hands. "Oh! I rolled out of bed and headed right into the garden! I didn't have to work today and that was a natural move for me. Digging and plucking."

"Then I'm just in time," he said, tilting the box so she could look inside. He pulled back a covering of cheesecloth revealing a small bed of white asparagus. "Sophia said you have been struggling with this variety and I have a good bed going. She was off with friends today and I offered to bring it to you."

"That's so nice," she said with some shock. "What a kind thing to do!"

"It's no trouble. Would you like me to help you find a good spot for it?"

"Sophia said you were a farmer," Marni said as if just remembering.

"In a manner of speaking," he said. "My personal garden is pretty small, but I have great luck with asparagus and some other heirloom vegetables and fruits. It takes about five years to establish a good asparagus bed."

"My garden is very small."

"Can I see it? Can I help you find a place for this?" he asked.

"Oh yes! Please!" she said, holding the door open and standing aside.

"I can go through the backyard gate…"

"Oh, heck no! I'm dirtier than you." And then she laughed. "At least you're in your clothes while it should be obvious, I'm in my pajamas. I *hope* it's obvious." Her pajamas were in no way revealing, so she had no worry there. Today's pj's were long pants and a top with short sleeves sporting sailboats against a powder blue background.

"I'm pathetic when it comes to fashion," he said. "I wouldn't know a woman's pajamas from a Versace gown."

That made her laugh. "No one is that out of touch."

"I assure you," he said. "When it comes to the latest fashion…"

He had a good voice. An exceptional voice. Not too deep, not too shrill, right in the middle with the slightest rasp. She also remembered that the first time she met him, at least a year ago, she found him a tad homely. Maybe ordinary looking was more accurate. His nose was a little crooked, his ears a little large and whatever was under that hat was a mystery. He looked like a farmer. Blue jeans, chambray shirt with rolled-up sleeves, all-weather lace-up boots, straw wide-brimmed hat.

He followed her through the house after wiping his feet on the doormat. The back doors stood open and the garden lay on the other side of the pool, bordered by hydrangea and fruit trees. The mountains sat all around beyond her yard.

"Beautiful!" he exclaimed. "Perfect."

He put the box down and began to walk around the garden. He looked closely at each row, bending to deadhead a flowering vine, sticking the dead blooms in his pant pocket. He wandered over to fruit trees and examined some of the early fruit. "Flowering plum is a favorite of mine but I admit I love the flowers more than the fruit."

"Does Sophia can for you? Plum preserves?"

"I'm afraid not," he said. "She works and goes to school and has a very active social life. I give away a lot of the things I grow in my garden. How about you?"

"My situation is so different. I use the garden for my show, especially in the summer recipes."

He bent at the waist to examine a very strong healthy tomato plant. "This is a solid plant; it'll yield good large fruit."

"Red sauce. Italian. I love to can. I have a wine closet but also a very large pantry for preserves. This is Brandywine." She stood a bit taller when she identified it.

"I'm growing Cherokee Purple. It never disappoints."

"I'm fighting aphids with dish soap and water spray and it works but it seems to need it every day, which is frustrating. I don't have enough time for my garden and sometimes I have to hire gardening help."

"I have a spray in my truck you might like," he offered. "It's nontoxic, natural and lasts at least several days."

"That would be wonderful. And I'd love a taste of your Cherokee Purple."

"Absolutely. Where are the herbs? A chef has to have her own herb garden!"

"Over here by the back of the house. It's very small, raised, gets morning sun…" As she walked around the garden to the spot where she grew the herbs, he followed. "I use my own fresh herbs in my cooking and this bed is good in spring, summer and fall. And it's close to the pantry where I dry herbs."

"And I think we've found the perfect spot for the asparagus. I'll leave the crate here against the house. I'll come back tomorrow with wood and soil and build a border to match your herb garden."

"You don't have to do that!" she said. "I can just call the gardener and he—"

"No, let me do it. You can blame me if it doesn't thrive. I believe it will, however. You don't have to be home…"

"Tomorrow is Sunday. I'm sure I'll be here," she said.

He dropped the crate and wandered off down the row. "Your lettuces and greens are so dark and healthy! And it's still so early."

"My own compost from the kitchen," she said. "I think it's feeding itself."

"I bet you've been cutting off this batch for weeks already."

"And I share with everyone. Except Sophia, who has her own garden."

"She has my garden," he said. "She doesn't work in it. She just enjoys it."

"Have you always been a farmer?" she asked.

He stopped where he was, sat on the heel of his boot and looked up at her. "I was raised on a farm in the Midwest. A different operation altogether, with the cold and long winters. Farming is easier here. I'm more interested in agricultural science than commercial agriculture." He stood. "My personal garden is for my own pleasure."

"Do you like to cook?"

"I like to eat," he said with a laugh. "My summer garden is my favorite. Except for a ham hock in the beans now and then, I'm mostly meatless. Beans, tomatoes, onions, squash. Or greens with a ham bone… You ever thin slice zucchini squash and soak it overnight in Italian dressing?"

"No! Sounds delicious. And you eat it with bread?" she asked.

"I buy my bread," he admitted. "As I said, I share a lot of the garden. In fact, it gives me almost as much pleasure to share it as eat it. Sustainable food is at the core of my study."

"Study?" she asked.

"I teach," he said. "I research more than teach. I study agriculture and hydroponics. Did your mother teach you to garden?"

"No, there was no garden where I grew up. I taught myself much later. I grew up in a very strange household. My father passed away when I was young and my two aunts moved in with my widowed mother so it was a family of women. It was my sister and me, my mother and aunts. It was a good life. I didn't realize until I was much older just how eccentric it was. At about the same time I learned there is no such thing as a normal family," she added with a laugh.

He was moving down the row to the root vegetables. He crouched. "Can I look?" he asked.

"Of course. Help yourself."

He pulled out a long skinny carrot. "Nice," he murmured. Next, a bulbous leek. "Ohhh," he fairly moaned. Then he carried on to the vines. Zucchini, cucumbers, beans, yellow crookneck squash. He held up two different kinds of cucumbers—one short and fat and one long and slender.

"Pickling and salads," she explained without being asked.

"I like your garden," he said. "It's logical and practical. And a very good use of space."

"But it's not beautiful," she said. "I lust after Ina Garten's garden. It's productive and a showplace."

"I think your garden is beautiful," he said, smiling quite handsomely. "What has prevented you from making it a showplace?"

"Only time and skill," she said just as her cell phone rang.

She'd left it on the patio table. "Excuse me." She looked at her phone, saw that it was Bella and answered. "Good morning, darling."

"Mom, I met the most wonderful man! His name is Tom and I think he might be just right for you. He's—"

"Hold on, sweetheart. I'd like to hear all about it but I'm just in the middle of something. Let me call you back in just a little bit." She glanced over at Sam and saw that he was brushing off his knees.

"What are you doing?" Bella asked.

"I'm all dirty from the garden. I'll call you right back," she said. Then she disconnected before Bella could argue. She didn't even stop to ponder why she didn't want to be distracted right then, though she could feel in her chest that she was enjoying talking with Sam about her garden and it was one of the more pleasant encounters she'd had lately.

"Take the call if you like, Ms. McGuire. I have to get going. I have a long list of errands," Sam said.

"Marni, please. Call me Marni. It's just Bella on the phone. We talk at least once a day. Usually two or three times."

"The same used to be true for me and Sophia, but her social life has picked up speed and lately she barely has time to check in. That's as it should be, I guess. She's twenty-two, so smart and busy."

"My daughter has decided it's time I thought about dating," she confessed, then wondered why she felt compelled to share that. "I bet you go through the same thing."

"Just the opposite," he said with a shy smile. "Sophia's mother passed away and I don't think she has even considered me spending time with another woman. Even though it's been years now."

"That's right," she said. "I'm so sorry for your loss."

"Thank you. It was pretty hard on Sophia. But I'd say she's come a long way."

"Even if she won't let you date?"

He just chuckled. "I'm very busy as it is. And by the way Sophia's social life is expanding, I expect her to grow out of that possessive stage soon. I think I'll get over here tomorrow morning to install your asparagus bed and I promise not to come too early. I'll let myself in through the back gate."

She plucked at her pajama top. "I'm usually up early, but tomorrow I'll make it a point to dress."

"Not just for me, I hope. Those sailboats are awfully cute." He grinned and headed around the patio. "I'll take my muddy feet out this way."

"Thank you, Sam. I'm so excited about the asparagus."

"My pleasure," he said, touching his straw hat.

And just like that, he was gone.

THREE

Marni called Bella back right after Sam left, but she had very little enthusiasm for meeting the man Bella found to be so nice, polite, not bad looking and very mannerly. "You do understand that I will never get married again unless I'm drugged," Marni said.

"I get that, but I think it would be nice if you had someone, you know?"

"I don't know," she said. "Why don't you explain why you think it's so important for me to meet someone new?"

"I just think it would be nice for you to have someone to talk to, someone to hang out with sometimes, so it's not always you alone or you and a couple of women. I know you get lonely sometimes even though you try to hide it. So I'm not trying to marry you off; I'd love to hear you say you're taking a man with you to this or that party you have to attend. Or that you're going overnight to the Bay area to see a show. Or that you're cooking for someone who might just stay over. You know, someone who fits into your life and you look forward to seeing. I understand why you don't want a full-time live-in partner. I do. Tom is a nice man, right about your age and he's very successful, but I can't remember at what."

"Has pregnancy damaged your memory?" Marni asked with a laugh.

"Absolutely! But the reason is I only met him briefly. His son is one of the lawyers in the prosecutor's office and Tom was just stopping by. We didn't talk long."

"Then what makes you so sure I should date him?"

"I liked him, that's all. So I asked Richard, his son, if he was single and dating. Then Richard thought it was a good idea and there you go. Two people set up by their kids."

Marni just sighed; this sounded more troublesome than being a room mother to six-year-olds or chaperone on a junior high field trip. "Why don't you get me a cat? The animal shelter is running a special."

"You can't talk to a cat," Bella said.

"But you can," she said. "I used to talk to Mr. Chips all the time, may he rest in peace."

"I'll just set up a coffee date for you. If you don't like him, fine."

But that made her feel that if she didn't like him, she'd be letting Bella down. Bella and some lawyer named Richard.

Marni said nothing more about it. In just a few months the baby would arrive and most of this dating insanity would die a natural death. Bella planned three months of maternity leave, then would go back to work. Between work and a new baby, she'd be too busy to worry about her mother's love life.

Marni didn't mention that she already had something to look forward to. She was very excited about her white asparagus bed and curious about the man who was installing it. Sunday morning couldn't come fast enough. She'd met Sam three or four times over the past several months that Sophia had been working with her but it was the first time they'd been alone and had a lengthy conversation.

Although Sam promised he wouldn't be early, Marni got up at the crack of dawn, showered, primped, even put on makeup.

Then she puttered around, tidying up her bedroom, watched a little cable news, paged through some favorite cookbooks and looked outside at least twenty times. She took some time to look over her calendar; it was packed. There were things related to being a public face that kept her busy—she had to keep up her nails and hair to be sure she was at her best on and off camera. She had a shopper who monitored her wardrobe and visited her with new items of clothing every month. And her cleaning and landscape crews came regularly. The housekeepers led by Julia came every week, every Monday very early, making everything shine and doing all the laundry, including the sheets and towels. The gardeners came every Friday, also early.

There were regular meetings with the cable network and production staff. The network offices were in Sacramento, a two-hour drive for her and she could see from the schedule she had a meeting on Thursday. Her job involved a lot more than just cooking. Hers was a complicated and competitive business.

It wasn't until eleven in the morning that she heard noise coming from the backyard. When she stepped onto the patio, Sam was there with a big bag of potting soil and several boards that looked as though they were made to match those of her herb planters. There was also a shovel, spade, rake and gloves.

"How did you get all that stuff out here without making a sound?"

"Maybe I didn't make any noise," he said cheerfully. "But I'm about to. You look very nice today, though the sailboat pajamas were a nice touch."

"It's going to be warm today but before it gets hot, how about a fresh cup of coffee?"

"If you'll join me," he said.

"Absolutely. Cream? Sugar?"

"A little milk."

She gave a nod and headed to the kitchen to fetch two mugs. When she returned, he was using his spade to make a square in the dirt, the same size as the herb boxes. She put their coffee mugs on the patio table, luring him away from the garden.

"Where is your farm?"

"My garden is behind my house. It started out as some lettuce and tomatoes and it grew from there. Now it's much too big. It's my guilty pleasure. I work another farm, not on my land. It's not the way I grew up; I remember rolling out of bed before dawn to start chores. My family grew corn and soy beans."

"But you met your wife in Argentina," she said. "Sophia said you were the clever American who fell in love with her mother. But why were you in Argentina?"

"Have you ever been to Argentina?"

"Briefly. I admit I haven't seen a lot of the country. It's a beautiful place. Was that what drove you there?"

"No, but it was one of the reasons I was happy to be there. It's a long story."

"I have lots of time. And Sophia is special to me."

"Well, let's see. A long time before I knew Sophia and her mother, when I was very young, I wanted to travel, but a farmer's son doesn't have those kinds of opportunities. So at my father's insistence, I went to college. It wasn't my idea. I majored in agriculture because I thought it would be easy. I thought I already knew everything about growing. When I got my degree, I looked for postgraduate programs that would include traveling to other countries to study agriculture. I visited farms and farming villages in Europe, Canada, South America and Central America. When I ended up in Buenos Aires, a city dependent on the crops they shipped to other countries, years had passed and I had switched my course of study to biotechnology and I fell in love with the mother of an adorable little girl." When he laughed, his face became bright and handsome. He had exceptionally good teeth. "I married Selena and adopted Sophia. I did a lot of traveling and studying in South and Central America, large commercial farms and small family farms from Guatemala to Costa Rica. We eventually moved to California and that's where we were living when Selena became ill. We lost her when Sophia was only fifteen. I took a job here five years ago. Now I mostly travel for pleasure and curiosity. Very seldom do I have to travel for business."

"Excuse me, what job brought you here?"

"Oh, I'm sorry," he said. "I never have been good at telling a story. I work for the university in the experimental research lab, agriculture. I wrote about my research and it got me a good job."

"How did you research?" she asked. "Pictures? Notes? Interviews? How?"

"All of that but most importantly, I worked alongside farmers." He began to describe some of the many farms he observed.

The big commercial farms were the most accessible; a fore-man would take him in tow, give him an in-depth tour and make sure he saw everything. But what he enjoyed the most were the smaller family farms. He described them to her by name. The Aguirre farm, the Sepulveda farm, the Soto farm. He talked about the family members; in one family there were seven sons. Though their farm was considered average to small, they were esteemed in the community because of the many sons. The Soto farm had daughters and while they worked just as hard, it wasn't until they married that the value of the family property went up. It was very old-world, very traditional.

These family plots were incredibly well tended. They ro-tated their crops so diligently, cared for their plants with a mother's love, used old and organic methods to combat pests. He named the children of each family and talked about their special talents and, importantly, who would take the farm to the next generation.

He told her about the houses, very small by comparison to those in the United States. She wanted to know about the kitchens. Much of their cooking was for a large number of people and done mostly outside in large kettles and pans with long-handled spoons and spatulas. He described the herbs and peppers that hung from the ceiling in the pantry and kitchen. The cooks, usually the women, would pluck off some leaves or seeds to add flavor or spice. They were wonderful hosts and spoiled him with pepián, tamales, mole, all with piles of rice and beans and tortillas. They all raised their own chick-ens and the potatoes, tomatoes, carrots and corn came from their own farms.

"I will have to learn some of those recipes," she said.

Then he described the beauty of the land surrounding each

farm from the magnificent mountains to the plentiful rivers and the rich soil. After a bit he moved from the patio table to the place he would build the asparagus box; Marni moved, too, urging him to keep describing. Soon he was talking about skiing and how much he loved it and how much Sophia loved to ski, one of many reasons he chose to settle near Reno. The university, skiing and farming.

"Experimental farming," she clarified for him.

"But tell me about you," he said. "You and cooking."

"Ah, it's not nearly so interesting."

"Try me. I'd love to know."

"It was a complete accident. In fact, I was also widowed. I was very young, my baby Bella only nine months when my husband was killed in a car accident. I always meant to go to college but I never got around to it. I started out as a server who handed out free samples in grocery stores. Bella was always with me, flirting with the customers. I give her most of the credit for my success. I went from samples to product demos to food preps. Bella went from the backpack to nursery school, but sometimes she went with me even when she was older. And I moved up the local ladder slowly but steadily. I filled in on a couple of morning shows until, like a miracle, I landed a spot three mornings a week. Live! It was terrifying! But it worked and it was over twenty-five years ago now that I was syndicated. *Marni in the Kitchen* or *Marni Cooks*. Through some stroke of luck, it caught on."

"It's a good show," he said.

"You've seen it?" she asked.

"Of course! Sophia works for your show! She loves the show! I think you might be the reason she's majored in communication. She'd like a career in television."

"I don't think she'll have much trouble making that happen," Marni said.

He finished his garden box, planted the asparagus, covered it with cheesecloth and loaded up the tools into his truck. She wouldn't let him go without first joining her for a sandwich.

"The best sandwich I've ever eaten, of course," he said with an appreciative smile. "You certainly have a gift."

They talked through a light lunch and finally it had to end. His tools already in the truck bed, they said goodbye.

He had been at her house for a total of three hours and all of that time they were talking. They fed each other questions while he built the garden and after he left she continued to hear his voice. She sat on the chaise on her patio, enjoying the sun and listening to his voice in her head. She could almost see him with her mind's eye, working alongside the families who tended their farms, eating at their tables, loading up their vegetables in trucks to take them to market. He had said, "Sustainable food is what binds families and communities and countries."

How had Sophia worked for her for six months and yet today was the first time she'd enjoyed an extended conversation with Sam? She kept silently repeating his words. He had such a kind spirit; such a strong heart.

He was inspirational.

She took his stories and his alluring voice to bed that night and wondered what he would think if he knew she was lulled to sleep by the sound of his voice.

Marni's first impression of Tom, the very nice man that Bella had picked out for her was positive. They met at Starbucks at ten in the morning almost a week after Bella had suggested it and when Marni walked in, a tall, balding man stood from a table in the corner and gave her a wave. She looked around, then pointed to herself and returned a questioning shrug, making him laugh. He took two steps toward her and put out a hand. "Hello, Marni."

"Tom?"

"Yes, of course. Take a seat over there and let me get you something. What would you like?"

"A vanilla latte, thank you." In just a few minutes he was back, smiling as he took the seat opposite. Aside from a woman with a book and a couple of other customers working on laptops, the place was deserted.

He passed her the latte. "It's nice to meet you in person. If you don't mind me saying so, you're even more attractive in person than on TV."

Remarkably she felt her cheeks grow warm. She was thinking maybe this wasn't such a bad idea at all! Marni was not immune to compliments. She wasn't in the least vain and considered herself just a smidgen over average-looking but that being said, she paid close attention to her appearance. She did have a public life, after all. And it was nice to be admired by someone.

"I have to admit, I've never watched a cooking show before," he said. "When Bella told me about you, her single mother, I had to have a look."

She lifted her brows. "That's reasonable. Do you like to cook?"

"There are one or two things I can make without embarrassing myself, but it's not one of my hobbies. But you were fascinating! How long have you been doing that?"

"On my own show? Over twenty years. The first few years I had two thirty-minute segments a week on one channel and later the show was syndicated. So how long have you lived in this part of the world?"

"Ten years, but I came from San Jose, then San Francisco, Sacramento and here. I've been in Northern California most of my life. I was a teacher, a sales rep and even a used car salesman, a very interesting combination of careers. I ended up in real estate in Reno, and it is clearly what I was always meant to do. I made my killing in it. It was the peak of the market but still, you had to know what you were doing and working with people was definitely my strength. I'm semiretired now but I still have my license. Every once in a while the bug gets me again. You know—the lure to make deals, to negotiate, to close on a big one. I had a house in Lake Tahoe—"

Then began a list of his achievements, down to specific deals and negotiations. He didn't offer his age but she asked and learned he was sixty-five and had been twice divorced. He laughed quite a lot—at his own jokes. His stories became punctuated by flattery. "You're fifty-seven? Good God you look many years younger!"

He went on about his favorite deals, highlighting how his cleverness in the clinch was his true calling. "I can't help it; I love it when the deal gets tough. That's when I really pull out all the stops and throw everything at the wall to see what sticks. Everyone has a tell and if you counteroffer enough, they'll show you their tell and you know exactly when and how to go in for the kill. I had a buyer once who wrote so much detail into the offer it brought the price down so far it wasn't worth it to deal. He was expecting an equally complicated counteroffer, but instead I didn't respond. I just let the offer expire which baffled him and threw him off balance. I was basically saying he wouldn't get the house at any price. I suggested I had a less complicated offer from someone else. And then, predictably, he came back. I like those deals; they're fun. But I've also had the stupid deals. You know, buyers who care more about the win than the end result. I had a buyer throw away a great deal over five thousand dollars." He laughed heartily at the memory. "I didn't lose any sleep over that, but I bet he did."

Marni wanted to look at her watch but sipped her latte instead. Somewhere between the tell and the kill, she began to grow bored. And Marni actually loved houses! She loved looking at them, imagining herself in them, and the house she lived in, she had built. She felt herself tempted to tell him all about it, it was such a great house, customized for her business.

She realized she was in trouble. She didn't know how to bring this encounter to an end. She should have quizzed Bella on how that was done these days. Was this the time to be brutally honest and say "I'm sorry, but I don't think this will work for me"?

"Um, excuse me, Tom? I'm afraid it's time for me to bring our coffee date to a close. I have—"

"Will you have another latte?"

"No, thank you. Actually, I have a meeting."

"A meeting? You didn't mention that when we spoke."

"I thought an hour would give us a chance to meet, and it has."

"What kind of meeting?" he asked.

"A business meeting," she said.

"What kind of business does a chef do?" he asked. She thought she detected a bit of sarcasm in his voice and she stiffened. This parting of the ways was going to be easier than she feared a moment ago. "I mean, I'm very interested, if you don't mind me asking."

"A production meeting," she said coolly. "My staff and the producer have a lot of scheduling to do before our next shoot."

"Of course," he said, backpedaling. "I was hoping we might schedule another date."

"I'll be happy to call you after I look at the calendar," she said. She stood. "Thank you so much for the latte. And the very pleasant conversation." She shook his hand. "Till later, then," she said.

"I'll walk you to your car." He followed her. "I'd love it if we could meet for a drink next time."

"I'll get in touch after I see the schedule," she repeated.

And then, remarkably, he reached for her as if to pull her closer. She stiffened and pulled away. Quite out of her control she said, "Ach!" and put a hand against her chest.

"Okay," he said. "Too soon."

"Goodbye," she said, opening her car door.

"I'll see you soon!" he called out.

Not if I see you first, she thought.

Marni did not have a meeting. She was glad to have some private time to think. She wasn't at all drawn to Tom, but then why would he need her to be. He seemed to be rather in love with himself. But spending an hour with him reminded her that she'd been too long without a man's arms around her.

It was such a beautiful day that she spent much of the afternoon on the patio. She was sitting there, paging through recipe books, when her phone rang. It was Bella. She was going to be forced to tell the truth.

"I heard from Tom," Bella said. "He said he didn't think he made a very good first impression. What happened?"

"Nothing all that interesting. He talked about himself and the only thing he asked about me was my age."

"No! Come on!"

"He also asked me how long I've been cooking on TV. Then asked me my age again."

"But did you like him?" Bella wanted to know.

"He seemed like a perfectly nice man but I don't want to date him."

"Don't you think you should at least give him another chance?"

"No. I think you're going to have to find another hobby. One that doesn't make your mother feel so awkward and uncomfortable."

"But why were you uncomfortable if he was perfectly nice?"

She sighed. "Because he talked about himself the whole time. Here's what I've learned about people who talk about themselves a lot. They're not listening or particularly interested in you—they're thinking of what they'll say next. That's the agenda. And sadly, they're usually only interesting to themselves."

"Maybe he was just trying to entertain you."

"Or trying to impress me with his many accomplishments. I'm sorry, Bella, but I was bored."

"Did he tell you about his trip to Africa? Or his cruise to Scandinavia? Or his son the lawyer?"

"No, none of that."

"Okay, I think you and I should sit down and have a talk about what you're looking for in a man."

"Nothing, that's what. Or maybe a Jason about twenty years older. Oops, I have to run. Someone's at the door. Probably a delivery…"

"I'm just pulling into the grocery store lot. I'll call you later."

Marni slid her phone into her pocket and went to get

the door. When she checked the peephole, there stood Sam Garner. He was the last person she expected to see. A smile came immediately to her lips and she opened the door. "Well, hello!"

"I hope I'm not intruding," he said. "I would have called but I don't have your number and I didn't want to ask Sophia for it. So I brought a bottle of wine and hoped for the best. Are you working?"

"No. And I wouldn't mind a glass of wine. I had a stressful day."

"Oven broken?" he asked with a grin.

"No, I had a date this morning. It wasn't promising."

"Let's open this and you can tell me about it."

He followed her into the kitchen. She wrestled open the wine. "Why wouldn't you want to ask Sophia for my number?"

"I wouldn't want to give her any ideas. You've probably noticed Sophia is nosy. She would start asking me a lot of questions and wouldn't buy the answers. Even after all these years, I can't predict her expectations. Like when I say I'm just visiting the asparagus, she would have more questions. I've had wives less nosy."

That made her eyes open wide. "You've had more than one?"

"I was married right after college. It was very brief. Hardly worth mentioning. It turned out we had nothing in common. We didn't even fight; it was that benign. We got a do-it-yourself divorce packet from the bookstore."

"But Sophia's mother—" she ventured.

"A farmer's daughter from Argentina, a lovely girl. Sophia was only six and Selena twenty-six. I was forty. Age didn't seem to matter. She passed away nine years after we married. She was far too young to die."

She passed him a glass. "So difficult for a young girl, too…"

"No matter what she has to deal with, fifteen is torture. The weather is perfect for me to visit the asparagus bed. Can we have our wine outside?"

"That's where I was when you rang the bell."

On the patio it was obvious where she'd been sitting. A pile of colorful coffee table–sized recipe books were stacked on the ground beside one of the chaise lounges and a small back support pillow was on the chaise.

"I think you were working," he said, taking the other chair.

"I read recipes to relax. What do you read to relax?"

"Action adventure. And a lot of history. Or seed catalogs. Besides the recipes, there must be something you like."

"Women's fiction. I love chick flicks, too. Books and movies with happy endings."

"You believe in happy endings," he said, and it was not a question.

"I hope for happy endings," she clarified.

"But Marni, one would assume you have your own," he said. "A beautiful home, a lovely family, a successful career…"

"I'm not complaining," she said. "I still like to read about happy endings. The most impossible situations are somehow resolved cleverly and everyone is happy forevermore."

"I admit, I like that idea."

"You've been widowed a long time," she said. "What do you do about dating?"

"My situation might be unique," he said, shaking his head. "My daughter is not playing matchmaker. I've heard her say 'my father will never love another woman.' Whether or not that is accurate, I don't know. In fact it might be even worse if her expectations were to find a stepmother for herself, even though no one could use a mother more than Sophia. She could use the wisdom of an older woman. Someone she could talk to about her own love life. The last young man she dated was abrasive and cold. Fortunately it didn't last long."

"That surprises me," she said, leaving it at that. Sam was anything but cold or abrasive. At least he seemed warm and charming from what she knew of him.

"I thought that, but maybe that's just a father's possessiveness. Sophia tells me I'm being silly, that if I knew him better, I'd admire him." He lifted one brow. "I doubt it. He showed no respect for her."

"My situation is also unique," Marni said. "My daughter is determined that I should date."

"Did you ask her why?"

"She doesn't want me to be lonely."

"But are you?"

She gave her head a shake. "Of course, everyone is a little lonely sometimes. But not enough so that I'm willing to risk another relationship. I've also been married twice and widowed once. My first marriage was also brief."

"I didn't know we had that in common," he said. "It would seem to me you'd have interested men swarming around you."

"Not even slightly, but then I don't find myself in many situations where I'm likely to meet single men of a respectable age. After a difficult divorce five years ago, I don't feel up to an adventure of that nature. And really, I'm going to get Bella off this kick. It sounds like way too much trouble."

"Agreed," he said with a laugh. "What happened on the date?"

"It was just coffee, set up by Bella, but I had no interest

in the man. He's nice but maybe he was trying too hard. I was bored. Then irritated. Then I couldn't wait to get away."

Sam laughed loudly.

"It was so awkward," Marni said with a groan.

"I meet a lot of women who think I should be married," he admitted, sipping his wine. "Frankly, I don't want to be married."

"Neither do I!" she said, sitting up straighter. "When you get down to it, I don't. I'm not even interested in a serious relationship—I'm perfectly content. I wouldn't mind having a friend, if we were compatible and had fun together, but I'm so busy! My work is important to me and it is actually very time-consuming. I put in at least fifty hours a week and I love what I do! Don't you? I mean, I'm not sure exactly what you do besides the farming part."

"That's mostly what I do. I do agricultural experiments. It can be dull to anyone who doesn't also do that."

"I don't know about that," she said. "I'm in love with my new asparagus bed."

"It looks like you've been in the garden a little bit," he said. "It's looking full and rich. And happy."

"It's a very happy garden. That stuff you gave me for the aphids is amazing. Where'd you get it?"

"I made it. When you run out and need more, let me know. How are you doing with the bunnies?"

"My fence is holding up but I do hit the popular edges with bunny repellant."

"Bunnies like the new tender leaves so if you can keep them away until most of your plants are mature, you'll have better luck." He took a breath and glanced over at the garden. "Fifty hours a week? Tell me, what do you do for fun? In the off time?"

"There isn't a lot but I'm good at independent play. I like to travel, but mostly for the art of studying cultural recipes and menus. As much as the food, I enjoy the people I meet."

"That's how it was with me when I was traveling from farm to farm."

"When I'm home and don't have to work, I still cook, try out new things. I read a lot. I love old movies. I enjoy the silence of being alone. I ski in winter. I go to the beach in summer."

"You've lived here a long time?" he asked.

"I grew up here or near here. Breckenridge is such a perfect little town, so clean and beautiful. My daughter works for the county DA and she wants to raise her family here, so I won't be leaving. My sister is here, teaching in Reno, married to a firefighter. This is definitely home to me."

"Your sister teaches?"

She nodded. "At the university in the English department. Nettie Carlisle. I mean, Annette Carlisle. Do know her?"

"I don't," he said, shaking his head. "Now I'll look for her. So, reading and watching old movies?" he asked.

"I have a bike. I like to take long walks, sometimes hike, get together with my girls. That includes Sophia, though not as often lately as her circle of friends grows. My sister, my daughter, my assistant, sometimes a few women in broadcasting."

"Do you get into the city often?"

That brought a spontaneous grin. "I love San Francisco."

"What do you like to do there?"

"Restaurants. Of course. But also live music, art galleries, shopping, import shops. I've never learned to sail but I've been deep-sea fishing a couple of times and loved it. Have you done that?"

"I have and I agree, it's great fun. We'll put that on the list of something we might do together sometime."

"But you won't mention it to Sophia?" she asked with a sly grin.

"You do whatever you want, but I plan to keep things uncomplicated on the home front. Sophia is a beautiful child with a sometimes fiery disposition."

"I won't tell her if you won't tell Bella." She chuckled.

"But before we make any plans to go to San Francisco, how would you like to see my garden?"

"I would love that! I have a feeling you'll put mine to shame."

"Look over your calendar and give me a day that would be good. If you have time, we'll grab a bite to eat."

"I'm sure there will be time!"

They talked for two hours, traded cell phone numbers and said goodbye at the door. They had laughed about their daughters, both only children and fiercely independent and entitled. They talked about everything but extraterrestrial life and religion, but it seemed it was only because they hadn't gotten to those subjects yet. They talked about their marriages and Marni was acutely aware they each focused on their second marriages—hers to Jeff, his to Selena.

There was one other thing they hadn't talked about. Love. Both of them had said they didn't want to remarry; both showed a real hesitancy toward another serious relationship. But neither had mentioned being in love. Marni felt this was a weakness in her character—that she longed to be in love again. There was nothing as thrilling and vulnerable as falling in love; nothing as frightening or devastating as fearing love was slipping away. And nothing as stimulating as feeling love fill the heart. It was so full of hope and promise. Despite her misgivings about marriage and her worry that it would be terribly risky to trust a man, she had to admit the idea of falling in love was delicious.

FOUR

Bella washed fresh vegetables and prepared a giant salad. If there was one positive thing the pandemic had emphasized, it was just how much work a lawyer could accomplish at home. With her phone and laptop she had staked out a space in her small living room and could even put her feet up while she worked. On the downside, her lap was fast disappearing.

She was going into the DA's office at least two days a week, usually three or four, but it was such a comfort to know she could retreat to her home. Her assistant, Shelly, was in the office nearly every day, ready by the computer and phone, taking care of the details and keeping her up to speed. Really, were it not for meetings, interviews and depositions, she wouldn't have to leave her house much at all.

Showing up to court was another matter—that was unavoidable. And since the pandemic had eased into becoming endemic, there was a lot of catching up to do. A great many court cases had been postponed and rescheduled. She hoped to be all caught up and ahead by the time the baby came. Then she planned to take three months of family leave.

Jason could take family leave as well but it was beginning to appear as if he didn't really want to. He said he'd be around more, but he didn't see the need to take extended leave. That was disappointing, but she'd live with it.

Just as he came to mind, she heard the door from the garage open. And the sound of him talking on his cell phone as he walked into the house was familiar and irritating.

"Yes, I'll get that taken care of first thing tomorrow," he was saying. "Have you checked all the available records for property closures on the Hanson case? And just to avoid any nasty surprises, do a wider search for warrants and arrests nationwide. No, just a feeling. Better to be safe than sorry."

Jason, also an attorney, worked for a law firm in Reno. He was a defense attorney while Bella was an assistant DA, a prosecutor. They met right after law school and had been together ever since.

Bella had set the table, her huge beautiful salad in the middle. She used placemats and everything. There was bread for Jason.

"Salad again?" he said, after he had changed his clothes.

"I'm trying so hard not to gain any more weight," she said. "I don't want to be round as a pumpkin when the baby is born."

"But I'm starving!" he complained.

"Well, could you make yourself a sandwich or something? I knew if I made a big dinner I'd just eat it all!"

"Fine. I'll make a sandwich. Or something."

They sat down and she heaped salad on their plates, then asked him about his day and told him what she could about hers. They had to be careful about what they shared—they were on opposing teams, after all. Jason was unusually quiet and she wasn't sure if he was mum because of a case he really couldn't talk about or if it was the salad.

"I'm still hungry," he said in what she judged to be a very juvenile tone.

She pushed the salad bowl toward him.

"Really, I don't want any more lettuce."

"I'm hungry, too! You promised to be supportive. After all, I have to be the pregnant one!"

He said nothing. He went to the refrigerator, opened the door and looked inside. She knew there wasn't much for sandwiches but there was always PB&J. Then he closed the door and went back to the bedroom. When he came out a few minutes later, he was wearing jeans, a light sweater, boots. He scooped his wallet, phone and keys off the table on the dry bar in the living room.

"I'm going to Bilby's for a beer." Bilby's was their favorite neighborhood bar and grill.

"I'll go with you," she said, beginning to rise.

"Why don't you let me go alone," he said. "I had a really frustrating day and I need a little space to shake it off. I won't be gone long and when I get home I promise to be in a much better mood."

"I could agree not to talk," Bella said.

"I don't think that will work. Just give me a little time to unwind and dump this funk I'm in."

"You've been doing this a lot lately," she said.

"There's no liquor in the house," he reminded her. Because she couldn't drink, she stopped buying it. When he bought it, she commented on how much she'd love a cold beer or a dry martini.

"There's wine," she said. "Would you like me to open a bottle?"

"No thank you. I'd like you to just let me step out for a minute, and when I get home, I'll be in a better frame of mind."

"All right," she said. "I had a long day, too, you know."

"I know," he said. "I won't be long."

He escaped before she could throw more roadblocks in his path. She finished loading the dishwasher and sat down, put her feet up and opened the book she'd been reading. It seemed like she'd been reading it for years but she was only on page 129. She read two paragraphs. Then she got up, found her shoes, grabbed her purse and headed out the door.

She drove the five blocks to Bilby's. It was a great little place with a friendly atmosphere where everyone knew the regulars. They had several such cozy hangouts in the extended neighborhood. They lived just two small towns over from Breckenridge, twenty minutes from her mother and an easy commute to either Reno or Carson City. Her little town had a great sushi place, a high-quality steak house, a small family owned Italian restaurant and an excellent hamburger joint, as well as Bilby's. She had not seen the inside of any of these places in a while because she'd been watching her weight. She'd gained too much weight in the first few months of her pregnancy and the midwife suggested she try to slow it down or she'd be an unhealthy weight by the time the baby arrived.

Jason was supposed to be supporting her efforts, even though he didn't have a weight issue. Lucky him! He also didn't have a hormone issue whereas Bella's hormones were as stable as a landslide!

His car was not at Bilby's. Had he had his beer and headed home that quickly, just as he promised?

She parked and went inside just to be sure. "Hey, Bella, you're looking good!" the bartender called.

She beamed. It wasn't easy and her pregnancy made her very proud. Not that long ago she feared they would never have a baby. "I must have missed Jason," she said. "I thought he was stopping off for a beer. He had a long day."

"I haven't seen Jason yet."

"Oh? Then I guess I'll see him at home. Since I can't drink, I'm not going to hang around."

"I can make you a green tea with French vanilla creamer," he offered.

"Oh. Yummy," she said sarcastically. "See you next time."

She drove by the other places Jason loved to go. No car. She drove a few blocks wider. She found herself looking in driveways and in the parking lot of a townhouse complex but there was no sign of him. She realized he could be anywhere and decided to return home.

She had been home about ten minutes when he walked in.

"Hi, babe," he said, dropping a kiss on her forehead. "Sorry if I was in a mood."

"Feeling better?" she asked.

"Much. Thanks."

"You weren't at Bilby's."

"I know. I changed my mind."

"Where were you?"

"Were you looking for me? Why didn't you call me if you needed me?"

"Why don't you tell me where you were?"

"Because I didn't want to upset you or fight with you. I went to Johnny D's and ate a pizza." He breathed on her. "Pepperoni!"

"Why Johnny D's? You don't even like that place!"

"No, *you* don't like that place. They have great New York pizza! And I was starving!"

"Did you eat with someone?" she asked, her chin quivering.

He shrugged lamely. "The waiter sat down a minute because it wasn't busy. He wanted to know if I was some local athlete. But I—" He had started to laugh but noticed the expression on her face.

"Hey! What's going on with you? I didn't tell you because I didn't want a fight! Look," he said, taking both her hands in his. "I know it's not easy being pregnant, especially the way we went about it, and I'll do everything I can to help, but, Bella, I have to have food. Food, not grass. All that lettuce just gives me the shits. If you want me to bring my own food home or stop off somewhere and eat it in private, I can do that. But I can't carry the baby for you and I can't lose weight for you. Okay?"

"Are you sure it was a waiter and not a waitress?" she asked, a big tear welling up in her left eye.

"Oh, Jesus, my Jesus," he said, dropping her hands and heading for the bedroom.

She didn't follow him. She sat there and felt sorry for herself for a good solid ten minutes before she went to the bedroom. He was lying down on the bed, a thick legal brief in his hands. He eyed her cautiously. She took off her clothes and slid into a nightgown. When she crawled into bed he gave a heavy frustrated sigh and pulled her into his arms and snuggled her.

He spooned her until his hand slid under gown, began to fondle her belly, her butt and eventually her breasts. Finally he pulled her on her back and kissed her. Then he made careful love to her and after that she was able to sleep soundly.

He was out of the shower early in the morning. He kissed her and said, "Early court. Are you all right now?"

"Fine. You?"

"I'm fine. Are you working at home today?"

"I'm going in for a few hours. Will you be late tonight?" she asked.

"I'll call you if anything comes up. Right now it's my plan to be home by seven at the latest."

"Okay. Have a wonderful day. And remember I love you."

"Bella, try to remember I love you." He blew her a kiss and went out the door.

She heard the garage door go up, the car engine, the door go down. She called her mother, which she did every morning. "Mama," she said, her voice soft. "Jason's having an affair!"

Of all the dramas Bella could throw at her first thing in the morning, this one was the most unexpected. "You *know* this?" Marni asked, aghast.

"He said he went out for a pizza, but I drove by all our favorite places and he wasn't at any of them."

"But why would he go out for pizza without you?"

"Because there are too many calories in pizza for me! And I need the roughage, so I made a big salad for dinner. He said he was going out for a beer and some space because he was in a bad mood but he didn't go where he said he was going. He's lying to me! There can be only one reason for him to lie."

"I bet there's more than one reason," Marni said. "Listen, I'd rather say this to your face, holding your hand for reassurance, but, Bella, you're a little high strung in the best of times but with this hormone overload you're dealing with, you're tracking on the high side. I don't think a man going out for pizza is evidence of an affair."

"What is then?" Bella asked.

"It took me a while to spot the signs with Jeff, Bella. But based on my experience, I'm guessing there could be all kinds of things. Lipstick on the collar, being out of touch for long periods of time, lots of texts and emails from the same woman, lots of phone calls from a woman? I bet if you suspect an affair, you look at his phone. Do you?"

Bella was quiet for a long stretch.

"Enough said," Marni said. "You do."

"We know each other's pass codes..."

"I think if Jason had something to hide, he wouldn't give you his pass code. I imagine his secretary doesn't have his personal cell phone pass code."

"His secretary is older than you and not what I would call attractive. I'm not at all worried he's flirting with Janine. Besides—"

"I think you should talk to someone," Marni said. "Call the fertility clinic. I remember reading through all that stuff you showed me and there was a therapist listed in there."

"A therapist?" she asked, sounding appalled.

"I'm just guessing, but they're dealing with a lot of women who have been pumped full of hormones so the in vitro will stick and there are side effects. Like maybe you get a little wackadoodle and paranoid."

"I'm not being paranoid! He said he would support me every step of the way and he shouldn't get me all upset! It's not good for the baby!"

"I was thinking of a counselor for you so you don't have to go through a lot of unnecessary anxiety. I didn't even get all the extra hormones when I was pregnant and I had bouts of crying for no reason, losing things, either sleeping all the time or having insomnia..."

Bella began to sniff. "I hope I'm not hurting the baby, being upset, getting overwrought..."

"Okay, this is not a medical opinion, but I think you can take it to the bank. If being upset while pregnant resulted in problems with the baby, there would be nothing but problematic pregnancies dotting the globe. Pregnant women are, by their very nature, worried about everything, yet the children keep coming. About that therapist..."

"Mom, I bet you have something wonderful and rich and calorific in the freezer that you could give to me. I'd like to cook something wonderful that Jason loves but I really don't have time, plus whatever I do is not as good as what you do. I can come and pick it up this afternoon."

Marni sighed deeply. "I have a fettuccine in the freezer, but I'll only give it to you if you promise to call the counselor."

"Momma, please..."

"I bet they've set aside several appointments for hormone-laced pregnant women who think their husbands are cheating when they were only sneaking out for pizza..."

"Okay, okay, I'll call and check it out. Do you have some garlic bread?"

"Yes..."

"And can you whip up a little salad? Or bruschetta? Yes, bruschetta with fresh basil and olives!"

Marni couldn't help but laugh. Bella had inherited none of her cooking skills but she sure could read a menu and her palate was impeccable.

"He'll probably know you made it, but that's okay," Bella said.

"It's okay because he'll be very grateful you called me. If he's starving, that is. Bella, you are so spoiled. Remember our deal. Call the counselor."

"Sure. Of course. I do have a very busy calendar."

This younger generation of lawyers never said busy day. They said busy calendar. "Me, too, sweetheart. I'll pack a little cooler. Do you suppose you'll find time to unpack it and warm it?"

She giggled because all her problems were suddenly solved, even the cheating husband had turned into a hungry husband.

"Any chance you have time to drop it off?" Bella asked.

"No! I also have a busy calendar! I love you. Settle down." And she hung up.

Marni was not foolish enough to think this would be resolved with a substitute dinner. This was probably going to go up and down, round and round, throughout Bella's pregnancy. Possibly for the first six years of her grandchild's life.

But what if Jason was cheating? Marni hadn't thought about this before but if there was ever anything that could hurt as badly as catching Jeff in an affair, it was finding her son-in-law cheating on her daughter. She counted on them to be happy.

But she got the fettuccine out of the freezer, pulled out a frozen baguette to thaw and checked to see if she had fresh salad makings. Then she went to her laptop at the breakfast bar to google *Affairs*. She had to remind herself for the millionth time that Bella's life was nothing like hers had been.

Her first husband had been a problem; she hadn't worried about her pregnancy as much as she had worried about her husband's temper. Her second husband had been somewhat overbearing, in her business every second, always giving her advice, right up until he started paying far too much attention to another woman, a younger very aggressive woman. What Bella was going through was fairly common: feeling fat and unattractive, overly sensitive, weepy. Add in the high doses of hormones to accommodate the IVF and kaboom!

How Do You Know if Your Husband Is Cheating was the first podcast. *What to Do if You Suspect Your Husband Is Cheating* was the second. She listened to both while waiting for Ellen to arrive to work. At no point in either podcast did they suggest you ask your mother to prepare a wonderful meal.

Ellen enjoyed her work so much more when their days were a bit shorter and there was no rush to get to the kitchen at the crack of dawn. She'd been up late doing some baking and slept in until eight. Then she packed up her tote with some cookies and other baked goods, her day planner and notebook and went into the garage. She pressed the starter on her late model Lexus and heard that awful sound—a muffled click. It was a quiet car to start with, but now it didn't even purr.

She walked out onto the driveway with her cell in hand and scrolled through the contacts. Her car was so dependable she wasn't sure she even had a number for a repair service. She thought that worst-case, she could always call Marni for a lift or the name of a good mechanic.

"Ellen!" she heard.

Looking up, she spied her neighbor in his drive. "Good morning, Mark."

He walked across their yards. "Got a problem?"

"I'm pretty sure it's the battery, though it shouldn't be. The car is only three years old."

"I think those batteries are timed to go out about six days after the warranty is up. Let me have a look."

"I can call someone," she said. "You probably have to get to work…"

"I have time," he said, going straight to her car. "Is the key fob in your purse?"

"Yes. Thank you. That's very nice of you."

"Not a problem," he said. He tried the starter, heard the same click and got out to lift the hood. "I'm guessing, but it sounds like and acts like the battery. How about if I take the battery to the service center, get a new one, bring it back and put it in for you?"

"I hate for you to go to all that trouble..."

"I'm happy to do it, Ellen. I don't have anything pressing."

"Don't you have to get to work?"

"I have plenty of time," he said.

"Well, gee, thank you. But of course I'll pay for the battery."

"Sure. Get what you need from your car and we'll go in my truck." And he proceeded to remove her battery from the engine block.

Mark Wascott had moved into the house next door about three years ago. Ellen introduced herself right away but it was a year before she learned Mark's wife had passed away and he just hadn't wanted to live in their house without her, so he sold the home they had lived in for many years and bought a slightly smaller one. He had a grown son and a couple of grandchildren who lived in Las Vegas. They visited, but rarely; she thought maybe Mark, being a single man, went to them more often. At least there were times she thought he had gone out of town for a bit.

They were friendly neighbors, hollering hello when they saw each other outside. If Mark was tidying up the yard, sometimes he'd blow leaves off her drive or there was once he shoveled her walk—right up to the door! They didn't get a lot of snow so it wasn't a big deal, but it was very kind and she took note. Once he asked her if she minded if he trimmed the branches of a bougainvillea that was invading his backyard, getting too close to the patio. Her empty trash bins were sometimes moved from the curb to near the garage, a gentlemanly gesture she appreciated. He was thoughtful and friendly—a great neighbor.

She'd told him she worked for the morning cooking show on Channel 40 and he said he was officially retired but worked part-time at a local grocery store for extra money and something to do. He didn't look very old. She guessed he was about sixty or so. And she had noticed he was in good shape, then scolded herself for even noticing.

As they drove to the auto supply store, after she thanked him three more times, she said, "You mentioned you were retired, but you didn't mention from what?"

"Firefighter. I put in over thirty years. I might have tried to stay on longer but Susan got sick and I decided it was time to quit. She was fighting cancer and the end was near for a long time. Too long."

"I'm so sorry."

"Thank you. I wish she'd lived long enough to enjoy some retirement."

"You were robbed," Ellen said. "That's just not fair."

"You're widowed as well, aren't you?"

"Yes, but my husband was disabled and I was a caregiver for a long time before he passed away. A part-time caregiver. I always worked. Or I might have lost my mind," she added. "He spent his last several years in a nursing home. There was never any hope that we'd have a retirement together. He passed six years ago. But I've lived alone a long time. Ten years."

"Do you ever get used to it?" he asked.

"Yes, I'm used to it. I'm afraid I'm very set in my ways. But my circumstances have been so different from yours. When Ralph went to the nursing home, he was physically and mentally disabled. I had a combination of grief and relief. I knew he wouldn't ever come home again. All I wanted was for him to get some rest."

"You've been through a lot. Any children?"

She shook her head. "We missed out on that."

"Too bad. My son and his family are great fun for me. Satisfying."

They didn't talk for the rest of the drive. When they got to the auto store, Mark cheerfully took in the battery and Ellen followed. The battery was checked and it was dead, but the warranty had a few months left on it so they replaced it free of charge. Once at home, Mark put it back in the engine, Ellen started the car and it revved up happily. They both laughed as if a great miracle had happened.

"I have an idea," Mark said. "How would you like to have dinner?"

She stiffened and actually gasped. "I don't even know what that means!"

He chuckled. "Well, let's see… It could mean we go to a restaurant together or it could mean one of us cooks for the other one."

"I'm a chef! I told you that, right?"

"I'm a fireman. I've done a lot of cooking myself, but I'm sure not a chef. It could mean we cook together. Tell you what—I'm off on Friday so why don't I cook for us on Friday night. How about six o'clock. Casual. Do you like lasagna?"

She just nodded, then she realized her mouth was open. She closed it. Then she shook her head slightly and said, "Listen, I haven't been on a date."

"Since your husband passed away?"

"Since way before that."

He grinned at her. If she could read it right, the grin said he thought she was cute. Girlishly cute. That was a bit heady for a sixty-year-old woman who'd had but one man in her entire life.

"We'll have a good time. I'll keep it simple. We'll have a few laughs. Okay?"

"Okay," she said with a shrug.

"Great. That gives me something to look forward to!"

FIVE

Marni knew that one of Ellen's favorite parts of her job was planning the next season's shoots. It took weeks of preparation and practicing, both the recipe prep, photos and set prep. And yet Ellen seemed somewhat quiet and distracted. More than usual at any rate.

The first phase was meeting to discuss the production plan, which included as many as a hundred recipes and whittling it down to fifty and then thirty. They looked at a lot of cookbooks with pictures, deciding on some that were quick and easy, some that were fancy dinners for two or four and more gourmet, some hors d'oeuvres and larger skillet or baking dish meals, and some that were complicated and labor-intensive. They had basic categories to consider like beef, pork, poultry, fish and meatless. Finally came the desserts. Next there was scheduling. They tried to achieve balance in the productions.

On this particular day Sophia had classes in the morning

and worked for Marni in the afternoon. "I have a project for you, Sophia, and I'm going to stay out of your way while you do it. You can use my office and computer—I'd like you to mock up a variety of sets. I'd like to have twenty different place settings, buffets, linens, serving trays or dishes, floral designs, background accessories, et cetera. We'll copy them or make appropriate substitutions for the actual shoot. Would you like to try your own ideas?"

"Oh, yes, Marni! I can do this!"

"I thought you'd like that idea."

"When the kitchen has less traffic, I can show you some layouts."

"Excellent. That will be good practice for a future producer."

Sophia couldn't wait to get started on her set designs. She enjoyed that far more than washing dishes, chopping and measuring ingredients or filling out paperwork. Ellen and Marni sat at the dining table with notebooks and stacks of cookbooks. When they weren't planning the next season, they were watching their competition. Gordon Ramsey, The Barefoot Contessa, The Pioneer Woman and others.

"High on my list is veal rollatini," Marni said. "It's labor-intensive but so pretty, delicious, and we could do it with our new white asparagus spears. I would put it with dinner for two or four, gourmet, an hour when prep is done in advance."

Ellen was looking away, thinking. She had been pushing this recipe for a long time and now she wasn't paying attention. "Ellen?" Marni asked.

"Hmm?" Ellen replied.

"You're quieter than usual," Marni said. "Are you worried about something?"

Ellen seemed to snap to attention. "Oh, sorry, I was thinking. Yes, rollatini, perfect. I was thinking we should do more gourmet entrées."

"I was thinking about a variety of bruschetta—pesto, balsamic glaze, garlic bread and tomato…"

"Mozzarella and tomato and basil; prosciutto, chicken and herb…"

"We could have fun with that. And it could make a nice visual and be easy to shoot. We agree on that so now why don't you tell me what's bothering you?" Marni said.

"Nothing, really." Then she sighed.

"After all these years, you expect me to buy that? Something's wrong. Don't scare me now…"

"It really is a big nothing. My neighbor wants to cook dinner for me. Lasagna. Friday night."

"Oh. What neighbor?"

"The one on the right. Mark. He's nice. He has blown away my leaves and shoveled my walk and pulled in my trash cans. But dinner is…"

"Is what?"

"I don't know. It's almost a date."

Marni was startled. "What's wrong with that?"

"I haven't had dinner with a man since my father passed away a couple of years ago!"

Marni asked, "Does he know you're a chef? Because surely you can out-cook him! Ellen, that could be fun."

"I'm going to have to cancel," she said. "I'm not good at this sort of thing. I've had an upset stomach since he suggested it."

"Ellen, come on! Be brave! Worst-case scenario, you have a new friend who will sometimes shovel the walk."

"He took me to get a new battery for my car," she said. "I just don't have any idea what I'd talk about."

"What did you talk about when you went for the new battery?" Marni asked.

"He talked. His wife died."

"Oh. Well, that sounds cheery… He invited you to dinner. Does that mean he likes to cook? Because you could talk about cooking until you're blue."

"He'll be so bored," she said. "I don't think I could stand that. You know, when he has to tell me that having dinner together is not working for him and when he thanks me politely and dismisses me."

"Aren't you getting way ahead of yourself?" Marni asked. "What if you have a wonderful time? Find you have lots in common? Maybe you'll have a lot to talk about. Maybe you'll find you're attracted to—"

"Don't even say it!" Ellen shot back.

"Well, come on! You're not dead yet!"

"Some parts of me are! The parts that haven't been used in decades, at least."

"There must have been a time when you were attracted? To Ralph? In younger years?"

"Long ago and faraway…"

"Don't you remember it fondly?" Marni asked. "Because that's the only part I do remember fondly…"

"I'm not sure, as a matter of fact," Ellen said. "I think Ralph talked me into it. He was very social. Lots of laughs, lots of jokes, lots of people around. Everyone loved Ralph. Whole groups of people were devastated by the loss when he had his aneurism and never recovered. But slowly they all drifted away. I couldn't go through something like that again."

"I understand. Believe me," Marni said, thinking of the many things she had no desire to go through again. Like a cheating husband or a violent husband, to name just two.

"But this is a whole new experience. You shouldn't reject it just because you're shy."

"There are not that many choices, though. Are there?"

"Yes, there are! You could find yourself a nice friend! You don't have to make a commitment! You don't have to pledge your life just because someone bakes you a lasagna! You can keep things simple and manageable, can't you? I would never get married again but I wouldn't mind rolling over in the night and running my big toe along a hairy leg! Is that asking too much?"

Ellen was quiet for a long moment. "It might get you into trouble."

Marni and Ellen did manage to get some work done despite what had become their mutual distraction. But Marni was now thinking about her own romantic life, which was nil. It caused her to look over her accounts and see if there was any way she could afford to loan Jeff money for his restaurant. She did so knowing she'd never see repayment and that bit deep. But they had history and she didn't want Jeff to suffer too much. In fact, she'd like it if he could be successful and secure.

Marni checked on Bella at least twice a day, not convinced that all her problems in her marriage could be solved by a frozen fettuccine Alfredo, even though she was a believer in the power of delicious food.

"We're getting along," Bella said. "But there's something wrong between us and I'm not sure what it is. I don't know if it's Jason's work—he does have a demanding job. And I suppose all couples bicker now and then. Did you and my dad fight?"

Marni wondered how they had made it thirty-five years

before that question came up. She was momentarily stricken. "We…ah…fought. We were young. We were young and inexperienced and stupid and… My young husband had a bad temper. Bella, Jason doesn't have a temper, does he?"

"Nah, he's passive-aggressive. He has a pout. I think I'm the one with the temper. And lately I can get upset about anything. Either that's the problem or else Jason is pouting too much, I can't tell. It just seems like he's…" She paused. "He seems distant. Very quiet."

"Did you call that counselor?"

"Not yet. But I will."

"Bella, you promised!!"

"I will! I've been so busy at work! Everyone from Carson City to Reno is in trouble and so much is landing on my desk it's not even funny."

"I can't imagine what is funny at the prosecutor's office! Now I want you to—"

"Listen, I have a favor to ask. It should be something you enjoy."

"It's very rare that a favor and enjoyment go together," Marni grumbled.

"Jason is sick of my low-cal dinners and he makes excuses to miss them—everything from meetings to working late, then he comes home with pizza on his breath. I thought, it's time for a girls' night out. I called Nettie. She's in. You can invite Ellen or Sophia or both of them."

"For dinner?" Marni asked.

"Yes, dinner. And Nettie suggested a show or something. She's going to check things out and come up with a suggestion. We can spend a little time together, have a laugh or two, and I get a break from Jason Cranky Butt."

"That's probably the best idea you've had lately. With ev-

erything you both have going on, you and Jason could probably use some time apart," Marni said. "When?"

"Friday night. Dinner at seven?"

"And then a show?" Marni groaned. "Can you at least make
it six for dinner? I'm just not up to late nights out."

Bella clucked disapprovingly. "Do not get old on me," she
said threateningly. "You've always been the life of the party!"

"I'm afraid that train has left the station," Marni said.

Marni floated the idea of a girls' night out to Ellen and
Sophia.

"Oh, that couldn't be more perfect," Ellen said enthusias-
tically. And that was most unusual as well.

"Really? You'll join us, then?" Marni said suspiciously.

"Can I join you for dinner and then excuse myself? I'm
planning to give my regrets to my charming neighbor but I'd
rather have a real excuse than make something up…"

"But why do you want to make an excuse to him?" Sophia
asked. "If he is charming?"

"Because it could be meant as more than just a neighborly
gesture," Ellen said. "I wouldn't want to give him the impression that I have any…you know…interest."

"Does he want to take you on a date?" Sophia asked.

"It's a long story, but he's offered to cook me a lasagna on
Friday night."

"It's not a long story," Marni interrupted. "He's been a very
good neighbor for at least two years, helping out with occasional leaf-blowing, snow removal, trash-can hauling and
most recently, car-battery replacement. They've been cordial
and he's single and loves to cook."

"That sounds so perfect," Sophia said.

"But not at all appealing to me, I'm afraid. And I wouldn't want to say that. I'd never want to offend him," Ellen said.

"Eventually you'll have to either spend a little friendly time with him or offend him," Marni said.

"I'm hoping to avoid both."

"You're very stubborn," Marni said. "Sophia? Would you like to go out with a few old ladies and one pregnant lawyer?"

"I'm afraid I have plans for Friday after work." Then her face lit up. "I have a date. With a man who is also charming."

"Well, now," Marni said. "Someone you met at school?"

"This time, no. I met him at a club when I was out with my girlfriends."

"Do your friends know him?"

"Oh, yes, they've seen him out before. He used to date someone's cousin. He's very handsome. Very."

"But do you know him?" Marni asked. "And do you know people who are connected to him?"

"I know him now. I talk to him all the time. He took me out for ice cream. I know all about him. He's so nice. His sister has a baby so he is also an uncle and is so sweet with the baby. I think he's a good catch."

"And has your father met him?" Marni asked.

"Not yet, but soon. His mama calls him Angel and I think he is an angel."

"You've met his family?" Marni asked.

"No, but he showed me a picture of the baby and he talks about him all the time."

"Sophia, how long have you known him?"

"Only a month, but we already have something. A connection. The first time he called me we talked for hours."

While Ellen and Marni went on talking about Ellen's date in hushed tones, Sophia fell silent and idly scrolled through the pictures on her laptop. She didn't want to talk about Angel anymore because she had lied. It hadn't been a month that she'd known him. It had been a couple of weeks. And it was wrong and she knew it. She just didn't know what about it was so wrong. It had been a very strange and peculiar night.

She had been truthful about meeting him in a club when she was out with her girlfriends and some of them knew him or knew of him. The moment she saw him, it was as if rockets went off and fireworks lit the sky as they sat in a dingy club. While her girlfriends danced, Angel, short for Angelo, sat at the bar and flirted with her for a very long time. Long enough for her to have a bit too much to drink. It was not typical of her; she blamed Angel for distracting her so she wasn't paying attention.

At one point a couple of her friends noticed she was looking drunk. When they came to talk to her, Angel offered to drive her home and make sure she was safe and she was so grateful. She woke up a few hours later, her head pounding. She was sitting in Angel's car in what must have been his driveway, and she had no idea where she was.

"It's okay," he said soothingly. "I didn't take you to your house for two reasons—one, you couldn't seem to give me directions. And two, I didn't think you'd want your father to see you being dragged into the house." From out of nowhere he produced a bottle of water. "Here, drink this. You'll feel better."

"What the hell," she muttered, opening the bottled water.

"I'd wonder if someone slipped you something, but you were with me all night. You put away a lot of wine."

She guzzled the water. "That isn't like me," she said, between gulps. "I apologize. Lo siento mucho."

"De nada," he said, smiling sweetly. "Would you like to go home? Can you walk a straight line if your papa is awake?"

"I'm feeling much better, and yes, I should go home. What time—" She looked at her watch. "Holy Virgin! It's four in the morning!"

He laughed. "You had quite a night. Want to give me directions now?"

She gave him instructions and he drove her home, walked her to the door, made sure she had her purse and phone, and gave her a very proper kiss. It was on the lips, but proper. "I'll call you to see how you're doing tomorrow."

"Do you want my phone number?"

He tilted his head and gave her a slightly perplexed look. "You gave it to me. At the bar."

"I don't know what's wrong with me," she said. "I don't do that! I take a number, not give!"

"I guess you trusted me not to hurt you. I can keep you safe."

And he called her the next day when she was feeling much better after her brief hangover. Everything else she told Marni and Ellen was true—they talked for hours, he told her everything about his family and asked her many questions about hers, and they seemed to have a very strong connection.

But there was one thing that bothered her. He called and texted her a lot. Too much. She made up a little lie and said that her boss, Marni, insisted her phone be turned off during work hours and, of course, if she was in class, the phone had to be off. And he said, "Oh, baby, you should have told me! I don't want you to be distracted. Tell me when a good time to call is."

Baby? She thought about the fact that he never called her

by her first name. He started to call her Chi Chi or Baby and said they were terms of endearment.

She knew he was moving too fast. Yet, once she was with him or talking to him, she wanted that. He told her she was the most beautiful woman he'd ever known, but that did not trigger her. That was a compliment. He said she was sweet, but she didn't buy it; she didn't think of herself as sweet. He loved her long dark hair and nearly black eyes. She didn't mind hearing these things. He admired her intelligence; she was working on a master's degree in fine arts, after all. But the thing that reeled her in was his proclamation that she would be a sensation as a news anchor, for that was her dream. "Tell me all about it; tell me your plan. I think you'll have your own news program someday. The sound of your voice hyp-notizes me."

That did it. She longed to be admired, to have someone believe in her dreams. And she thought maybe she had found him.

Before leaving for work on Friday morning, Ellen walked across her front yard to Mark's house with a note card in her hand. It was her seldom-used stationery, embossed and bor-dered with a matching envelope. She was just about to wedge it into the front door when it opened. She jumped back in surprise and said, "Oh!"

"Good morning, Ellen," Mark said.

She waved the envelope. "I didn't want to disturb you so I wouldn't have called even if I'd known your number. I'm afraid something has come up. I have a business dinner to-night. I'll be home too late for another dinner. Plus," she added, trying to laugh lightly, "My waistline can't take it!" She could feel herself blushing.

"I understand," he said. "How about tomorrow night?"

"Uh. Oh. That probably won't work for me, either."

He folded his arms across his chest and smiled. "Okay, either you don't like me or you have some issue that keeps you from having dinner with an interested man."

She sighed deeply. It was the word *interested* that got in her way. "Mark, I like you fine. I think you're very nice. And I love having you for a neighbor. You're so thoughtful. But I've been single for a long time and when I was married, my husband wasn't well. It was a slow and difficult road. I find I'm not very well-equipped for anything more than a wave across the yard. I hope you can understand."

"Of course," he said. "At the risk of offending you, I wasn't planning to propose," he said with a laugh. "As for marriage, I also lost a spouse after a lengthy and difficult illness and the thought of doing that again doesn't appeal to me, either. But after being alone for a few years, I am thinking I really miss a little female companionship. I'm not looking for anything complicated, of course. What I mean is, I wasn't thinking about commitments or long-term plans. Frankly I was thinking, if it worked out that we hit it off, that would be nice. And if we didn't...?" He shrugged. "You're the first woman I've suggested such an idea to."

"But I won't be the last," she said. "You're a very good-looking man."

"Thank you. And you're a beautiful woman."

"Oh, please," she said, both amused and irritated. "I know better than that!"

"Apparently you don't. But never mind. Just have a good time at your business dinner and think about tomorrow night or even Sunday night. You can cross out your excuse, if you can think of one, and bring me a new note. I can freeze the lasagna. It's very good," he said with a grin. "It might be as good as yours."

"I don't know about that," she said.

"There's only one way to find out."

Friday night, girls' night. Nettie showed up in her out-to-be-seen clothes with a big smile on her face. Bella was looking glorious in a black sheath, her cheeks rosy, her eyes sparkling and her dark hair thick and shiny, like an advertisement for pregnancy. Ellen came from work so she was still wearing a comfortable pair of pants and lightweight V-neck sweater. Marni had changed into something a bit more of the evening-out mode—she wore comfortably fitted black pants and a pink-and-black tunic that sparkled and dropped below her hips.

This foursome had a favorite hideaway called Rosa's owned by a delightful Basque family and it was not on what would be called restaurant row but rather tucked away in an inauspicious strip mall. It would go unnoticed to anyone not familiar with the place. It sat between a sushi bar and a tattoo parlor but there was a red carpet to the curb and two Grecian urns filled with plastic vines on either side of the door. The little strip mall also boasted a dance studio, a submarine sandwich place, a caterer and an alterations business. Most of the non-restaurant shops were closed by six so parking for the eateries was plentiful.

Marni loved trying new foods, but she also loved dependably delicious things and Rosa's was a favorite. It gave her great pleasure that she had given Rosa's her thumbs-up when she had not given Jeff's restaurant the same endorsement. That also made the food even more appealing.

Marni ordered, as always. Sometimes when they were all

out together, one of the other women would suggest something but they usually just let her take charge. She was the expert, after all. And they also let her pick up the check. Though it was never spoken of, except on Google, Marni was clearly a millionaire by now while Bella was a new young lawyer working for the county, Nettie was a professor at a state college and Ellen was a producer for a cable network.

Marni ordered a cold shellfish platter served on ice, then a round of salads, bread and olive oil, a vegetable marinade platter and a side of pasta to round it all out. Then they caught up on the latest—Ellen had to fill them in on her conversation with Mark and his insistence that they try dinner another night. Bella had much to contribute about her growing pregnancy and it seemed she was feeling a little more tender toward Jason today. Nettie talked about the current politics in the English department. They ate and laughed and ate more. With a great deal of food still left on the table, Marni ordered Basque cheesecake for dessert.

"Why don't we do this more often?" Marni asked.

"Because you resist," Nettie said.

"I always think I just want to stay home, go to bed early, but then once I'm out with you women, I come alive!"

"Wait until you see the show I picked out for us! We're going to Miss Ruby's," Nettie said.

"That club we went to last year? With the comedians?" Marni asked.

"Same club," Nettie said. "It's open mic night but I don't know what kind of talent."

"I hope it's comedians again!"

Ellen said good-night at the restaurant, leaving Marni, Bella and Nettie to go on to the club. They piled into Bella's new minivan and headed for Reno, the south side. Miss Ruby's was tucked in the back corner of a large hotel. They worked their way across the main floor of the casino, through the noise of the slot machines and the laughter of hundreds of patrons.

There was a line holding at the front of the club, people queuing through the gambling tables and slot machines. A sign on the front door of the club said Impressionists Tonight. In smaller script right under that, it said Open Mic, indicating it would be anyone's guess who was performing. There were so many people waiting it took quite a while to get inside and find a table. Then it took time to get settled and even longer to order drinks.

The room was large and dark with an impressive stage in the front and a beautiful long bar along one side. There were booths in the back of the room and tables filling the rest of the floor. On the stage was a beautiful baby grand piano and a microphone. The house lights were up as the waitstaff weaved through the tables and the bartenders were putting on their own show by flipping bottles in the air before pouring. A young man and woman in waitstaff livery came to their table, fun and animated. "Ladies' night?" asked the young woman.

"We don't have any men good enough for this table," quipped the young man.

"We'll look, though," said his partner. "What are we drinking tonight?"

Marni felt unexpectedly alive. It was nice to be among people so energetic. She always thought she'd rather have a quiet evening, and she was rarely right about that. She went along reluctantly to many events and in the end was almost always glad she had.

Laughter rang out from the surrounding tables, drinks arrived and people ordered doubles, as experienced showgoers did, knowing the waitstaff would retreat when the show started. It seemed a long time before the lights dimmed and a comedian came to the stage, opening the show with a few jokes and announcements. He was dressed as a ringleader for the circus and he gave a rundown of what was to come. "All our impersonators and performers have appeared on this stage before, the best of the best, and we hope to see them again and again. We're starting out tonight's show with the Rat Pack!"

The performers leaped onto the stage from behind the curtain, Frank Sinatra, Dean Martin, Joey Bishop, Peter Lawford and Sammy Davis Jr.—amazing look-alikes. Their voices were so purely recognizable; heads were turning throughout the crowd as people tried to determine if they were lip-synching from old recordings. The group performed for almost fifteen minutes.

Next, to the thrill of the audience, Elton John came strutting out in full vintage Elton regalia, including platform shoes and oversized glasses. Next up was a ringer for Barbra Streisand. Her voice was stunningly on target, her hair and makeup absolutely exquisite. Bella leaned over to Marni and said, "Is that a man?"

"I honestly don't know!" Marni answered, but surely the performer was a female impersonator. And the best she'd ever seen.

Next came Elvis, and the audience went crazy.

Then, silencing the crowd with her amazingly authentic husky voice, was Adele. She wore her thick hair down, her gown a glittering masterpiece.

"Hello," she sang. "It's me."

The singer was enchanting and the audience was clearly as mesmerized as Marni. The voice was spot on, as was the smile and the hand gestures. But there was something about her that caused Marni to frown as she tried to figure out what it was. She was heavily made up, of course, but the shape of the eyebrows and nose were familiar. At the end of the song when Adele smiled, Marni gasped. She knew that smile, or at least most of it.

Yes, it was definitely him! Tom. Her coffee date.

And what talent! He was undeniably gifted. He carried the song with passion and style.

Finally, the last performer to close the show was Cher and this was undeniably a female impersonator, reed thin with a discernable Adam's apple. Her voice was glorious and the way she strode across the stage with those long legs was nothing short of perfection.

Marni said nothing, she just clapped and cheered along with the rest of the audience. It was the best Vegas-type show she'd seen in years. The house lights came up and the ringmaster brought out the performers one at a time and the whole audience rose to cheer. Marni stood, adding a hearty woo-hoo to her clapping. She grinned her biggest grin. They locked eyes and she could see Tom freeze momentarily.

She nodded in his direction, smiling her warmest smile. She gave him a discreet wave and was suddenly filled with emotion. What a talent he had. What she didn't know was, is this something he kept private? He sure hadn't mentioned it during their coffee date. He'd been all about his success in real estate, his great negotiating skills. He certainly looked shocked to see her.

She would say nothing. She felt an urge to brag about knowing him. He was so good! But until she knew whether or not this was something Tom was open about, she'd be quiet. But something she had not seen coming—she now found him much more interesting and was going to make a point of calling him. She would compliment him, for sure.

And she'd ask him if his friends and family knew about his talent. If the answer was no, she'd assure him she would keep it to herself. But she would make sure he knew that would be disappointing. Talent like that should be on the stage!

"That was the best," Bella said. "Did you enjoy it, Mama?"

"Totally! We'll have to do it again!"

SIX

Sophia spent over an hour primping after work. She wanted to be beautiful for Angelo. Tonight they could be alone because her papi had a function at the college and wouldn't be home for dinner. Angel had told her, rather sternly, not to mention that he was coming over—he said there was no reason her father needed to know. "We'll play it loose, pretend it was last-minute and I just dropped by. If you tell him ahead of time, he might decide to come home early."

"But that is like lying," Sophia had argued. "That is not something I do with my papi. He respects my decisions and he might not if I start to lie to him!"

"Let's just try it my way and see how it works."

But she had told her father the truth, anyway. She had mentioned her friend Angelo might drop by; they might watch a movie. "Is this a boyfriend?" her father had asked.

"We will see," she answered coyly.

But in her heart, she was thinking, *Yes, Angel is my boyfriend.* She hadn't had many. A few young men had caught her attention, but not like this. Angel was not only handsome and clever, he was also so bold. She hadn't realized what a difference that would make.

When he came in the front door, he immediately pulled her into his arms and devoured her in a deep penetrating kiss. She hadn't realized until that moment how much she enjoyed the feeling of being overwhelmed by passion. He held her tightly against him, running his hands through her long hair, whispering against her lips. "You didn't call me back," he said.

She giggled. "I listened to your messages; you didn't ask me to call you."

"I called you twelve times today," he whispered.

"I was working..."

"You didn't even text!"

"You knew I was working," she said. "Marni doesn't like me to use my phone while I work. I explained that to you."

"Who is this Marni?"

"The chef I work for," she said. "She's very important and it's a good job! I am an intern in television production and it's not a small thing. I am paid and get credits in my college program. I can't call you during work unless it's an emergency. But it wasn't an emergency."

"How do you know? It could have been."

"If it was, you would have said."

"We're going to have a problem if you're going to leave me hanging like that," he said, adding small kisses to her cheeks. He moved his hands to her butt and pulled her hard against himself.

She pushed him away. "I didn't leave anybody hanging," she said. "You were not hanging for anything!"

He pulled her tight. "We decided I wouldn't call you unless I needed to, and if I called, you would answer or call back!"

She put her hands against his chest to make some space. "You didn't leave a message to say you needed anything! I thought you understood I wouldn't answer because I was working. Weren't you working?"

"Not today, because I got fired! I wanted to tell you but you weren't there for me! So is that how it's going to be? When I need you, you're not there? Because other things are more important? And I mean nothing?"

"I didn't know," she said. "How could I know?"

"You could know if you called me back." Suddenly he pushed her away. "I'm so disappointed. I thought I could count on you."

"Of course you can count on me! But you have to tell me if you need something. I thought you were just...you know... checking in. Because you wanted to. I can't read your mind, Angelo."

"Were you busy with someone else? Maybe you don't care about me as much as you say."

She frowned in confusion. She couldn't recall telling him how much she cared. But she hated that he would be disappointed in her, as if she'd done something wrong. "I don't like to argue," she said. "I made us some hamburgers. We can have something to eat, watch a movie or something, and there's ice cream for later. Why fight? We have nothing to fight about. We can eat and you can tell me what happened with your job."

"I can't talk about it," he said in a sulking voice.

As far as Sophia knew, Angelo was working at a local restaurant as a busboy, cleaning up, wiping off tables, hauling heavy bins of dirty dishes. He told her he expected to be added to the waitstaff soon, to be a waiter and make more in tips. She had praised him for working hard and trying to better himself while inside she was thinking it wasn't much of a goal. But still, at least he was working. "If you don't want to talk about it, okay. Do you want a hamburger?"

"I'm not that hungry anymore. I think I should just go. I don't think you're that happy to see me…"

There was a voice in her head telling her to say he was right, he should just go. This was absurd, acting as if she'd done something to apologize for when, all things considered, he had been the one in the wrong. He was being ridiculous and unreasonable. But she just wasn't made that way, she wasn't brought up that way. First of all, her mother had always stressed kindness and excellent manners. And then there was that thing with some Latino men. They were raised to believe they owned the world. A woman must handle a man's ego with care. That's how her mother and entire extended family had behaved.

She was no longer as attracted to him as she had been. But, for reasons she could not identify, she wanted him to be happy with her.

"Let's see if a hamburger makes you feel better…"

He shrugged, looked down at his feet as if he wasn't sure. "I suppose. Since I'm already here."

He didn't say since you've gone to the trouble, he said okay because he was here. She wondered if that was a signal, but she couldn't quite let herself believe that. She said nothing. Instead she took his hand and pulled him toward the kitchen. He found himself a place at the kitchen table and sat.

Sophia began to get the hamburger patties and condiments out of the refrigerator—lettuce, tomatoes, pickles. "I can put some frozen French fries in the oven if you think you'd eat some."

"I might. Put some in. That would be good," he said. "Your father has a rich house," he said, looking around.

"He's a very smart man," she replied.

"He must have been born to money to have such a nice house."

She laughed lightly, beginning to become more comfortable again. "Not so much," she said. "His people are from Iowa. He grew up on a farm. The farm is still there and he says it will pass to his brothers. Just as it was in my family, in Argentina, except I have no brothers. My papi is a teacher. And he is also a scientist. He teaches at the college."

"You said he was a farmer!"

"He would tell you he is a farmer first. He is a very educated man and he does experiments with crops."

"And is not Latino," Angelo said.

"My mother was Latina. My papi is multicultural; Irish, Swedish, Welsh, German and he says probably other things also. He studies agricultural science. That's how he met my mother in Argentina. He was studying there."

"So he is rich," Angelo said.

"I think he is important at the college but teachers aren't usually rich."

"But you will be rich," he said.

That made her smile, not because she hoped to be rich but because she wanted to be a successful television journalist. That was one of several reasons she was so grateful to be interning with Marni. She was learning all about television and programming and development.

"I want to have my own program someday, like Marni. I don't think I'll be a cook. It will be some other kind of program. But Marni says to keep an open mind. She didn't start out as a chef. But she also didn't start out in television. That fell in her lap. She was doing demonstrations using items in the kitchen, the home. Kitchen tools, cleaning products, like that."

She slid the fries in the oven, sliced up a tomato, some cheese and onion and picked up the platter of hamburger patties. "I'm going to put these on the grill. Would you stay here or come outside?" When he said nothing, she added, "Do you want to cook the meat?"

"I'll help you," he said.

He followed her out onto the patio. She put the platter on the counter beside the grill and lifted the lid to start it. She heard his long slow whistle. She turned to see him taking in the yard. He used a flat hand to shield his eyes from the sun as he looked at the garden. "This is his farm, then?" he asked.

"It's my papi's garden, yes."

He shook his head in what appeared to be sheer wonder. "My mama would die for a garden like this. You are very lucky."

"Papi gives away most of his crop," she said. "We can make a basket for your mama if you want. Does she like to garden?"

His face went dark again and he muttered something unintelligible. She ignored him and began putting the hamburger patties on the grill. After a few minutes he came up behind her, reached around her for the spatula and took over, pressing the burgers down to flatten them and then turning them.

"I'll go put out plates. You can do this if I leave?"

"Of course," he said.

Although it hadn't been a part of her plan, she went to a little extra trouble putting out plates and utensils. She used placemats and cloth napkins, even though she'd have to launder them later.

When Angelo brought in the burgers, he seemed visibly happy. As though something had gone right for him. She saw that he was waiting at his place and so she served him some fries and put a burger on his plate. He said, "Ahhh," as he began building his burger with layers of mayo, onion, pickles and lettuce.

She began doing the same.

When he bit into his burger he moaned in ecstasy. She felt a lift of success in her heart, though she wasn't sure why.

She cut her burger in half and almost gagged. It was raw in the middle. Of course he had never asked her how she'd like hers done. From what she observed, he wasn't all that familiar with a grill and wouldn't have been able to deliver in any case. She nibbled around the edges where the beef was well done as he devoured his, but he never noticed even though there was a puddle of bloodied liquid gathering on her plate, wetting her fries.

"Tomorrow, we should go to the lake," he said. "The water is still cold but the temperature is supposed to be in the eighties. It'll be great."

She didn't say anything. She was busy wondering how people could eat raw meat.

"I swear, even my mama can't make a hamburger like this. Chi Chi, you are the best. I didn't even know I wanted a girlfriend, then you came along and I am a new man."

He finished his hamburger, leaving not a speck, and she picked up their plates, taking them to the sink.

"My day started out so bad but I think it's going to end pretty good, thanks to you spoiling me. I felt like crap when I woke up, then even though I hurried, I was late to work and they had a big breakfast crowd." She rinsed the plates and he came to the kitchen, hoisted himself up on the counter and sat there. "I was late because my sister used the car last night and it was on empty this morning when I had to get to work. My boss caught me coming in the back door and was yelling at me before I could even tell her the reason. She's such a bitch; I wasn't about to explain to her, anyway. So I just went back home and back to bed."

She turned off the water and looked at him. "And you're fired?" she asked.

"It was a crappy job," he said. "I hated it, anyway. You done there? Let's go get cozy on the couch. Or better yet, the bed."

"I don't think the bed," she said, scooting away from him. "We can watch a movie. Or we could go out…"

"We could watch a movie in bed," he suggested.

"But what if my papi comes home?"

"He's out, right? You didn't tell him I was coming over, did you?"

"I had to," she said. "He asked me what I was doing tonight. I told him the truth, to lie would be dishonest."

"I told you not to! Now you've ruined everything!"

"How do you know that?" she asked. "He trusts me because I never lie to him!"

The words were barely out of her mouth when she heard the garage door rising and a moment later the door from the garage to the kitchen opened.

"Shit," Angel muttered. "See? Maybe next time you'll listen to me!"

Her father walked in and put a stack of books on the kitchen counter. "Hi," he said casually. He stuck out a hand to Angelo. "Hi, I'm Sam."

"Angelo," he replied stiffly.

"Sorry to interrupt your evening, my friends, but I was able to escape after the hors d'oeuvres. Thank God. It looked to be a long boring night. I didn't really need to be there. What are you guys up to tonight?"

Sophia started to respond. "We had a couple of hamburgers and now I think we're going to watch—"

"I have to get going," Angelo said. "I have to get gas on the way home."

"Nice to meet you. I'm sure I'll see you around," Sam said, gathering up his books and leaving the kitchen.

"Oh," she said to Angelo. She knew she should be glad he was leaving. He was angry again and his mood swings were wearing her out, but she couldn't help it, she was disappointed. She was secretly asking herself why she was disappointed and she couldn't quite figure it out. When he was happy, he was so fun and sexy. But when he was unhappy, she felt oddly guilty, as if it was her fault. Of course, it wasn't.

He was pouty as he left, hands plunged in his pockets, looking at his feet, shuffling along. "I'll call you later," he said. Then out the door he went.

That left Sophia to try to find something to watch alone on television. If she had known the evening would turn out this way, she would have found something better to do.

Ellen was glad she had begged off early, though she usually loved getting together with the women for girl time. As she pulled into her neighborhood at about eight that night, it seemed so peaceful, as if everyone had gone to bed, although it was early, the summer sun still struggling to say good-night. When she approached her drive, she noticed a box sitting in front of the garage door.

She parked in the drive and had a look at the box. Inside was a fancy bottle of Crown Royal and two glasses. The note read: *If you're not too tired after your dinner meeting, let's have a nightcap.* And beneath that, there was a phone number.

Well now, she thought. This might be a good idea. Better than committing to a whole meal. She and Mark could have a drink together. That would only take a half hour. Like a trial run. There was that screaming voice saying it was a terrifying thought, getting friendly with a man, no matter how innocent. But there was a warm and fuzzy voice that said a drink would be nice. What harm could it do?

She pulled her car into the garage and took the box into the house. After turning on the lights, she got out her phone and texted him.

It's such a lovely evening, let's meet on my patio for that drink.

And then she began to tremble. *If this goes badly, I'll have to move,* she thought.

She got out two tall glasses for water, wiped out the cocktail glasses with a dish towel and distributed ice into all the glasses. She lit the candle on the patio table and just as she did so, she heard the clang of the back gate. By the time Mark came around the corner of the house, two full water glasses, two cocktail glasses and the bottle sat on the table.

He grinned handsomely. "Perfect." He opened the bottle and asked, "Two fingers?" while he held two fingers against the glass.

"Sure."

He raised his glass to her in a toast. "Here's to perfect summer nights."

It was a beautiful night. It was almost relaxing.

"How was dinner?" Mark asked.

"It wasn't what you would expect. The woman I work

with is a television chef. I'm her assistant and have also studied the culinary arts. When we go out to eat, we go out to taste. Marni always orders. She chooses a selection, asks for extra plates and everyone is expected to have a sampling of their choice. I had a beet salad, cold shellfish and a warm pasta with tomatoes, ham and capers. It was delicious."

"I think I'd like that," he said. "If they'd make the portions smaller, every night would be a buffet."

"I bet you love the casino buffets," she said.

"I admit, I've indulged. But it sounds better the way you do it. I always enjoyed cooking at the firehouse. Now that gets competitive! We're all trying to outdo each other. How did you get started in cooking?"

"My mother's kitchen," she said. "I was barely a teenager when I was put in charge of big family dinners. I come from a large family, lots of aunts and uncles and cousins, all in this northern Nevada part of the world. I studied education but never worked as a teacher. I went directly into a restaurant kitchen and spent many years as a sous chef. I've worked with Marni for over twenty years, since she was appearing on a local morning show on Channel 3."

They talked then about what drew Mark to firefighting. He was young and restless, wanted to do something challenging and took the test and applied when he was twenty-one, loved it, stayed with it. Next thing he knew he was married, had a son and rose through the ranks. "For me, it was a lucrative, exciting career. I didn't even think about retiring until my wife got sick."

That led to him asking about Ellen's husband, Ralph. Before long they knew each other's stories and to Ellen's surprise, they had many things in common, not just the fact that they'd both lost their spouses. There was the cooking, the love of the outdoors and hiking, their closeness to family. Ellen had her siblings and nieces and nephews; Mark had his son and grandsons and also a brother and his family.

They had a second drink, a very short one, and before long it was after ten. Neither of them yawned and Ellen was not at all bored. She thoroughly enjoyed his company and began to dread the end of their evening chat.

"It's past my bedtime and I bet it's past yours," Mark said. "Thanks for letting me invade your evening."

"I enjoyed it," she said.

"I put that lasagna in the freezer. I'm working at the grocery store Sunday to Wednesday but any other day I can pull it out and we can have a dinner. If you're interested."

"I can make a Caesar salad," she said, surprising herself. "I make my own dressing. It's pretty garlicky."

"I tend to overdo the garlic sometimes," he said.

"Do you still want to try tomorrow night?" she asked.

"I'd like that."

"I'll add some bruschetta to the meal," she said.

He laughed. "We better watch it; we'll get fat. We both love food too much!"

"How about six?" she asked.

"Perfect."

And she thought, *Yes*.

The inside of Bella's van was full of chatter, but only from Bella and Nettie. They were laughing and carrying on about the show, which was thrilling. Marni was in the front seat and a bit quiet.

"Who was your favorite, Marni?" Nettie asked.

Without a doubt it was Adele! "I was partial to Elton John," she said.

"The way you were staring at Adele, I would have guessed that was your favorite," Bella said.

"You're right. I loved her. Did she look familiar to you?"

"No, why?"

"Bella, that was Tom. My coffee date? I wasn't going to say anything but there I go, blurting it out. By the way he was looking at me… He was shocked when we made eye contact. I bet his son doesn't know about his special talent."

"Oh, my God, really? I did think Adele was awfully tall!"

"And where did he get those boobs? They were splendid," Nettie said.

"She," Bella corrected. "She identifies as female when she's dressed female, like tonight. I think."

"Just tonight?" Marni asked. "He was a man at our coffee date. Right down to talking about himself and how successful he was."

"I go by the Tootsie rule," Nettie said.

"The movie, *Tootsie*?" Marni asked.

"Yep. When she was dressed as a woman, no one knew her as a man. It doesn't matter what might be under her bloomers; she was Tootsie. Besides, what's under her bloomers is no one's business, just like it's no one's business what's under yours."

"What's under mine is a Gymboree class and The Bump is in first place. I think he enjoyed the show. There is no question, Adele was a star tonight. Wow, " Bella said.

"How about you?" Marni asked. "Did you have fun with the old ladies?"

"Hey, speak for yourself," Nettie complained.

"I did," Bella said. "It was a good break from Mr. Crabby Pants."

After dropping off her mother and aunt, Bella headed home. For no reason she could fathom, her mood sank as she drew closer to home. Her energy plummeted and she was suddenly fatigued. As she approached the door to her condo, she realized she dreaded seeing her husband.

She thought she might be losing her mind. Jason was darling and good-natured and she had been putting him through hell lately. Her mood swings were killing them. It wasn't her fault, she knew this. It was a combination of the hormones she'd taken for IVF and the wacky hormonal world of pregnancy.

Then she opened the door and all her logic flew out the window. There was an empty pizza box and several empty beer cans on the kitchen counter, Jason's shoes and sweaty socks were on the floor, his smelly workout shirt was draped over the chair, his open briefcase on the coffee table, piles of briefs on the floor, chair and coffee table. And there was Jason sprawled on the couch, asleep. The TV was on, the volume low. It was on a news channel, probably because he'd been watching a ball game that was now over. And he was snoring.

She started to cry. She had no idea why. She wasn't one to cry over a messy house. She began to gather up the trash, noisily tossing it in the trash bin.

He stirred. "Oh, hi, honey." He snorted and sat up. "I didn't hear you come in. Did you have fun?"

She didn't answer him. Suddenly she knew it was not the hormones or the pregnancy or the mess that irked her and made her cry. It was the fact that he had enjoyed a large pizza and several beers while she'd been out with her mother and aunt and had eaten salad.

"I'll get that, Bella," he said. "I was going to clean up but I fell asleep. I went to the gym to get some exercise, then had pizza and beer and… Well, you can see. It did me in."

"Pretty inconsiderate of you," she said. "The house was immaculate when I left."

"I'll take care of it, okay?"

"If you'd been on a diet for six months, you'd understand."

"Are you crying?" he asked. "Come on, baby, don't cry. I'll clean up. Don't get all emotional."

"I can't help it!" she wailed. She dropped the trash and blew her nose. "I just feel so unappreciated. Just leave everything. You can clean up the house tomorrow."

"Um, I'm going to play golf tomorrow," he said. "But I'll be home early."

Her jaw dropped and she was statue still. "Let me get this right—you want me to look at your dirty dishes and trash and mess until you get home from the *golf course*? You'll come home sweaty and tired and want a nap. Maybe we can pick our way around your papers and clothes and shoes until Sunday? I didn't know you had plans to play golf. I thought we were going to look at baby furniture!"

"Steve called tonight. They need a fourth. I forgot about the baby furniture. But I'll clean up tonight and I'll be home early tomorrow."

"I'm going to bed," she said, sniffing all the way to the bedroom. "You don't care one bit that I'm big as a cow, uncomfortable, starving and have to clean up after a grown man."

"Here we go again..."

"You don't even want this baby!"

"Don't be ridiculous! Didn't I agree on all that miserable infertility shit?"

She gasped. "You think I enjoyed it? I did it for us!"

"Who do you think I was doing it for? I sure wasn't doing it for me!"

"You don't want the baby now?"

"Of course I do! You're pregnant, aren't you? But does everything have to be about you and the baby? Can't I eat a pizza and fall asleep on the couch without it being some giant insult to the freaking baby!"

"You immature ass!"

He started picking up all his papers, grumbling. Bella went to bed. She closed the bedroom door. She headed to the bathroom and brushed her teeth, even though she was whimpering. She looked in the mirror and decided her face looked round as a pumpkin. She pinched her cheeks and started to cry harder.

She could hear Jason moving around out there, throwing away his trash. Out of nowhere, a storm of self-pity assailed her. She felt fat, clumsy and unbearably cranky. She thought her hair was considerably thinner than it had been; it looked limp and sad to her. Her face was fat, and she was plumping up everywhere! She pulled off her dress and when she was down to her bra and panties, she looked in the mirror. Using a handheld mirror, she looked at her back. Her ass was huge and she had back fat! She cried harder. She put on her nightgown, crawled into bed and pulled the covers around her.

She cried herself to sleep and slept like the dead, never feeling Jason come to bed. When she awoke it wasn't just morning, it was eight thirty! That was the latest she'd slept in a long time.

The bed was still half made. She didn't move around much when she slept but Jason was usually all over the place. "He's left me," she said. "I'm going to have to raise this baby alone, all over a pizza box and smelly tennis shoes!"

She hurried out of bed before her straining bladder gave way. She made it to the toilet just in time for what felt like Niagara Falls. Either that or a cow peeing on a flat rock.

She wondered if he'd left her a note. She imagined it would say, *Dear Bella, I can't take any more of your mood swings but I'll pay child support...* She braced herself before opening the bedroom door. He would have left the mess...

"Well, hello, sleepyhead." Jason closed his laptop. "I thought I was going to have to hold a mirror under your nose to see if you were breathing!"

The house was practically shining it was so clean. There were even vacuum-cleaner tracks on the rug and the faint smell of Windex and furniture polish. And Jason was cleaned up—shaved and everything. He wore a clean pair of jeans and a light sweater.

"Aren't you playing golf?"

"I begged off. I texted Steve last night."

"What did you tell him?"

"I told him I had forgotten that I promised to go baby-furniture shopping today and if I didn't, someone would have to hold the baby until we could get a crib delivered. He has three kids. He understands."

"I thought you had left me," she said. "You didn't come to bed."

"You were upset; you had fallen asleep so I slept on the couch so I wouldn't disturb you. I think you must have needed the rest." He stood and went to her. He kissed her forehead. "I'm not leaving you, Bella. And you're right. I'm an immature ass. And lazy."

"Oh, Jason," she said, hugging him.

"I'll take you out to breakfast, then we'll buy some furniture. How's that?"

"That would be nice," she said. And then, she thought, *I'd better call that counselor before Jason does leave me.*

SEVEN

Marni's feelings became utterly clear upon answering the phone. "Hi, Marni. It's me." He didn't say his name; he didn't say it's Sam. He just said *me*. And she knew exactly who it was and that he was calling to make a date. There was something wonderfully intimate about that.

"Hi, Sam." She didn't know what kind of date but Marni, who had not wanted to meet any men or date, knew she would say yes. She knew she wanted more of him and there was a bit of a thrill in it.

"How's your day look?" he asked.

"Wide open," she said, even though she had been mentally compiling a list of things she should do. She had no employees coming over today, it being Saturday, and since Bella was shopping for baby furniture, the day was clear.

"I'm going to visit one of the experimental farms. Would you like to see it?" Sam asked.

She had no idea what he was proposing. "Absolutely!" she said.

"I'll be there to pick you up in an hour. Unless you need more time."

"I should be fine. How does one dress for an experimental farm?"

"Comfortably. There will be a lot of walking involved."

"Miles and miles of crop rows?"

"Not exactly. Think of it as a big day at Costco."

She laughed, then she said, "Okay." Her mind was telling her that description took some of the romance out of the idea, even though she liked Costco.

But she knew she wanted to be with him.

She wore knit pants with a matching short-sleeved hoodie and her favorite slip-on Sketchers with very cushiony soles. She pulled her hair back in a clip and took a little extra time with her makeup.

Sam drove a late model Ford extended cab truck and she was astonished by how clean it was. She had a vision of farmers trailing dirt along in their path, but not Sam. Even his hands were soft and clean.

He asked her about her week; she asked him about his. "My week seemed occupied by meetings. University people love meetings and I think everything after the first ten minutes is usually redundant. I thought online teaching and Zoom meetings would improve that but I think it became a little worse. People were so hungry for companionship, they hated to let go."

She hated meetings as well and had long been of the opinion you could get your business handled and decisions made much more efficiently by not gathering people in a room to go after each other. "There are always two people who feel they have to get the last word to be relevant. Sometimes three, but always at least two. We have a lot of meetings about production. If they're brainstorming sessions, I'm good; I take lots of notes. But if it's scheduling or acquisitions or HR issues, I admit I lose interest," she explained. "We must be about the same age, within a few years. Have you thought about retirement?"

"I'm asked that a lot, which forces me to think about it. And my answer stays the same. What's the point? I have as much time off as I need. If I don't work, I don't know what I'll do. My work isn't finished, so there's that. What about you?"

"I have a grandchild coming," she said. "There may be many changes in my schedule because of that." Then she told him all about Bella, her only child producing what could likely be an only child since it had been difficult for her to get pregnant in the first place and Bella and Jason were both attorneys, successful for their ages. And busy, given their demanding jobs.

They talked about their careers. Sam had associate professors, researchers and staff who were his responsibility and aided him in his work. Marni had her own studio—her kitchen—and the cable company's support staff. While they chatted about their jobs, Sam kept driving. Marni was expecting them to make a left turn and head south where most of the valley farmlands existed, but Sam kept heading west, past the UNR campus, past the airport, west toward the Sierra Nevada mountain range. They drove through a heavily populated Reno suburb, where there were lots of businesses, and finally he turned into a big parking lot that fronted an industrial park.

She thought very briefly perhaps they were headed for Costco, after all.

"Here we are," he said, parking right against a building as big as an airplane hangar. There were dozens of cars in the lot, but his space was reserved. There were glass doors just a bit toward the middle of the building that said Visitors, but he escorted Marni in through a single door in front of his parking space. He used his key to unlock that door.

"Where are we?" she asked, thoroughly confused.

"This way," he said, taking her by the hand and leading her down a long narrow hall that opened into a lobby. There were a couple of groupings of chairs, giving the impression of a waiting room. On the wall was a huge world map, painted in many colors. "This building is the hydroponics lab. This map indicates the arable land in the world. Only twenty-nine percent of the world is land and less than half of that is suitable for farming or grazing. And we're losing land mass constantly. But we're growing more in this warehouse than we can get from a healthy twenty-acre farm."

"You call it a lab?" she asked.

"We're always conducting experiments to improve our crops, making them larger, stronger and better tasting. There's controversy between the soil farmers and hydroponics farmers, stemming from the question of whether doing it without soil is equal to the task, measuring the stability of the vegetation and the flavor. But this idea of growing with ninety-five percent less water in stackable trays is not meant to be a replacement for the farm. Rather it's an alternative, providing sustainable food supplies in the worst of times. Let's walk around. I think you're going to love it."

He held open the door for her and she stepped into a vast warehouse with aisles lined with what looked like shelves that stood at least eight feet high in some places. The shelves were trays that could be pulled out. They were overflowing with greens. Upon closer inspection she found spinach, several varieties of lettuce, kale. There were smaller trays holding herbs like basil, mint, dill and rosemary.

The shelves bulging with rich green plants seemed to stretch for miles. There were a lot of people, roaming through the aisles, grooming plants, carrying trays, even some on raised platforms that took them up to the top of rows of plants. And it was pristine. Immaculate.

She reached out and tore off a piece of kale, popping it into her mouth without thinking. "Oh! I'm sorry! Is that allowed?"

He laughed. "It's encouraged. How's the flavor? Bitter?"

"Yes, but not overly. Is it a young plant?"

He pulled it up to expose the roots. "It's almost ready to be harvested. The trays below this one have been harvested and new seedlings installed and the trays above this one are just behind in growth. We generally begin harvesting at the bottom, always replenishing on the way up. This is most obvious with the tomato vines, the tomatoes closest to the floor ripen first and by the time the uppermost fruit is picked the bottom is almost ready again. The rotation is constant."

She noticed that some of the workers wore white lab coats and gloves. "Who are these people working?"

"Some are students, some are scientists, some are full-time farm workers. We have an outdoor farm just south of Breckenridge that is university property. We gauge the differences in the crops in everything from size to flavor. Our soil grown crops have to contend with weather whereas here we can control the climate with a switch."

She heard a faint rumble and saw a fine mist engulf the greens. "Just like the produce section of the grocery store, as if the fruits and vegetables can hear." There were long hanging lights that descended from the ceiling in some places and in other places they were stacked on pillars on wheels.

"Watch your step," he said, grabbing her elbow and pulling her out of the way of a tall metal elevator that was operated by a man in a lab coat who was standing on the top tier, pushing the levers to take it up above the trays at the top.

At the end of one long corridor of plant life, the greenery exploded into what appeared to be giant bushes that stood at least twenty feet tall, peppered with red and green fruit. Tomatoes! Just as Sam had said, they were ripening from the bottom to the top. It appeared they'd been harvested to about halfway up. About twenty feet away there were yellow and red peppers. "Sweet peppers," he said.

There was a man on a ladder with a gizmo that looked almost like a spray paint gun but with a finer nozzle. She pointed at him and Sam said, "We hand-pollinate here. Once we brought in bees. It was healthy but awkward; our workers had to wear gear they found to be hot and heavy, some people were allergic, it became stressful. Besides, hand-pollination allows us to be more precise. It's labor-intensive but it's the perfect solution in a place like this. We have a lot of fruit from melons to berries."

"Hey, Dr. Garner," someone said.

"Arturo," Sam greeted. "Meet my friend, Marni McGuire."

"It's a pleasure," Arturo said. "Have you visited this lab before? Because I think I know you from some place."

"She's a television chef, Arturo. Maybe you've seen her on TV." Then to Marni he said. "Arturo grew up farming in the central valley but studied agriculture at the university. He was the perfect recruit for this lab and is now an associate professor. The past year he's been experimenting with fertilizer additives. Arturo is a chemist and under his supervision the pH is checked daily and he develops his own cocktail of macronutrients."

"I only want the fruit to smile," he said. "Big, healthy and proud."

"What kinds of things do you add?" Marni asked.

"Epsom salts, phosphorous, zinc, other things that might be found in the soil—we add them to the water," he said. "We reevaluate all the time. It has been adequate for a long while, but we want more than that. We want flavor and presentation and perfect texture. I want a fruit that begs to be bitten into. My grandmother used to say a garden feeds the stomach and the soul."

"Aw," Marni said, her hand to her heart.

Sam thanked Arturo for his time and continued explaining things to Marni. "We established with the astronauts that we can deliver nutrients in a tube filled with a tasteless paste, but real food? Real beautiful, delicious, crunchy, amazing, sustainable food. That's what we're after. Sustainable food filled with taste and calories and beauty—that's our mission. Come with me." He led her down row after row of crops.

They walked down the rows for a long time. Marni touched the fruits and vegetables, smelled them, squeezed them. They even stopped at worktables now and then to cut them open and taste them. She was surprised and delighted by the quality and flavor. She loved the smell of the place; it was ripe with life and fresh produce but minus the dirt. Her palate and nose were well trained; she could pick out a single spice or herb and identify it.

In an hour Sam was following her as she wandered through the warehouse, stopping to introduce her to people they passed. It was not lost on her that when people came upon him, their eyes lit up and they were so happy to see him. It was also very clear that he showed the same amount of deference and respect for the janitor as the CEO. And yes, there was a CEO because there was a commercial arm to this hydroponic farm; they supplied a couple of grocers in Reno. They also had a large section of their garden dedicated to the development of heirloom fruits and vegetables of a more rare variety, the kind that might be used in five-star restaurants. "This is a special project. I'm growing the same varieties at home and comparing them. So far they're neck and neck, but my garden will have to contend with seasonal changes. Not so in here."

When Marni looked at her watch, she was only a little surprised to see that three hours had passed. She'd had a million questions about where the food would go, how much could be produced in a year, how many such warehouses could equal an acre of farmland, what was the approximate cost of the irrigation and lighting.

"Are you getting hungry?" Sam asked.

"Well, I can always eat," she said with a laugh. "But I have done a lot of nibbling all day, tasting your produce. So I'm not starving. What do you have in mind?"

"At the risk of boring you, how does a hamburger sound? It's a special hamburger. I know a place on the river."

"Perfect!"

Given the time of day, the café on the river was nearly deserted. And there weren't many university students around in the summer. There were only half a dozen patrons and they were able to sit outside with a view of the river. There were lots of houses and condos along the river walk, a very upscale part of town. People were strolling along the river, sitting on benches not that far away from them, gradually filling up the restaurant, but Marni and Sam were not mindful of them.

Sam ordered a beer, Marni had a glass of wine and they ordered burgers. While they waited, they talked.

She asked him what it was like growing up on a farm. He told her about living in a small farming community where there wasn't much of a town—a church, a bar, a feedstore, a rural police department. They had an elementary school but for secondary education the children were bussed out; the school was in the next town over. "I asked for a set of weights for Christmas and my father gave me a pitchfork and told me I'd build more muscle baling hay than lifting weights." He had been in 4-H and raised a bull from a puny little calf to a big mean bull who fathered most of the herd and his father swore he took his life in his hands every time he had to turn that bull loose on a cow.

She told him about growing up in a household of women and one man, her beloved father, who died when he was only fifty-seven. "Because my mother and aunts dominated the household, I didn't hear him speak a whole sentence until he was on his deathbed when he said, 'Marni, don't let them push you around.' But they did. They were a force to be reckoned with."

He told her about his accident with a baler and how he could have lost a leg, but it was only broken. She told him she nearly died of appendicitis when she was twelve. When their burgers arrived, she said, "I think this is my favorite meal."

"You're a well-known chef! That's some kind of blasphemy naming a hamburger as your favorite meal!"

"It's beautiful in its simplicity. I love a good burger. And the brioche bun is an excellent choice."

Their conversation eventually wound back around to hydroponics and he told her about some of the research papers he'd written recently, some of the studies they'd conducted in the lab, such as the crop differences between the hydroponic and soil beds. "What do you prefer?" she asked.

"That's not a fair analysis. In a perfect world, where the soil is rich in nutrients and the air is clean and the seasons don't torment us with extremes, I would chose a cozy farm in a moderate climate. But we don't have a perfect world. It is good to have alternatives so we can all eat healthy food. Sustainable food is the goal. More than food that will keep us alive but will also feed our spirits, our souls. Food that welcomes us to the table and rewards our hard work with joy. I loved watching my father. He did three hours of chores before a big breakfast of meat and eggs and oats and he gave thanks but not because he was a religious man. He said it was because he knew he had been in balance with the world. He gave and he received. It was, to him, a perfect life."

Their hamburgers were gone, their drinks finished, but Marni didn't want it to end. "Everyone should be talking about this more. About sustainable food and balance and feeding the mind and the body. I think you're working on saving the earth."

"You've identified the problem. The earth just needs to be left alone. I'm working on saving the people. The earth won't die. The people will."

She was brought up short by that truth. "And long after the people are gone…"

"I'm no climatologist but farmers are close to the earth. My limited knowledge suggests the planet will restore itself. It's our population we have to save."

As they were leaving the restaurant, she said, "I think that was the best burger I've ever had."

"Want to walk along the river for a little bit?" he asked.

"That would be perfect," she said, offering her hand.

They strolled along the crowded path, crossed the bridge and passed a few more sidewalk cafés before he suggested they turn back. Although Marni had lived around here all her life, she couldn't remember it ever being so beautiful. The flowers that bordered the sidewalk and fell gracefully from window boxes were lush and colorful. Bees buzzed around their heads and Sam talked about his parents and how rich their poor life on the farm had been.

They finally reached his truck and headed for her house in Breckenridge. He finished his tale about the family farm by mentioning that his two older brothers were both farming there. They had each picked up some neighboring acreage and were talking about selling out to a corporation, but they were still just talking. When they pulled into her drive, she turned to Sam. "I had the most wonderful day. I don't want it to end."

He put a hand on her knee. "Are you expecting company?"

"No. Why?"

"You could invite me in. I'm not working today."

"Please!" she said, brightening. "Come in!"

Her mind was whirring with what to offer him. They'd barely walked off that late lunch or early dinner! She didn't have any beer. Maybe tea? No, he did not look like a tea man. Or a soda? Or she could open a bottle of wine, but then he'd just had a beer and he was driving. *Oh, stop,* she scolded herself! There was no need to get so worked up. Maybe they could just sit on the patio and talk some more. She loved his stories.

She opened the door, walked in ahead of him and found herself immediately scooped into his arms and his lips hovering close over hers. He held her like that, her body flush against his, his lips just about to drop onto hers. "Is it too soon for this?" he whispered.

"No," she said with a little squeak. In fact this was everything she wanted, right here, right now. All she wanted to drink was him. Her arms went around his neck, his arms tightened around her waist, his mouth touched hers and then... He devoured her. Her lips opened gratefully to take him in and he turned with her in his arms, flattening her back against the front door. It took only seconds to realize how much she had missed this physical contact. Being in a man's strong arms again was more delicious than she remembered. She ran her hands over his broad shoulders and when he pushed against her, she pushed back. She moved her hips slightly and was so happy to feel he was ready for lovemaking because she was full tilt on her way. She never even considered turning back now.

She took him by the hand and pulled him toward her bedroom. She heard a rather girlish giggle come from herself followed by the deep rumble of his laugh. They tumbled onto her bed and the undressing began—he pulled off her top, she untucked his shirt—their lips barely left each other while tugging at clothing. They kicked off shoes, pulled off trousers, embraced for more kissing.

"I haven't had sex in more than five years," she whispered.

"I hear it's like riding a bike," he said.

"I haven't been on a bike in a while, either," she said.

He slid a hand over her hip, pulling her close. "We'll be fine."

And she answered with a deep moan.

She was fascinated by the mat of hair that covered his chest, dark and thick and spun with silver. "A farmer without a farmer's tan," she said, combing his chest hair with her fingers.

"I take off my shirt in the garden on those rare hot and sunny days. And you stay out of the sun. Your skin is as tender and flawless as a baby's." He pulled the clip out of her hair and fanned it over the pillow. "Let's pull back the covers."

"And find the sheets," she added.

They rolled, kicked away the duvet and were immediately back in an embrace. He pulled off her underwear, she pushed his down and then they were locked together, kissing and moaning and touching. His hands on her were so soft, his caresses so tender but firm, his exploration of her body bringing mounting desire. He thrust a knee between her thighs and she opened up for him. He did just a little searching to find that most sensitive knob of clitoris and her moan was louder and more heartfelt. "Yes," she whispered. "Yes, yes, yes."

He gave her a gentle rub, heightening her pleasure. She briefly thought she might faint for want of him so she closed a hand around him, massaging, very pleased by the sounds it brought from him. Lips engaged and hands working each other's bodies, tongues at play, they came up with a language all their own; groans and sighs and soft whispers.

He finally pressed toward her and she opened wider, urging him on. He entered her slowly, bit by bit, until she swallowed him up and felt the fullness of him inside her. It felt so good, like the fulfillment of a promise. When he moved, it was gentle at first, then a little harder. Finally, while in possession of her lips, he thrust into her and she grabbed onto his shoulders. A meek whimper escaped her and she held tightly to him as she felt the build up of passion. Finally she burst into a shower of pleasure. And she arched against him.

"Oh, God," he said. "Oh, God."

She had no answer for that. She just let herself fall against the sheets.

He gave her just a little time to enjoy the aftermath and then he took his in long deep pumps. She loved the sound of his quickening breaths that eventually caught in his throat as he came. There was a moan, deep and sexy, then he lowered his lips to her neck and treated her to a good deal of kissing and licking and stroking.

He seemed in no hurry to leave her body, which pleased her. She stroked his back, met his lips, massaged his butt, tangled her feet with his. His feet were soft as well. Soft and warm.

A mournful little sigh escaped her as he rolled over. He didn't go far. He held her hand.

"That was nice," he said. "Very nice."

"Unexpected," she said. "And welcome." Then she laughed.

He rolled onto his side, propping his head up, looking down at her. "I wonder if I should start giving regular tours of the hydroponic lab."

"Is this going to be complicated for us? With Sophia working for me?"

"A couple of weeks ago I might have worried about that, but she's involved with someone and busier than ever. I wouldn't suggest lying or covering up, but we don't have to get her permission. And I want to see you again."

"I think you're suggesting discretion."

"I just don't want anyone to mess up my plan!" he said.

"You have a plan?" she asked, sitting up in bed, pulling the duvet over her breasts. "Do tell."

"It's not much of a plan." He sat up in the bed, leaning back against the pillows. "I'd just like a little time to get to know you better, time for us to enjoy each other, before we're up to our necks in outside influencers."

"And if someone finds out?"

"I'm not suggesting secret-keeping. I'm just saying until we get comfortable, this can be a table for two. For a little while, as we check each other out."

"I think you should know, I will never marry again," she said.

"Most people our age make that choice, I think. I'm not looking for a wife."

"I'm not looking at all," she said.

He grinned handsomely. "Well, if you tripped over someone who measures up, do you think you could enjoy his company? Asking for a friend."

She thought for a moment. "If he amuses me," she said. "Possibly."

He put a hand on her bare shoulder. "What should we do now?"

"Ice cream," she said. "Now we should have ice cream. Stay right here. I'll get it."

Ellen thought herself very clever. When Mark asked her where she'd like to meet for the dinner he'd made for them, his house or her house, she quickly said, "Let's have dinner at your house. I don't want you to have to cart over food, that's too much trouble." Her strategy was multilayered. The man lived alone and she would be able to judge his housekeeping, even though she didn't expect to see much of his house. She had some work she wanted to do for the show and she wouldn't have to spend the whole day cleaning her own house in preparation for company. And the third and most important reason—when she'd had enough, she could leave. She could feign a headache or something but it was easier to leave than to kick him out.

But the joke was on her. First of all, his house was charming. Very welcoming. She had expected Mark to replace his wife's furniture with a recliner and a pool table, but it appeared very much a family home—a long cinnamon-colored sectional with a matching ottoman and some very rich wood accent tables. The dining set and twin buffets matched the living room furniture.

"You have a lovely home, Mark."

"My late wife gets the credit," he said. "This is furniture she picked out. I painted the walls in colors she had chosen for our last house."

"Does it feel like the same house?"

"No, but it's just enough like our house to be comfortable. It's a different floor plan, entirely different yard, and I replaced the furniture that was getting old." He chuckled. "I ended up buying stuff that was just like what we had, which made me wonder who had done the choosing in the first place."

His home was immaculate. And the aroma from the kitchen was heavenly. Her nose told her it was just the right amount of garlic and oregano. "Let's warm up this bread," she said.

"Great. And let's have a glass of wine while the lasagna sits. With your Caesar salad, it's going to be a garlicky meal. I hope that's okay."

"It's perfect."

"Come and sit right here," he said, pulling out a chair.

Ellen lifted a plate. "This is beautiful. I think you got out the good dishes."

"After Pam passed away, I gave away a lot of the things she used. My son and his wife took a lot of stuff and my nieces and nephews took a few things. It took me a long time to get it done but after a couple of years I had given away most of Pam's things. I still have plenty of stuff we used—all the pots and pans and flatware. But the linens are all new." He blushed slightly and turned away. Ellen wondered if he was trying to inform her she would never be sleeping in his dead wife's bed.

He pulled something out of the fridge and slid it into the microwave, warming it. "How long have you been widowed?"

She had already told him most of this so she kept her response short. "A few years, but my husband was in and out of nursing homes most of our marriage. And you were also a caregiver?"

He took the plate from the microwave and placed it on the table. "This is a crab spread on baguette. See if you like it. Yes, I took care of my wife."

Ellen took a bite. Crab, garlic, cream cheese, parmesan and something else. "Green onion?"

"Close enough. Chives."

While he tossed the salad and served the lasagna and bread, they talked about their dead spouses. Pam was quiet and shy while Ralph had been a social butterfly, a funny and outgoing man with many friends. In Mark's marriage, he had been the more social one, but he feared he had lost some of that when he lost his wife.

They ate and talked about their careers. Mark had loved being a firefighter and was still involved in an organization focused on helping people and Ellen explained her culinary studies and twenty-year relationship with Marni. "It's like being a personal chef. It's creative and challenging and there is only one other person in the kitchen. She has all the stress of being in front of the camera and there's no competition for power. I have the freedom to cook and create without pressure."

"And you love it?"

"By now you know I'm an introvert. I love cooking for

people but I take people in very small numbers. Being stuck back in the kitchen is the perfect place for me, but I can't tolerate a kitchen in a big restaurant. Too many people; too much rushing around and yelling. I have no interest in jockeying for position in a busy, competitive restaurant—that's brutal work. It drives the creative joy out of cooking."

"I enjoyed cooking for the guys." He laughed. "Let me correct that—they are not all guys. They were when I started over thirty years ago. Now there are an almost equal number of women. I like the crowd at the table; I love the praise. Having people happy with my meal means everything."

His lasagna was divine; his crab-spread appetizer was delicious. They talked about food, their favorite crowd-pleasers and party foods. They listed their showstoppers and their quick and easy favorites. Neither of them entertained much these days but they still had preferred menus. "I get to contribute my ideas to the show. *Marni Cooks* has very high ratings on the cable networks."

"I'm working on an idea of my own. You know Chef José Andrés?"

"I don't personally know him but I know all about him," she said.

"Then you know he travels with a large crew to places where disaster has pummeled the population and he feeds people. I've been working on building a foundation that does something like that but on a smaller scale."

"Really?" she asked.

"I'm not really interested in retirement yet and I love staying busy. I've been learning about writing grants and running nonprofits. I've been active in Friends of Firefighters for a long time now, but there's still a lot to investigate. That would give me something productive to do with my time."

He rose from the table and surprised Ellen by pulling a cheesecake out of the refrigerator for their dessert. He kept talking while he served her. "I've laid the groundwork and registered a foundation and investigated the necessary licensing. I have my food handler's license and compiled a list of commercial kitchens for rent. I'll need a climate-controlled truck, which is harder to come by than you think. But I've compiled a hefty list of volunteers who are ready when I am."

"How long have you been working on this?" she asked while devouring the cheesecake.

"A couple of years. The year after Pam died, I thought about it a lot. The next year I talked to an attorney who handles estates and foundations. He directed me to the state's community foundation. They were extremely helpful and assisted me in finding a good sponsor. It turned out to be a match made in heaven—if I commit to the work, they'll commit to the funding. I am already in touch with philanthropists interested in my project."

"Where will you start?"

"I'm going to convene the board of directors and take out a loan that we can repay with grant money. My CPA is a firefighter and he can help me with the accounting. And, it's almost fire season. The need will present itself."

Ellen couldn't speak. She was too impressed for words. "It's June," she said. "Can you be ready in a couple of months?"

"For jobs that aren't too far away," he said.

"What's your range?"

"I'm not sure. We'll know what we can do when we try to do it. Or when we have to say no."

"Something tells me you're not the saying-no kind of guy."

He laughed with some embarrassment. "Not while there are things to do."

"What are you doing tomorrow?" Ellen asked.

"I'm going to work for six hours or so, then I'm going to squeeze in a nap. You?"

"I'm thinking of slow-cooking a pork roast in kraut and beer. Are you interested?"

"That sounds good. I don't think I've done that."

"Well, you should think about it. Pork and sauerkraut are priced right," she said. "That's another thing—have you been pricing groceries lately? It's one thing to cook for hungry people and another to be able to afford it during a recession."

"I've been looking for not only financial donations but also grocery donations," he explained. "Most of the best prospects are going to make me prove myself first, show that I'm a reliable guy. I have the reputation of the fire department to back me up."

"What's your big ambition with this food service?" she asked.

"I want to fill the gap. Where there is no food service, I'd like to bring food. I'm not the Red Cross, I'm not the food bank. You know that in the Paradise, California, fire, fourteen thousand homes were obliterated? People whose homes turned into a big pile of ash were camping in their trucks and cars because the shelters nearby were full. Those people needed a hearty meal to get them to the next day." He gave a nod. "I know how to do that."

She was quiet for a moment, absorbing this. Then she looked at her watch. "I have obviously thoroughly enjoyed dinner. Will you let me return the favor tomorrow night after you've worked and napped?"

"I'd love that."

"Let me help with the dishes," she said.

"I'll clean up. There's not much to do. But can I walk you home?"

"It's just next door!"

"I don't want to scrape you up off the driveway tomorrow when I go out for the Sunday paper. Let me see you into your house. Thanks for having dinner with me. It was so nice."

"Dinner was amazing," she said. "You're such a great cook!"

"Coming from you, that's a huge compliment. Come on," he said, cupping her elbow in his hand. "Let me get you home. I think it's way past your bedtime."

"Hours," she said with a smile. And the date she had dreaded was transformed into the time of her life.

EIGHT

Sam was in his bedroom, reading. He heard the door open and close. It was very late. He didn't usually wait up for Sophia, but tonight he had. He had texted her at about nine and asked when she'd be home. She had replied that she'd been at the lake all day and would be home soon. That was three hours ago.

Of course he got up, book in hand.

"Oh, Papi, I woke you!" she said.

"What is this?" he asked, pointing to the small ice pack she held against her cheek. She slowly pulled it away and there was, unmistakably, a purple bruise. "Sweetheart! What is this?"

"I tripped; I fell. We shouldn't have stayed so late. It was dark and I fell on the rocks around the lake. It's nothing."

"You're going to have a shiner. Where did you get the ice pack?"

"We stopped at the drugstore. Really, it's nothing. Just a stupid accident."

He put down his book and looked at her hands. She hadn't reached out to break her fall; her hands and knees were not scuffed or scraped. "Who were you with?"

"A bunch of people. Friends. I was not drinking."

"I can see that," he said. "That wasn't what I was thinking. Were there a bunch of kids or just you and one other?"

She didn't respond to the question immediately. He knew and she knew he knew. "There were six or eight. Let me think…"

"Should we go to the ER and get a CT scan to be sure you don't have a concussion?" he asked.

"Please, no! Really, I'm so embarrassed!"

"Didn't any of your friends suggest that? And what friends, by the way?"

"Heather and Sean…you met her. Jasmine and her boyfriend."

"I'm trying to find out if a certain young man was with you. Angelo."

"Yes, he brought me home. He took me to get an ice pack."

"And is he the reason you're out of sorts?"

She grimaced and shook her head. "I just want to go to bed, Papi."

"Okay, okay. If you have any trouble in the night, a headache or anything. Wake me."

"Si. Of course."

He gently kissed her forehead and let her go to her room.

Sophia had lied to her father. She knew he wouldn't be able to understand the truth because she didn't understand it. She hadn't been with friends at the lake because Angelo had wanted them to be alone. At first that was fun. They went on a long hike around the lake, laughed and poked fun at each other, found a secluded spot and made out like teenagers for a while, then had an argument about her turning off her phone. Then he was depressed because they'd had an argument he couldn't win. It was true she'd fallen on the rocks at the lake's edge but it hadn't been a total accident because he was angry and had given her a little shove, which he claimed was just playing around. Then he'd actually cried because she'd gotten hurt and he called himself stupid and unworthy. He carried on until she swore it was all right and she wasn't mad and she'd never tell anyone.

She wasn't sure how she'd gotten to this place. And so fast! She'd been seeing him a couple of months and it seemed like years and she enjoyed about half the time they spent together. It was June and the summer days were long and warm, perfect for spending time with the one you love, but it wasn't going that well for Sophia. Angelo could be charming and complimentary, then make a switch to moody and unhappy. He was ridiculously unpredictable! She found herself almost flinching when the tone of his voice changed, suddenly so uneasy about what might be coming next. Then everything would be all right and she'd chastise herself for creating problems where there were none.

With regularity he would say, "You're just going to break up with me, aren't you?" Instead of telling the truth, that she didn't think this relationship was working out for either of them, she would turn herself inside out trying to convince him she wasn't planning to break up with him. "But do you love me?" he asked. "Because you said you did." And even though she hadn't volunteered that she loved him, she would insist that she did and he should stop being paranoid before he ruined everything.

★ ★ ★

Sophia had to go to work on Monday with a black eye. She did her best to cover the bruising with makeup, but there was no way she was getting away with it. Ellen gasped when she saw Sophia but Marni did not react.

"What in the world happened?" Ellen asked.

"I was at the lake with friends on Saturday and I slipped on the little hill and fell into some rocks. I'm fine. It looks worse than it is."

"Did you do anything for it?" Marni asked.

"Yes, I put ice on it but I don't think it did much good."

"You never know," Marni said. "Without the ice it might be twice as swollen and discolored. Did you think about the emergency room?"

"My Papi did. He thought I should have an X-ray to be careful but I didn't want to. I just want it to go away."

"Did you trip on something?"

"There was a dirt path to the lake. Down a little hill. Some big rocks. I slipped on the path and fell and hit my head right here on my eyebrow. It's so ugly."

"You didn't lose consciousness, did you?" Marni asked.

"No, no. I just hit hard. I'm so happy I didn't knock out my teeth."

"Oh, Sophia, poor girl. You have to be careful! Were you with your boyfriend?" Ellen asked.

No way was she going to admit she was with only Angelo. "Yes, and he took me to the drugstore to find an ice pack for my eye. He was so sorry he didn't catch me, but he couldn't. There are places it's really steep."

"Are you all right to work? Do you have a headache? Dizziness?" Ellen asked.

"I'm okay. I want to work. This will be over in a day. I hope your weekend was more fun. I ruined the day getting hurt."

"Mine was definitely good," Marni said. "Yesterday I went to Bella's house to see baby furniture for The Bump! It's getting so exciting."

"Are they going to choose a name for that baby or will he be receiving his high school diploma as The Bump?" Ellen asked with a laugh.

And that fast the attention was off Sophia and her black eye.

"Tell us about the baby furniture," Ellen begged.

"I can do even better," Marni said, getting out her phone. "I took pictures! Since Jason has a big truck, they brought everything home rather than waiting for delivery."

"What did you feed them, because you never go anyplace without food?"

"I brought a breakfast casserole. And they gobbled it up like starving children. I almost didn't get any!"

Ellen was having trouble paying attention and more than a few times she missed what Marni was saying and had to ask her to repeat herself. "My stars, are you just so worried about Sophia that you're completely unfocused?" Marni asked.

"That's probably it," she said, knowing that wasn't the case at all.

The night before, Sunday evening, she and Mark had cooked dinner together. She taught him how to make her veal rollatini. He was thrilled about it. It was the first time Ellen could ever remember anyone being so excited to watch her demonstrate a recipe, and certainly the first time in her life a man had shown this kind of interest. Also the first time any man had participated in the meal prep. He seemed so comfortable chopping and slicing and creating little dishes of ingredients.

She was equally interested in his dream of starting a food service available to the victims of natural disasters in the area.

Having been a fireman his whole career, he was particularly sensitive to the needs of wildfire victims, and there were so many. She had so many questions about how he was planning to set it up.

And he had a million questions that she could answer, like how to go about cooking large amounts of food in a relatively small space and how much by way of transport vehicles would be required. What she could not answer with facts she was more than excited to research for him.

Amidst it all there had been history sharing and a lot of laughter. She'd been up till midnight, about three hours past her bedtime. She wouldn't see Mark again for at least several days as he was going to work at the grocery store, stocking shelves. "It keeps me in shape and adds a little income to my pension." Because also, until his nonprofit became a known and trusted entity, he was going to have to beg, borrow and steal to get it up and running, emphasis on the borrowing.

She had never wanted to tell someone something more in her life. She wanted to tell Marni that she had this wonderful new friend and it was none other than the man next door. But she was keeping the news to herself because she just wasn't sure how long it would last or if it would become more than a friendship between a couple of cooks. But it was definitely having an impact on her because she felt like her brain was visiting another planet. Several times a day she would have to pause just to steady herself—she felt like she was floating!

Sixty years old and a woman alone for how many years? And now she felt like a teenage girl! It was embarrassing!

And she'd never felt more fit or energetic in her life.

On a Tuesday after work Marni got a text from Sam. He said he could sneak away from the house for a while if she was open to receiving company. Sophia was going to a study group with some of her friends from school and would be out until eleven. Marni responded with an enthusiastic yes! And she lifted the garage door so he could pull right into the garage, parking beside her car. He drove into the garage and came into the house through the back door. As soon as he walked in, she threw herself on him. Holding onto each other for dear life, stuck in the hallway, devouring kisses consuming them, they were possessed. Relieved and eager to be together again.

Then Sam chuckled. But he didn't let go.

"Is it normal for people our age to act like this?" she asked.

"I don't know," he said. "I've never been this age before."

"Where exactly is Sophia?" Marni asked.

"She said her friend's apartment is near the campus. My truck is in the garage—are we hiding?"

"A little bit, yes," she said, laughing. "If someone comes and we're in a situation, it will look like no one is home. It feels a little naughty."

"I'd like it to feel naughtier," he said. "Can we get out of the back hall?"

"Right this way," she said, leading him to her bedroom.

In no time they were undressed and rolling around in the sheets, whispering and laughing and moaning hungrily, clinging to each other. Eventually they lay still and exhausted under the sheets, but of course they were still touching.

"Are you hungry?" she asked.

"I could eat," he said with a shrug. "Are you?"

"I could throw something together. Let me lie here for a minute more."

"It might take me more than a minute. I didn't come over here for a booty call. Please believe that."

"You want me to believe you came for my mind?" she returned with a teasing tone in her voice.

"No, but certainly for your heart and humor. And maybe food. Don't blame me, since you're famous for it."

And then, against all odds, her doorbell rang. She sat bolt upright in bed. "Dear God, who is that? Where is my phone?"

"You're asking me?" Sam said. "I don't even know where your clothes went!"

"Here it is, right here." She picked it up off the bedside table and clicked on the security camera app. And there stood Jason. "Jason? What are you doing here? Is Bella okay?"

"Yes," he said into the camera. "Sorry to bother you. I should have called but it was a last-minute thing. Are you busy?"

She glanced over at Sam, the sheet covering him to the waist. His salt-and-pepper hairy chest was inviting her fingers to comb it. Funny, she'd never been particularly drawn to a hairy chest before and at this moment all she wanted in the world was to bury her face in it.

"Just give me a minute," she said into her phone. "I was just changing clothes. I'll be right there."

"Take your time."

Marni ran a hand through her hair and just looked at Sam in exasperation. "It's my son-in-law. Do I look like I've just been ravished?"

"You look delicious. Do you want me to hide in the closet for a while?"

"He won't stay long, but my daughter is almost six months pregnant and I should see what's up. Can you wait awhile? Then I'll fix you something to eat."

"I'll get dressed," he said.

She turned on the TV for him and went into her closet

to find fresh clothes. She walked into her bathroom to run a comb quickly through her hair and put on a little lipstick. Then she pulled the bedroom door closed and went to the front door.

"What a nice surprise," she said, opening the door for Jason. "To what do I owe the pleasure?"

"I was on my way home from court in Reno and I thought I'd just stop to see if you need anything moved or lifted or... Since I was passing by."

"I think I'm all set," she said. "Is everything all right?"

"I guess." He put his hands in his pants pockets and rocked back on his heels. "I called Bella to tell her I was on my way and she said she'd made me a big salad. Marni, if I have to eat one more head of lettuce, my colon will explode."

"Come with me. You're in luck. We were experimenting with a roast chicken with a spiced rub and I didn't freeze what's left. Unless you're in the mood for something more gamy...like pizza or something?"

"I've been stuffing down so much pizza, burgers, tacos and other fast food on the sly that I'm starting to crave decent food..."

"I have your back," she said with a laugh. "Tasty, nutritious and quick. You'll be able to go home and partake of the salad like the supportive man you are. But don't you think you should talk to Bella about this issue?"

"Ah, I should probably keep my mouth shut," he said. "Lately I'm just a big fuckup. I can't do anything right. If I try to be affectionate, she cries that I don't really mean it, I just feel sorry for her because she's so fat. If I don't go near her, she cries because I'm avoiding her because she's fat. She's not even fat—she's pregnant!"

"I don't think it's really about being fat or thin," Marni

said. She pulled out half a roast chicken, sprayed it with olive oil and slid it under the broiler. "I think her hormones have gone insane. Which is intensified given the in vitro." She deftly slid asparagus, spiraled zucchini and yellow squash into a pan and lopped off a hunk of a stick of butter to sauté it.

"Yesterday I brought home flowers for her and of course I brought the ones she's allergic to. Have you ever heard of anyone being allergic to daisies? She started to sneeze, peed her pants and threatened to leave me."

Marni laughed. Then she popped the top on a bottle of Sam Adams and handed it to Jason.

"I probably shouldn't be talking about my problems with my wife with my mother-in-law."

"I'll never tell." She shook a few quartered and cooked new potatoes on a plate and microwaved them. "I'll be the first to admit, Bella is a little bit spoiled. It's not her fault. She was raised by four women and no men. By the time she was nine months old my husband was dead, my father had passed and it was me, my mother and two aunts. Bella was royalty." Within five minutes Marni had half a chicken, potatoes and vegetables professionally arranged on a plate. She slid it across the breakfast bar, produced a knife and fork, and said, "Mangia."

"You're good! You should do this for a living."

"I'll think about it," she said. "Have you told Bella you're not counting calories?"

"She doesn't want to get fat while she's pregnant. She wants me to be supportive. It's torture. I've tried mentioning that I don't care if she gets fat. That didn't go well. I told her I'm starving and she said so was she!" He cut a slice off the chicken. "I'm better off just constantly telling her she's beautiful and eating salad."

He took a couple of bites, closed his eyes in ecstasy, looked like he might faint. "This is just chicken but it's unbelievable."

"Butter and spices. Rich and tasty but, I'm afraid, pretty caloric."

"Thank you! I should have eaten a bigger lunch, but we were too busy. I'm in the middle of a trial."

"Pregnancy is usually hard on the whole family," she said. "Forget the movies or TV commercials—most women do not feel special and beautiful while they're pregnant. They feel bloated, queasy, gassy..."

"I can vouch for two of the three..."

"And yet the women who can't get pregnant feel horribly cheated. It's primitive, I think—that strong urge to reproduce. God knows, you and Bella went to a great deal of trouble to get this far."

"I don't regret a day of it. But sometimes I wonder if Bella does. She knows she's moody as all hell. She can't help it. But I'll be honest, Marni. If this is how she's going to be for the next forty years, I don't know if I can take it."

Marni almost said she didn't blame him. Instead she made a silent decision to speak to her daughter.

"Pregnancy and early motherhood will be stressful. I strongly recommend you get a little expert advice to cope. I've already suggested counseling to Bella and now I'm going to suggest it to you, also."

"I'm really proud of her, you know," Jason said. "Except for these issues we've had lately, she's been so brave. All those injections she had to take just to get pregnant, all the mood swings from hormones, the discomfort of gaining thirty pounds. She's been strong."

"That's very sweet."

He finished eating and pushed his plate away. He smiled.

"She's stronger than I am. Look what happens to me when I get a little hungry."

"Feeling better?"

"You have no idea. You're the best."

"You'd better get back to Bella and that salad."

"I don't know how you did it alone," he said. "And you were so young. No husband…"

"But there was my mother and the aunts. I dreamt of being alone. It was a very long time before I could support myself."

"And look at you now. One of the most well-known chefs in TV land."

"Jason, you have to go now. I have things to do."

"Oh, you should have said something. You have plans? Are you working?"

"No, I have a handsome and exciting man locked in the closet waiting for me to be done entertaining you." She laughed. "It's a good book, actually. I'll never get to the good part if you hang around any longer. Seriously, though, I think you have to get home to your wife. But feel free to stop by anytime. It's always wonderful to see you. Really."

He leaned down and gave her a kiss on the cheek. "Thank you for dinner. You saved my life. I feel ready to take on the salad now."

"I'm just going to say it. If this is your biggest problem…"

"I know. I know."

She told him to drive carefully. When the front door closed, she locked it. Seconds after the click of the bolt, the bedroom door down the hall opened and Sam stepped out. He was wearing a very handsome, sly smile.

"A good man, brought down by a salad," he said.

"You were listening?"

"Not intentionally. Mostly I was watching the news. The news was not as interesting as your son-in-law."

She stepped into the kitchen. "Do you like salmon?"

"I love it."

"Are you willing to try something new?"

"Of course. But don't go to any trouble on my account."

"You don't really mean that," she said, beginning to pull out food and putting it on the counter. Salmon fillets, garlic, butter, spinach, capers, cream. She glanced over her shoulder at him and saw him smile. "Warning. It's very rich."

"I'm already imagining it."

While she seared the salmon in olive oil and garlic, she put a pan of water on to boil for pasta. It could be a side dish or the creamy salmon could be served atop the pasta.

"Do you ever get tired of cooking?" Sam asked.

"I have had days I don't feel like working, but I always feel like cooking. Or baking. I'm good with desserts. And breads. Do you ever get tired of farming?"

"Having a farm is like having a baby. There's always something to do; it always needs tending. Do family members stop by often? And hungry?"

"It's kind of a gathering place, but not during working hours. Everyone knows I'm working from nine to five, unless I'm not here. I do go to the station in Reno or the cable headquarters in San Francisco. Not often, but regularly. But my family usually knows if I'm going to be in meetings or out of town. My sister and brother-in-law come by, but they call ahead. My son-in-law, though rarely. My daughter, about once a week. I'm far from lonely. And remember, people I work with are here all the time. Sometimes I can't wait for some time alone."

She removed the salmon from the pan and stirred in butter, cream, spices. While the sauce thickened, she opened a bottle of cold pinot grigio and poured two glasses, passing one to Sam. She poured a healthy dollop into the sauce as well. Back in went the salmon, spinach, capers. She drained the pasta and added it to two plates. "I've only made this once before but I think it's going to be a favorite."

"It could be a favorite of mine as well."

She put out placemats and flatware. Then she tested the sauce. "Hmm," she said appreciatively, letting her eyes close briefly.

"I'd love to be as organized as you are," he said. "I'm very excited about this salmon. What will we do if the doorbell rings now?"

"That's easy—we'll admit to being friends. We can answer the ring as long as we're dressed. But I don't think anyone will drop in now. It's getting late. Come over to the table."

"But this is a gathering place," he said.

"Sometimes at the end of the workday we'll have a cup of tea or glass of wine together. When my sister, my daughter, my assistant Ellen and Sophia are all here, relaxing, gossiping and chatting, I'm in my happy place. We work hard and remain very professional while we work, but social time is let-down-your-hair time."

"Do you have any idea how much Sophia admires you?" he asked.

"And I admire her. She's smart and strong. She makes good choices."

"I'm a little concerned about one of her choices," he said. "It's possible I'm just being overprotective but I don't think so. Sophia has had boyfriends before and they never seemed to get so serious so quickly. And this one...? It feels like her mood has changed. From the first day she mentioned him, she has not seemed happy. Isn't true love supposed to make you giddy and perpetually happy?"

"I wouldn't know..."

"Not even your husband?" he asked.

"My first husband, we were too young. My second—we met through work. He was a newscaster and I liked him. We were good friends. Buddies. He was the most logical partner I could possibly choose, but I was never giddy. I do believe I loved him. I know I was loyal and he was not."

"I'm sorry, Marni."

"It's long in the past and we had a few good years. As for Sophia, if she ever confides in me, even a little bit, I'll get in her business and see how she's doing. I'm the mother of a daughter. I'm pretty sneaky."

He grinned. "That would be so appreciated. I want her to be happy, but safe."

"I do understand that, believe me."

"And how can I return the favor?" Sam asked.

She lifted one brow and one corner of her lips. "Taste the Tuscan salmon."

He did so and chewed very slowly, moaning in appreciation. He finally swallowed. "You are a sorceress."

She sat back in her chair. "Thank you."

Sophia's girlfriends were still in undergrad, due to graduate in the spring, one more year. Both had a syllabus for their senior year, so they knew what they were up against and were determined to do well. Sophia had graduated with honors and had been accepted into the masters of fine arts program. Clarissa was studying special ed and Lia was majoring in English and was hoping to go to law school.

They called this little get-together a study session but they only talked about studying. They all worked and went to school and hadn't seen each other in a while and came together like long lost lovers. They met in Lia's apartment, a small and expensive two-bedroom that she shared with a roommate who was out for the evening. They had a glass of wine, shared a pizza and caught up on the latest news.

Hardly any time had passed before they had exchanged the latest gossip about some of the professors and mutual friends and were laughing like little girls. They moaned and groaned about the work they had to complete for school and commiserated about the toughest assignments in college life. Then, of course, they had to exchange updates on their romantic lives. Clarissa reported that she and her boyfriend of a couple of years, Brad, were talking about getting engaged. Lia said the new guy she'd met had great potential and she was really falling for him and Sophia said Angelo was very sweet and attentive but moody.

"Moody how?" Lia asked.

"Unpredictable," Sophia said. "I don't think I will put up with it much longer. Everything is going along okay and then all of a sudden he gets cross. Then he gets upset with himself because he was cross and we have to go through all the making up. He is a lot of work."

"That's not good," Clarissa said. "Does he have a temper?"

"Just cross, but sometimes when I see his number on the phone, I don't want to pick up. Because, Dios, he can make me so tired."

"Do you cook for him?" Lia asked.

Sophia laughed. "I don't cook for anyone. I did make him a hamburger once."

"Haven't you learned great cooking from Marni? They say the quickest way to a man's heart is through his stomach!"

"I am her support staff. I do a lot of chopping and dicing and shredding. I look at the recipe and make up the ingredients in small dishes and bowls. To be honest, I don't even pay attention to how she puts it all together. But lately I've been helping with the sets for the productions. It's like every recipe gets its own soundstage and that is my job. I think I'm more of a set decorator than cook." She straightened proudly. "She is very happy with my work. And I am learning from the videographer. He is so good. He's going to show me his editing work for the next season."

Soon it was after nine and Lia suggested they go to The Library, the name of a bar near the campus. It was a place they had often gathered with friends from school. "Just one glass of wine and then I'm going to have to get home," Sophia said. "I have both work and school tomorrow."

When they walked into the bar, they were immediately surrounded by friends from school because that's exactly who gathered there. They were invited to join a large gathering of girls who had pushed some tables together and they were happy to be so welcomed. Drinks were ordered and the reunion spirit continued. There were a few young men, dates of some of the girls. There were also small groups of men scattered around the bar, but Sophia was only interested in reconnecting with her girlfriends. It didn't take long for her to feel a sense of coming home and she realized how much she'd missed spending time with them.

"Masters of fine arts?" a voice said. Sophia looked up to meet eyes with a young man who rested his hand on Lia's shoulder. "Literature? Writing? Film? What's your specialty?"

"Right now my specialty is chopping and slicing for a television chef, but I'd like a career in television."

"News?" he asked. "Shouldn't you be in journalism?"

"Not necessarily, since I did have some journalism in undergrad. Now I'm thinking of doing my dissertation in South American literature, but it's early." They talked for a while about literature and then football and finally hockey. A couple of girlfriends spotted her and said hello, made her promise not to be so invisible and in her heart she was thinking the very same thing—she was not going to give up all these lovely, fun friendships. She'd been seeing Angelo for a while and he was not a friendly guy; he had no interest in her friends, even though they were quite well established.

She felt a hand on her shoulder. Speak of the devil.

"Great study group," Angelo said.

She looked over her shoulder. "Have you followed me?"

"No! I come here sometimes. For a beer."

A glass of wine appeared before her. "No," she said to the waitress. "I didn't order that."

"I don't know who ordered it, but it's paid for." And the waitress left it.

"Someone's trying to pick you up," Angelo said. "Maybe that guy over there," he said, indicating the guy she'd been talking to.

"That's Lia's boyfriend. We were talking about school. You don't come here! I think you followed me."

"Now you insult me?" he said. "What? I can't come here because it's a campus bar and I'm not a college student?"

"I just never saw you here and I came here with my friends a lot. I met you down in Breckenridge. Not a lot of students hang out there."

"So you're good enough for the college bar but I'm not?" He lifted his beer, took a long pull and put it down on the table so hard the glass broke. Some of the young women around the table pushed their chairs back sharply, squealing as they tried to avoid the spill.

A bartender was at their table instantly. He was more of a bouncer than a waiter. "Got a problem, buddy?" he asked.

"Nothing's wrong," Angleo said. "Just mind your own business."

"It's okay," Sophia said. "I was just leaving."

"We were just leaving," Angelo corrected, grabbing her elbow and standing from the table.

The waiter threw down his towel and came around the table quickly. "You don't have to leave with him," the waiter said to Sophia. "I can make sure you have a safe ride home."

It was at that moment, just when the waiter, who was muscled and bulky, said she didn't have to leave with Angelo that she realized for the very first time she wanted great distance between her and Angelo. Forever!

"Hey, watch it! She's my girl!" Angelo said and then he lunged at the waiter. Before he could register what had happened, Angelo was suddenly sitting on the floor in what was left of the spilled beer.

Clarissa and Lia and Lia's boyfriend were all at her side. "I have to get home," Sophia said.

"We'll follow you home. We'll make sure you're okay."

"Good. Thank you. I'll call my father, make sure he's home," Sophia said. Then looking down at Angelo she said, "You stay away from me. I mean it."

Lia rode with Sophia while her boyfriend followed.

"What exactly happened?" Lia asked when they were alone in the car.

"I'm not sure. He was angry. He said he saw me in the bar, said something like it didn't look like a study session. He said he just happened to see me there but I think maybe he followed me and I didn't know it. I don't know what's the matter with him. One minute he's sweet and loveable and the next minute he's mean and nasty."

"That's not normal," Lia said.

"He was going to fight that big waiter."

Lia laughed. "That would have been fun to see."

"Why do I think that would somehow be my fault?"

"Sophia, you better tell your father what happened."

"I hate to do that," she said. "I'll never get out of the house again."

"That might be a good solution. For a while, anyway."

NINE

Marni had noticed that her house and kitchen, her business, had grown very quiet. Ellen was never much of a talker, but now she'd grown oppressively quiet. And Sophia, usually bubbling over with life and laughter, was withdrawn and silent. Since Marni talked to Sam every day, sometimes a couple times a day, she asked him what was going on.

"She hasn't volunteered anything and when I've asked how school and work are going these days, all she has to say is that the reading list she has for her class is intimidating. And she's working on enunciation—I think she's ready to lose the traces of her accent, looking for a life in American television. But I will tell you what I suspect. I suspect this is all about a young man. The recent boyfriend. She hasn't mentioned going out with him and he hasn't been around."

"Ah, maybe there's a breakup. That would put a strain on her mood."

"And it would lighten mine. I can't say there was anything wrong with him. He was polite around me. But there was something about him. I can't put my finger on it."

"Then there was something wrong. Men are just not as good at trusting their gut as women are. Has she been spending time with her girlfriends?" Marni asked.

"Not since their last study session, and she was home from that earlier than I expected. She's been doing a lot of reading. How can I complain? It's what she's supposed to be doing."

"One of these days, if I see the opportunity, I'll reach out," Marni said. "But I warn you, if I offer her confidentiality, I'll honor that promise."

"It's appreciated just the same," Sam said. "I know you'd give her good advice and sound counsel. I wouldn't have asked," he added. "Not because I wasn't tempted, but because that would seem an overreach. Right now the girl could use her mother. Selena was wise and patient."

"I don't know that anyone will ever say that of me!"

"Oh, I bet they already do. You've raised a smart and well-adjusted daughter of your own and on your own."

Marni laughed ironically, as Bella was now seeing the reproductive therapist every week. At least she was getting along a little better. Marni was worried that this hormone mania she was experiencing was perhaps a premonition of issues to come after the birth of the baby they'd worked so hard to have. She kept the fact that she was worried about postpartum depression to herself. She was afraid that naming it might make it so.

She chatted with Sam for a while, finally moving on from the subject of their daughters to their work and even the weather. It was summer in Breckenridge and the peaks surrounding their town had at last lost the topping of snow, the weather was perfect, the rain was moderate, the crops and gardens were flourishing.

"I've been spending a lot more time in the garden lately," Marni said.

"I can probably sneak away for a couple of hours tomorrow night, if you feel like a little company," Sam said.

"Do you feel guilty about misleading everyone around us?" she asked. "Our closest friends and family don't even realize we're friends!"

"I don't feel a bit of guilt," he said.

"Well, good. Neither do I. What I feel is young. And I like it."

Marni couldn't remember when she last felt like this. Certainly not with Rick, who very quickly took over her life. Nor with Jeff; he had seemed perfect for her and they fit together like best friends and partners from the start. In fact, in no time she began to depend on him always being there, always having her back. It was the shock that he'd betrayed her more than the betrayal itself that stung the most. In fact, after a couple of years, after giving him far more money than he deserved to end the marriage, she had grown bored with anger and bitterness and chalked it up to yet another good life lesson. After all, most of her success came after he left. And he had proven himself unable to spin what she had given him into a viable living.

He'd managed to lose everything, even the woman he'd sacrificed his marriage for. She'd be lying if she claimed it didn't give her a bit of dark satisfaction. She'd also be lying if she said she didn't feel sorry for him. It was impossible to figure out how the man could have been so stupid.

Of course she'd been that stupid once. But she'd been seventeen.

Now she had met this wonderful farmer. An intellectual who was fully invested in the future of sustainable food, which meant they had many things in common. And he rang all her chimes, but she wasn't about to say the word *love*. Love for her had been a poison and she might be accident-prone but she wasn't stupid. She wasn't about to be led by some emotion she clearly didn't trust or understand.

But there was no denying the thrill it gave her to lift the garage door for him to drive his truck in and conceal it from the world. That feeling was matched when he grabbed her in his arms and kissed all the worries out of her, right there in the hall. They couldn't keep their hands off each other; they were mad for each other. She didn't care if he loved her or not. It was certainly gratifying that he wanted her and there was no faking that.

"Do you think this insanity I'm feeling will pass?" she asked him.

"If it doesn't, I won't live as long as I expected. Did I tell you my father is eighty-five? And doing great. My mother is eighty-four. They've had very few health problems. I could last a long time. Unless this wonderful madness kills me."

She couldn't help it, she laughed. "At some point, we're going to be found out."

He laughed. "We're over twenty-one."

"True."

"And we've been single and independent for a long time."

"And parents."

"Didn't you say your daughter wants you to be dating again?" he asked.

"Dating, yes. But what we are doing might shock her."

Sam laughed again.

This was her favorite part of her life now. Conversation

with a smart man, nakedness and passion, laughter. At some point before he left, they might have a drink together. Maybe something to eat. And when it was time to part ways for the evening, they would linger at the back door and find it hard to say goodbye.

Sophia had been through the full gamut of emotions since the night she went out for a glass of wine with her girlfriends. It had been a very rocky week. At first she was genuinely shaken from her confrontation with Angelo. When she got home from the bar, she was greatly relieved that her father was home. She told him she was exhausted and went straight to bed, where she could not sleep. The next day she pleaded a stomach bug and missed work and school.

She was initially afraid that Angelo would call or even come to the door so she put her car in the garage, made sure the doors were all locked and huddled fearfully in the house. Her Papi called to check on her a couple of times and that reassured her.

In that long day of worry, she came up with a plan. First she was not going to take any calls from Angelo or, to be safe, from any unknown number. Lia called to check on her and they talked for a long time about Angelo's anger and his flimsy grasp of control. "I don't think you should go out with him anymore," Lia said.

"I just don't understand how he can say such loving things and then accuse me of such terrible things, like insulting him or thinking he's not good enough to be in a campus bar because he hasn't gone to college."

"There's only one way to never have that experience again," Lia said. "Stay away from him. He is one giant red flag!"

Sophia was already there. She was definitely done. She

wasn't interested in trying to figure out why Angelo behaved the way he did. She was officially afraid of him. Well, she was at least very nervous about his unpredictable moods. He could make her feel so bad about herself. But a couple of days after telling him to go away and leave her alone, she began to feel better because he seemed to have moved on.

She did have one little slipup. She'd told Marni she couldn't come to work because she had a little stomach bug but when she was back to work and feeling fine, Marni remarked on her improved condition.

"I think it was a migraine and it was terrible. I'm fine now," Sophia said. Of course Marni questioned that and said something about a stomach issue.

"Ah, I wonder if the migraine upset my stomach," Sophia said, quickly trying to cover her mistake.

"I've heard that can happen," Marni said. But her expression made it clear she wondered if Sophia had really been playing hooky.

By the time a week passed, Sophia was feeling so much more confident. She was lively and humorous again, back to both work and school, diving into both. It being the summer session, she had a very light load—one class that met three times a week and was made up of a book and writing critique group and the occasional guest lecture.

She had a very long list of required reading to be completed by the onset of the fall semester. She had always been able to lose herself in books and did not mind the assignment. The days ticked by nicely.

There was one little thing that went on for weeks; whenever her phone chimed, even with just a text, she froze until she could see that it was not Angelo. Then she would breathe a sigh of relief and get right back to feeling confident again.

She did wonder how many more weeks would have to pass before she stopped looking over her shoulder. She and Angelo had no mutual friends; a couple of girls she barely knew claimed to have had a friend who dated him once, but there was nothing to share, no warnings or tips.

Since that incident at The Library, all had been quiet. It appeared Angelo had disappeared. Most of the time she felt the misery had passed, that it was long ago and far away. But there was still a small kink in her neck when the thought crossed her mind that he might find her at some point in the future and become a darkness, a threat.

She had grown lonely during this isolation and when Clarissa called and said a bunch of them were gathering over Fourth of July for a cookout, Sophia was thrilled. There would be about twenty kids, including Lia. And the gathering would be at Clarissa's parents' house on the lake. It sounded perfectly safe and secure.

"Don't worry about me," her dad said. "I've been invited to some friends for ribs, but I won't be out late. You go, have fun, call me if you need me."

And God, it felt so good to dress for a party, dress to be seen and not worry about being at risk. She wore her shortest shorts over her bathing suit, blew out her long thick dark hair, lathered on the sunscreen and did her eye makeup. She had new sandals that had wraparound straps to mid-calf and she felt pretty!

Once she got to Clarissa's house, carrying a basket of fresh cuttings from her father's garden, she checked one last detail. "You didn't invite Angelo, did you?"

"God, no! Is he still giving you trouble?"

She shook her head. "I haven't heard a word!"

"Good. I guess he finally got the hint."

She had a wonderful day. They ate barbeque, Clarissa's mom was thrilled with the fresh fruits and vegetables, Sophia had a couple of beers, helped in the kitchen and even enjoyed the attention of a couple nice young men, though she was very cautious on the latter. They swam, sunned, ate, drank, played, and life became normal again. But just like a timid rabbit, she called to be sure her Papi was home before she headed that way.

"Oh, Papi, did I wake you?"

"Not yet," he said with a laugh. "Call me again in fifteen minutes and you might!"

So off she went, headed home with the car doors locked, got to her house, parked in the garage, went into the house through the kitchen, found her father nodded off on the couch with the TV on, and all was right in her world. She kissed him good-night, went to bed, slept the sleep of the happily tired. And she felt like her worries had long disappeared.

Until the next afternoon.

Monday was a holiday and Sophia had neither work nor school, but having taken the weekend off, she planned to stay home and see if she could get ahead on some of her required reading. She was determined to do well in her courses because her father was not only a professor but the head of a department and she knew without being told she'd better not embarrass him. Sam was not a high-pressure kind of guy but Sophia was a perfectionist. She lived for him to be proud of her.

She had gotten a good start on the plays of Arthur Miller and was also indulging a novel, *Christy* by Catherine Marshall, which was not required. The day was hot and sunny and she was tucked into the corner of the sofa, a light wrap draping over her bare legs. The doorbell rang.

Her first reaction was to stiffen with anxiety. Without moving too much, she reached for her phone. They had a video doorbell. She clicked on to have a look and gasped. It was Angelo, standing on the front step, holding a large bouquet of flowers. She couldn't move. He rang again. She sat very still, barely breathing.

She was determined not to answer the door. She didn't want anything to do with him, and she sure didn't feel confident about being alone with him. She didn't want to argue or bicker and she didn't want to put up with his senseless anger. After what seemed like five minutes had passed, she looked at her doorbell camera again. There was no one there. She would eventually peek out the front window to see if his truck was anywhere around, but not right away. She was afraid he might be lurking near the house and see her.

Her book was closed in her lap. So much for Arthur Miller. She felt the prickle of tears behind her closed lids. It was so frustrating because she didn't really know the cause. He made her nervous. He was like a sleeping dog—not a good idea to confront him or startle him. One never knew which Angelo would come out. He'd done a little acting out but he hadn't done anything so terrible as hit her. He gave her a little shove and she fell, but if she hadn't been on a hill, she wouldn't have fallen; it hadn't been a hard shove. He broke his glass at the bar, but it could have been an accident, like he said. And following that incident he had left her completely alone. Then why this ripple of fear? She closed her eyes and took deep breaths.

It seemed as if only a moment passed when she heard his voice. "I thought you might be here."

Angelo! In her house! Standing beside the couch, looking down at her. She gasped and sat up, clutching the throw to her chest.

"Why didn't you answer the door?" he asked, like it was the most normal question in the world.

"I didn't want to! I wasn't expecting anyone so it could have been the delivery of a package! How did you get in here?"

He glanced over his shoulder. "The slider is open. Listen, Chi Chi, we have to talk." He put his giant bouquet of flowers on the cocktail table and sat on the end of the couch. She pulled her bare feet away from him.

"I don't think we have to talk, Angelo. You just broke into my house!"

"No, baby, no! I was worried about you. I knew you were here. I came around the back and walked into an open house."

"You had to climb over an eight foot gate and wall!"

"That gate wasn't locked, either. I only came over to talk to you. The last couple of weeks have been terrible for me. I thought maybe we could work a few things out. We were so happy. I know I screwed up. I didn't mean to. I just wanted to make sure you're okay."

"I'm okay," she said, scooting away from him. "You should go."

"Are you saying you won't even talk to me?"

"There is nothing to say," she said bravely, but her voice wobbled. "I can't deal with your anger; I am tired of your little tantrums. I am not the only person to see it! The bartender offered to get me safely home! No, I don't want to talk about it."

"But can you just listen to me? For just a second?"

"Please be quick about it because I don't feel safe with you anymore."

"Oh, Chi Chi, that kills me! I would never let anyone hurt you! I live to be sure you're safe. I know I have to work on my anger. My mother tells me this all the time. I never really knew my father but my mother says I got it from him. But being without you is so terrible. I'll take an oath never to let my anger get the best of me again. Try to imagine, my Chi Chi, what it must be like for me to constantly fight the ghost of my father, trying to be a better man."

She swallowed and lifted her chin.

"At least say you forgive me."

"Of course," she said very softly.

"And we can try again," he said.

She shook her head. "I wish you well. You'll be so much happier if you conquer your anger, but I don't think it will work for us. Me. It won't work for me. I am sorry but that is the end of it."

"You break my heart," he said. He looked so sad, forlorn and lost. "I hoped we could at least be friends. Can't we be friends?"

She was quiet for a moment. Finally she said, "I think we could be friends. If you don't get angry."

"I swear to you!" he said. "So, I will take you out to a nice dinner on Friday!"

"No! No, I said we can be friends! I'll say hello, I'll give you a wave, I'll see you somewhere and you'll tell me what you've been doing and ask me what I've been doing, and that's how we are friends. I am not dating you, Angelo. We tried that and it didn't work out!"

"It was working for me," he said in a morose tone. "Can we meet for a beer some time?" he asked.

"Maybe, but please remember I work and go to school and have piles of homework. I told you before. My work and school come first. It's very important to me. You said you understood."

He sat quietly, his elbows resting on his knees, looking down in a very dejected manner. Of course she felt guilt at disappointing him but her instincts were telling her not to lighten up.

"Okay. I get it," he said. "Is it okay to call you sometime?"

She started to say yes, of course. Then stopped herself. "If I'm working or in class, you'll have to leave a message. That's how it is. At work we are taping and all our phones are off. And in class, no phones."

"Sure," he said, but he said it in a way that indicated he didn't really believe it. He got up, leaving the flowers on the table, and shuffled to the back slider.

"No, please go out the front door. I'll walk you out."

She tried to keep her distance as she followed him to the door. If he turned and grabbed her in an embrace, she thought she might freak out. His steps were slow, but he finally made it through the door.

"Goodbye. Be well," she said. And she firmly closed the door, throwing the latch. She then ran through the house, out the slider and all the way around the house to the metal gate. The yard was completely enclosed in a wall with a locked gate on each side. That gate was locked. It was locked with a key! It wasn't as if Angelo could have found it open and locked it himself. That was proof he had climbed over.

She went back in the house, locked the slider. She checked all the other doors and windows in the house, then she threw away the flowers.

Holiday or not, the hydroponic farm needed care every day. Sam had gone by in the morning, checked on things, answered some emails, looked at the schedule, then spent a couple of hours with Marni. When he got home, the house was quiet. He looked in the refrigerator and the contents were a little bleak. Sophia must have forgotten about running to the grocery store to shop for supplies. He blew it off and checked the pantry. There, in the trash can was a bouquet of beautiful white lilies, roses and baby's breath.

He carried the basket to Sophia's room and knocked on the door.

"Come in," she said.

He opened the door and held up the trash can. "If it's none of my business, just say so."

She laughed and her cheeks flushed slightly. "I told Angelo I didn't think it was working out with us, but he must not have heard me clearly."

"I see," he said, the corners of his mouth twitching. "I trust you clarified for him."

"Yes, I explained it again."

He was quiet for a moment. "Let me know if you want to talk about it."

"It's fine now, Papi. Don't worry."

Jason had been in love with Bella for a long time. They'd been married for five years and had been together a couple of years before that. He fell in love with her because she was smart, funny, deep down good in her heart, stable, honest and maybe the sexiest woman he'd ever known. And she had been reliable. Predictable. He never worried about her being in a weird mood. He had never been thrown off balance by her emotions.

Until in vitro and pregnancy.

The doctors did warn them both that there could be some

serious emotional swings, but there was no way he could have prepared himself for what his marriage had become. He was never sure what he'd be coming home to at the end of the day. Bella could be Mother Earth, warm and fuzzy, nurturing and soft, or she could be a fire-breathing dragon. She could be giggling about the size of her ankles or sobbing about the size of her butt. Her nipples itched and she had a hemorrhoid. She had gained more weight than she wanted and so she'd taken to starving him. She had discovered lean meals, mostly salads. But, of course, he was gaining weight as well because he was fearfully loading up either at lunch or on his way home from work. So afraid of the hunger pains, he would stop and wolf down a whole pizza or a couple of Big Macs. And he wasn't getting much exercise; Bella wasn't as active and resented his occasional outings with the guys to golf, bowl or shoot a few hoops.

When he looked at his profile in the mirror, he wasn't optimistic about the future.

He was torn every day. He wanted to get home to her or he didn't want to go home at all. He had a big defense case brewing and that would go to court in a couple of weeks, which also had him stressed out. It was a sketchy one, a custody fight that involved criminal domestic abuse. Jason was representing the man accused of felony domestic assault and it was weighing on him.

He entered their townhouse and saw that Bella was lying on the sofa, her swollen feet elevated on a pillow. He went to her directly and kissed her forehead. "How are you feeling?"

"Bloated. You were supposed to call on your way home."

"I'm sorry. Just when I was about to I got a call from the office that had me tied up. I'll be happy to go to the store if there's anything you want."

"That's sweet, but my blood pressure is a little high. How about we go out to Friday's for a bite to eat. I can get a broiled chicken breast with some vegetables and you can get whatever you want. I'll run by the store tomorrow. We don't need much."

His mind ticked off—score one for Jason. He wasn't in trouble. "That sounds perfect." He looked at her swollen ankles and felt like a dog. He had done this to her and she was miserable. "I'm sorry about the cankles."

"It'll be over soon. My friend Stacy said after the baby is born it's like someone puts a pin in you and you deflate."

The mental image of that made him laugh. Sadly that wouldn't work on him. "I'm ready whenever you are."

She groaned and sat up.

As they drove, she was describing her very boring day. Given advanced pregnancy, she wasn't being assigned any long cases. Instead she was doing a lot of paperwork for the DA's office, proofing warrants, doing research, interviewing witnesses, following up on evidence.

Then she asked him what he was working on.

"I can't talk about it with the DA's office, even if it is different counties."

"I hear nothing, I see nothing."

"It's a pretty tough one. A woman has alleged spousal abuse in a suit to grant her custody and with that, increased child support. The defendant says not only is he completely innocent but that she beat herself up. And he says it's not the first time. He says she's a complete narcissist and a dangerously good gaslighter. There's a real dearth of evidence, but there is a shy, brilliant six-year-old involved. I'd hate to rely on her, but I'll do what I have to do."

"I would ask her one question," Bella said. "Where do you

most like to sleep at night? She might say Momma's house, she might say Daddy's house. She might say Grandma's or even Aunt Jane's. Or maybe a friend's house. From that you will know which way to go next."

They talked about it for a while and Jason was reminded of one of the many reasons he loved Bella. She was insightful and had great instincts. Discussions like this had long been the seasoning on their marriage, giving it flavor. He loved it.

He was feeling pretty good when they got to the restaurant. Typical of this place, it was crowded and noisy but they were able to get a booth that was tucked away. He looked over the menu.

"How are you guys tonight?" the waitress cheerily greeted, slapping down a couple drink napkins.

"Doing great, how's your night going?" Jason returned.

"Better all the time. You want a drink to start you off?"

"A light beer, whatever is on tap," he said.

"Ma'am?" she asked.

"Just water," Bella said.

"I think we're ready to order, unless my wife wants another look."

"You know what you want?" Bella asked.

"I'm going to have what you're having."

"Oh, that's so sweet! This is a man who came prepared," the waitress said, beaming. She did have a beautiful and engaging smile. "Ma'am?"

"Broiled chicken breast and steamed vegetables, whatever is available. Maybe a small salad with dressing on the side."

"Does that sound okay to you?" the waitress asked Jason.

"Perfect. Pass on the salad, though. And can we have some bread?"

"Absolutely," she said. "I'll get your drinks. Be right back."

Bubbly, Jason was thinking as she bopped away. Bounce in her step. Easy laugh. When he finally pulled his eyes away and looked at Bella, she was frowning.

"Are you okay?" he asked her.

"Fine," she said, unconvincingly.

He wisely chose to keep his mouth shut. Their waitress was back with a couple of waters and Jason's beer. "I thought you might like a water, too," she said. "Now if there's anything else you need while we're waiting for your dinner, I'm Tiffany and this is my section so I'll never be far away."

"Thanks, Tiffany," Jason said. "You can go ahead and bring my bread anytime. No hurry. Just when you get a minute."

"Absolutely! I'll do it right now! I don't know why I didn't think of it."

She whirled away and nearly sprinted across the restaurant. He couldn't help it; he watched her go. When he pulled his eyes back to Bella, her expression was dark.

"Come on," he urged. "We were having such a nice time! Don't be grumpy."

"Maybe we can order a few more things so you can watch her wiggle across the room again."

He had been watching her ass but he'd be cold and dead and in the ground before he'd admit it. "I wasn't watching her wiggle."

"You were."

"Come on, Bella, don't be ridiculous."

And poof, like magic, a small basket of bread appeared. "Oops, I forgot the butter. Be right back."

"Take your time."

Tiffany flashed him a lovely grin, whirled and headed back across the room. Jason stubbornly fixed his eyes on Bella's and did not so much as blink.

"You're being pretty obvious, the way you're now not looking at her."

"I only have eyes for you, my love."

"Well, there's a lot more of me to look at."

"You are more beautiful to me every day." He watched as her expression began to soften and he felt like taking a victory lap. Bella never used to be so hard to please. *Pregnancy*, he reminded himself. *Hormones.*

Tiffany returned to their table. "Butter! Now can you think of anything else you'd like?"

"I think we're good," he said.

"Your dinner will be up shortly. Holler if you want me!" Then she giggled. Jason felt his cheeks grow warm. A quick glance told him his wife snickered.

He buttered his bread. He stared at the bread, not Tiffany's butt.

"She's flirting with you."

"If that's true, it would be a total waste of her time," he said. Then he wondered how he was going to get through a whole meal without looking up.

It seemed like an eternity before their meals arrived but it had only been a few minutes. "Here we go," Tiffany said cheerfully. "That looks wonderful. Is there anything else I can get you?"

"I don't need anything. Bella?" he asked.

"I'll take an order of French fries and some ranch dressing."

"That's ranch you have on the side. Do you want some more?" Tiffany asked.

"Yes. I want more."

"Sure thing," she said, bouncing away.

The tension eased between them as they ate. Bella was starving and feeding the monster within calmed her. Jason could relate. He was starting to take on some of her predilections. He was thinking he needed to stop force-feeding himself in the middle of the day and find time in his schedule to work out.

As they ate and tensions calmed—and Tiffany stayed away—they had an enjoyable if quiet dinner. He drained his beer and thought he'd like another but he wasn't going to chance it, not with Bella on the watch.

"Can I get you another beer?" Tiffany, who appeared out of nowhere, asked.

"No thanks. I'm good."

"Is there anything I can get you?"

Tiffany was pressing her luck. Bella was a wife, a pregnant wife, and a gifted prosecutor. She might look soft tonight in this setting but she was a badass. "No, thank you."

"Holler if you change your mind."

Jason decided at that moment he was going to find a way to get better control of this situation. First of all they were going to start having adult beverages in the house again. He shouldn't be going out for a drink in the evening. He'd rather have a drink at home, with his wife, after a long stressful day. That she wasn't drinking, he appreciated, but he didn't overdo it and it was better to stay clear of the Tiffanys of the world. And he was going to get back to the gym; it helped his body and his stress level. It helped him sleep better.

He thought these silent but important decisions would change everything. Then the bill came. It was slipped into a leather sleeve and, of course, Jason reached for his wallet and credit card. He didn't even notice it at first. He just glanced at the bill, then glanced over his shoulder, then back at the bill. He slid his card in.

Bella, having looked over her shoulder, looked back at Jason. Then she said, "Let me see that."

"I've got it," he said. And he immediately thought, *Great lawyer, Jason.* Now it was going to go down all different; now it was going to seem he was hiding something.

Bella snatched the leather sleeve out of his hands, flipped it open and glared. "Not on my watch," she growled.

Tiffany had stupidly scrawled her phone number on the bill. Tiffany was soon to be toast.

There was a time Bella would have laughed and said something like, *Want to tell her fat chance or should I?* But Bella was over six months pregnant with ankles the size of her thighs and drunk on hormones. She slid out of the booth and charged to the hostess station. He watched helplessly. She clearly asked for the manager. A man appeared in just seconds. She waved the bill in his face. He spoke; she spoke more. She was using her prosecutor's voice. It was soft but firm and there was no smile. After a few words were exchanged, she returned to the booth to gather her purse. "Dinner is on them," she said. "No tip."

He followed her out of the restaurant. His step was slow and he didn't dare look at Tiffany, not because of what he might see in the girl's eyes but because of Bella's reaction. When they were in the car, it was dark and silent. He didn't start the car; he sat there stewing.

"You could have stopped that before it went so far," she said.

"How?"

"You could've said, 'I'm married, this is my wife, let's not flirt.'"

"I didn't flirt. And I didn't consider what she was doing as flirting. I thought she was friendly and bubbly."

"She put her phone number on the check!"

"I would have tossed it in the trash!"

"And said nothing?"

"Why would I say anything? I certainly wouldn't have called her!"

"That was *wrong!*" Bella said.

"I'm not the flirtation police! Does the girl still have a job?"

"That's not my problem," Bella said. "If she gets fired for flirting with the married customers, maybe she'll learn an important lesson about being professional. But you could have put a stop to it, nipped it in the bud, put her in her place."

"Or we could have ignored it and laughed about it later! Jesus!"

"Was there any concern about how that might make *me* feel?"

"I figured being a grown-ass woman who puts away hardened criminals for a living, you could let it roll off your back, maybe make fun of it later. That's what I would have done if a good-looking young waiter was flirting with you!"

"I once saw you grab a bartender by the front of his shirt and threaten to throw him in the street if he didn't stop undressing me with his eyes."

It was true. He had. "I was much younger then," he said.

"And maybe much more in love with me..."

"Not possible. I definitely love you more now than I did when I was younger, but I know how to conduct myself better now. I was ashamed of my behavior that night." He gulped. "I was pretty ashamed of that bartender's behavior as well, but he was a bartender. I was a lawyer. I should have been more controlled."

"And tonight?" she said. It sounded like a jab.

"For a few minutes, until you started to seethe, it was kind of fun. A silly young girl thought I was a catch!"

Bella was quiet. "Sorry I ruined your fun."

"And I'm sorry that wasn't you, flirting with me."

And he started the car.

TEN

Sophia didn't hear from Angelo for several days. She was just starting to get her mojo back, feeling a bit more positive and confident, and then he texted her.

How about a beer after work on Friday night? I have a new job. A good job! I can't wait to tell you about it!

She texted back that she had commitments with family and had to pass but congratulated him on his new job. Then she held her breath. When he didn't shoot back an angry text, she breathed again.

A few days later he texted again asking when she might be free to grab a beer.

She didn't respond to his message. But she was concerned, remembering what happened the last time he grew impatient.

In less than twenty-four hours she got another text message. When are you free to get together?

She texted back that her schedule with work, school and family commitments was packed and she would be in touch when she could. But her mood sank. She didn't have to be psychic to know that was going to piss him off.

While she was at Marni's house, working on the set designs, she was distracted and unusually quiet. Marni was busy in the kitchen but Ellen brought it up. "Sophia, I can see something is upsetting you. Do you want to talk about it?"

"No, I have to figure this out. But thank you."

"Sometimes just talking about things helps," Ellen said.

"I haven't wanted to bother anybody," she said. "It's a boy problem."

"Oh, dear, I'm not any good with love. I have no experience with romance."

"It's not romance!" Sophia said. "I went out with a guy a few times and now he thinks he owns me! I don't know how to break him away!"

"Is he bothering you?"

"It's my fault," she said, looking down. "He asked if we could be friends and I said yes to that, but his idea of friendship and mine are very different. He wants to go out for a beer and he's going to ask and ask until I do and I don't want to. I don't know what to say to him. I don't want to make him mad!"

Ellen took Sophia's hand and pulled her over to the dining room table, just out of Marni's view. "What happens when he gets mad?" Ellen asked.

"Well, he sulks…"

Ellen chuckled. "Do you have to be a witness to his sulking? Can't you just ignore that?"

Sophia looked down at her hands. "A few weeks ago I turned him down because I was getting together with girlfriends for a study session. When we were done, we went to a bar for a glass of wine and he happened to be there. He was mad; he said, 'is this how you study?' He slammed down his beer so hard he broke the glass and the bartender wanted to throw him out. I don't even remember what I said that made him do that! I wasn't with another guy or anything! I was with my friends! So I told him to stay away from me and I left with my friends. After about a week, he came to my house with flowers. He wanted to work things out. He said it was all a misunderstanding and we should try again."

"Oh, Sophia, you shouldn't have let him in," Ellen said.

"I didn't! I didn't answer the door and he came in through the back slider."

Ellen blanched. "He…came in?"

"I was on the couch, reading, and he was suddenly standing there. He said the door was open. It might've been, but the gates to the back garden were locked. I checked after he left and they were *locked*. He must have climbed over."

"Sophia, I don't think he happened to be at that bar and he sure didn't happen to find the back slider open. I think he's stalking you. I think he wouldn't have found the back slider open if he hadn't climbed over the backyard wall. And before we go any further, you can't *make* someone lose his temper! It wasn't something you did! Have you told your father about this?"

"No," she said. "I don't want him to think I can't handle myself."

"It sounds like you're handling yourself just fine but this young man is not! It is not a good situation and it's not your fault."

"I don't know what to do."

"He scares you, doesn't he?" Ellen asked.

"Yes, but he hasn't done anything to hurt me. Not really."

"That black eye? That had nothing to do with him?"

She gave a helpless shrug.

"Was he involved in some way?" Ellen asked.

"He was angry because there were so many people at the lake and he thought we should be alone. He gave me a little shove to hurry me along but we were hiking down the hill and I tripped. Really, I did trip."

"But would you have tripped if he hadn't pushed you?"

Sophia didn't respond because she didn't know the answer. She bit her bottom lip.

"That's what I think, too. Okay, I will tell you what to do. I have a little experience in this. First, do not call him. The next time he calls you if you're in a position to speak to him, take the call. Tell him very firmly that you're not going to be dating him anymore, not even as friends. Tell him to lose your number. He was quite rude, especially coming into your home without being invited and no, it cannot be worked out. Goodbye and don't call again. You have to be polite but very firm."

"He'll say he just wants to talk…"

"And you'll say no, there is nothing to talk about, your mind is made up. Sophia, this guy has shown you who he is and believe me, he's not going to change. He will only get worse."

"Has this happened to you?"

"No, not to me. My younger sister had a serious problem with a man she was dating. And she was divorced and in her early thirties, so it's not as if she knew nothing about men. Her first husband wasn't perfect by any means but she fell hard in love with the guy who came next and he terrorized her. He never touched her that I know of. At least she insists his abuse was all emotional and verbal. Yet, she was completely harassed. He would park outside her house to watch her coming and going, show up at restaurants where she was meeting her friends, call and call and call her, cry and threaten to kill himself if she wouldn't take him back. The police couldn't help her because he didn't threaten her specifically.

"You must hear me, Sophia—if this young man is making you frightened and uncomfortable, you have to push him away. And you have to tell your father. You need his protection now."

"I'm afraid it will only worry him."

"It worries me!" Ellen said. "I've seen firsthand how dangerous this sort of thing can get."

"How did your sister get out?"

"It took her a long time and great perseverance. It felt like it went on forever. My brothers got involved. I think it was a year and then she was looking over her shoulder for another year."

"What did she do to get the attention of her terrible man?"

"That's the thing you must understand—it wasn't anything she did, just as it isn't anything you did. He picked her. And I bet your young man picked you."

Sophia felt as if she'd just swallowed a boulder. "He bought me a drink and then he drove me home after I'd had one too many. I'm not going to pretend I've never had a little too much to drink, but it's not something I'm known for! I fell asleep in his truck. He said he was keeping me safe!"

Ellen frowned. "I don't know if I'd believe that. Sweetheart, it's important that you think hard about this and be determined not to take any chances. Be careful not to be alone with this man. I will drive you to and from work and school, if you need me to. And promise me you'll talk to your father tonight."

"I will try," was all she said. Because she just didn't know how! "Please don't say anything to Marni."

"Sophia, Marni is your friend!"

"I'm so embarrassed that I let this happen!"

"No, no. This happened to you! You're going to have to be strong to make this go away because clearly he doesn't like taking no for an answer. This is no time to fear your friends! We're here to help."

Ellen was quite concerned about Sophia and it brought back memories of when her younger sister had a bothersome man in her life. It was over twenty years ago but still the memory could send prickles up her spine. Had she thought *bothersome*? He was dangerous, though he never actually did anything. He threatened, he dropped creepy innuendo, he was an expert gaslighter. He never crossed the line but he regularly charged right up to it. He stalked her, called her and said scary things like "I know where you were last night" or "I know how late you were out." She would spot him sitting behind her in the movie theater when she was leaving. He said threatening things but once she had a recording device installed in her phone, he stopped so she couldn't prove it. She wasn't able to get a temporary restraining order from the police because he toyed with her, seemed to enjoy scaring her but hadn't threatened her life outright.

Ellen remembered how difficult it was to get anyone to do anything, even going so far as to ask, "Are we being told that he should actually try to kill her before we can help her?"

After that, a police officer agreed to speak with the stalker but that seemed to make matters worse for a while.

Back when it was her sister's challenge, the expression *gaslighting* was not commonly heard, but now it was the subject of every other talk show or podcast. But that's what it was—it was a power struggle in every way. In fact, as Ellen had learned, most abuse cases were about power, about gaining and keeping control. If what happened to her sister happened now, Ellen would handle it differently than she had back then.

She drove home, wishing she could talk to Mark about this. What she had been so surprised to find in him was the kindest most sensitive man, who loved children and animals. If he weren't so busy setting up his foundation, he'd have a dog.

They'd been having dinner together at least three nights a week for a little more than a month, and while cooking might be a common interest, they found they had so many other things to talk about as well.

But right now he was out of town for a few days, visiting his son, a Las Vegas firefighter. She had his cell number but wouldn't dream of bothering him while he was visiting his family. She still hadn't even mentioned to Marni that she and Mark were seeing a lot of each other. And Marni asked all the time.

When Marni came to mind, Ellen thought of Sophia. Ellen was going to give her three days to tell Marni and if she didn't, Ellen would. Women should stop trying to shoulder these things alone!

Once again she realized how much she wanted to talk to Mark. In the few weeks they'd been meeting for dinner she'd been very careful not to have expectations, but here she was, wanting only him. In a few weeks he had touched her shoulder, put a hand on her back or gently grasped her elbow, nothing more. But their conversations had been so deep and pure.

When she pulled up to her house she was surprised to see

an RV with a trailer attached parked in the street in front of his house and hers. She gasped because it must be his and she had no idea it was coming. It could only be his traveling food truck.

His caravan was blocking her driveway so she parked on the street right behind the trailer. She didn't see him anywhere so she went to the RV's door, which was standing open. "Mark?" she called.

He appeared suddenly in the RV doorway, a grin as big as the sun lit up his face. "What do you think?"

She was stunned and excited. "Is this what I think it is?"

"Almost. It still needs some work. I need refrigeration in the trailer and more storage. But according to my calculations, what we can do with this setup can feed twelve hundred people a day. We'll need additional space for meal prep but I have fire department connections and you'd be amazed what we can do with a parking lot and tent." He stopped talking and frowned. "Ellen? You okay?"

"Oh, Mark, look what you've done."

He stepped down from the RV doorway and opened his arms so she could step into his embrace.

And she lost it. She hugged him and sobbed into his shoulder.

"There now," he said, with a little chuckle. "You're gonna have to tell me why you're crying so I can help."

That did nothing to stop the crying.

He gently moved her hair away from her face. "Does this mean you missed me?"

She pushed back just enough to look into his eyes. "I wanted to talk to you and had no idea how much until just now."

"You have my number," he said. "You've only used it for

logistics, like what time is dinner and where will we eat. But you can call for other reasons. Like if there's something heavy on your mind."

"But you might be busy and I hate the thought of bothering you. I thought you were visiting your son."

"My son helped me arrange for this kitchen caravan. So yes, I was with him and he helped me put all the details together. Now what's got you all upset?"

"It's been a long day," she said.

"Sounds like time for a glass of wine while you tell me about it."

"That would be perfect," she said. "My house?"

"We'll come out and rearrange the vehicles later. Come on, Ellen. Much as I like holding you, I think it's better if we talk first."

"Oh, my God, I threw myself at you!"

He laughed lightly. "Yeah, that was wonderful." He took her hand. "You must have had a rough day at work!" He led her up the walk. "It's only been a few days but it's nice to be back home."

They went into her house and straight to the kitchen. "Are the RV and trailer safe on the street?" she asked him.

"I'm sure of it. This is a quiet neighborhood. After dinner I'll back them into the driveway side by side and locked." He sat down while she took a chilled bottle of chardonnay from the refrigerator and uncorked it. "You're turning out to be great to come home to. That looks good."

"Are you starving?" she asked him.

"Not at all. I had a snack basket in the RV. My daughter-in-law made me a lunch with lots of extras. It's a whole new ball game to drive your kitchen and bathroom around. All I had to do was pull over on a wide space in the road for a little break and to refresh my drink and get food. We'll put our heads together and come up with a plan for dinner in a bit." He patted the chair. "Talk to me."

"You haven't met Sophia but I've told you about her. She's Marni's intern. She's still in school, hoping for a future in TV production."

"The Argentinian girl?"

"The same. It turns out she has a problem with a young man she's been seeing. He's becoming a real pain. Something like that happened to one of my younger sisters. It was a long time ago now but it was awful."

"What kind of pain?"

"The way she put it, they went out a couple of times and he thought he owned her. Reading into it and asking a few questions, it seems he immediately became controlling and domineering. He expects her to be available, to answer her phone if he's calling, no matter what she's doing. And if she doesn't respond to him, he has a little tantrum. It's exhausting."

"Is that what your sister went through?"

"Yes, times ten. Her boyfriend became more and more obsessed with her until eventually he was literally terrorizing her. He was jealous, became angry over nothing, followed her. He would park at the end of her street and call her to tell her he was watching her. He never laid a hand on her but there's something so terrifying about being stalked like that."

"But that didn't ever happen to you, did it?"

"No, not to me, but I think I felt it almost as deeply, because I was afraid for my sister. She finally left town and went to stay with friends for a couple of years! She was divorced and had a couple of little kids. It's not as if she was young and naive. And she hadn't led him on—he picked her out and focused on her."

"But Sophia is so young. What did you suggest she do?"

"I explained as best I could how manipulative this is, urged her to be very firm in telling him she is not interested and suggested she tell Marni. And her father! It's just Sophia and her dad right now. He's a professor and she's a student at the same college. I told her if she didn't tell them, I would. She shouldn't be alone with some deranged young man stalking her."

"Maybe he's just really stupid and infatuated..."

"That would be good," Ellen said. "But he still has to go away!"

"You've had a very hard day, haven't you. And you're so worried about Sophia you fell apart."

"Oh, no! I mean I am worried about her, but that's not what made me cry! What made me cry was realizing how much I had missed you in only a few days! I had this rush of emotion when I saw you! I had a little problem and even though I've been close friends with Marni for twenty years, the only person I wanted to talk to was you! Oh, Mark, I'm scared. I don't want to become dependent on you! That wouldn't be good for either one of us!"

He frowned slightly. "Why not?"

She gave a huff of startled laughter. "Says the man who lost his wife to a woman who buried her husband? Both of us after years of caretaking?"

"Well, there's another way to look at that. Maybe we both deserve a break. Ever think of it that way?" He laughed in spite of himself. "Susan confessed she was planning that I would die first. She said she'd been writing my eulogy for years. And she was very disappointed to be going ahead of me."

"What? She said that?"

He nodded and continued to laugh. "It was one of her good days and she was getting close to the end. She said she was furious about it. After all, she'd been getting up at dawn for long walks, meditating, cooking and eating balanced meals and taking all her vitamins for years while I was running into burning buildings. Plus, she said, she didn't trust me with her eulogy at all. She admitted I might be a better cook but I was certainly not a better writer." He wiped his eyes but it wasn't sadness he wiped away.

"How could she say that to you?" Ellen asked.

"Because Susan was one of the funniest women I knew. And she was right. I'd lived such a risky life while she lived such a cautious, balanced life. It was all wrong. But you can't cheat death. Or health. She had health issues. Her mother and sister had health issues; there was family history. On my side of the family, everyone had better health and lived longer than they deserved. Sometimes the best way to a long life is just dumb luck."

"I'm so sorry about that," Ellen said. "I also had a healthy extended family. But my husband had a stroke in his early fifties."

"Sometimes life is a crapshoot," he said. "You can do your best but you can never exactly predict what's coming. Poor Susan. She lived a healthy, responsible life and yet..." He shrugged.

They were quiet for a moment. He sipped his wine and with his other hand, he squeezed hers. "We should talk about food. I have some corned beef from the deli, some rye bread in the freezer that will thaw in nothing flat and a brand-new jar of sauerkraut."

"Reubens!" she said with a clap of her hands. "I have Swiss

cheese and mustard if you don't. I don't have any potato salad to go with it."

"We'll have to rough it," he said.

"So, Mark? The eulogy. How was it?"

He looked down. "It was pretty awful. My part, at least. It's on video somewhere. I'm not showing you."

Then, unexpectedly, they both burst into laughter until they were holding each other up.

August came and signaled the end of summer. The days were still hot, in the eighties with humidity in the valley. Gone was the snow on the mountaintops and the crops were high. During this time Marni had started spending more time at the hydroponic warehouse and was mentally putting together a show in which she could feature organic fruits and vegetables from Sam's secret garden while cultivating her own garden. But since filming had to stay ahead of the calendar, they were already working on holiday meals, and menus for holiday parties and celebratory gatherings to mark the New Year.

At the same time Marni and Ellen worked on a large group of internet shorts to flush out their cooking presence online. In these demonstrations Kevin, their videographer, would edit the films down to five to six minutes, cutting from prep to taste. The subjects were cookies and breads, hors d'oeuvres to desserts. While all of this was enough work to fill every day, they had to plan a dozen live cooking shows. Those had to be well thought out by what was available and in season. Marni was partial to seafood and they prepared and shot cioppino and Maine Shore seafood bake and seafood gumbo. And thanks to the hydroponics made available by Sam, they planned to also shoot spring and summer picnic and bar-beque shorts.

Because of this new attachment to the hydroponic farm-ing, Marni and Sam had begun the process of coming out. Obviously they had food in common. Sam began dropping by to help Marni with her garden, which had grown beauti-ful and lush under the loving touch of Professor Garner while his own garden was left untended for much of the time. But he was a presence at Marni's house and in her kitchen. He brought new samples all the time.

Nettie was stopping by every week to load up on her sister's offerings from items they prepared, either as shorts for the in-ternet shows or rehearsals, and it became routine for Marni's house to receive a lot of visitors at the end of the workweek.

"Thank God my sister has a talent for cooking," Nettie said as Marni and Ellen filled a cardboard box with a beautiful selection of meals and desserts. "This saves my life. Marvin finally thinks he married up."

Bella was dropping by more often as her load grew heavier. She shared the news that The Bump would be a son for Bella and Jason. "A boy," Marni said. "That figures. I know noth-ing about boys. I come out of a family of women and raised a daughter."

"We'll figure it out," Bella said. "Nettie has boys. And Jason has two brothers."

"Thank God. I can't even throw a ball."

Ever since the arrival of her white asparagus bed, Marni had been sneaking around to grab a minute or an hour or two with Sam. She felt seventeen again. In fact she couldn't remember a time she'd been this stirred up. They hadn't said I love you yet but they had both mentioned they didn't expect to be revisited by all this emotion in their fifties. When they weren't panting, they were giggling like high schoolers.

"We're going to have to tell the truth soon," Sam said. "Sophia hardly leaves the house. She only has three classes a week but is trying to get ahead on her reading so she can do both work and school in the fall without too much pressure."

"And she told me about having an issue with the boyfriend."

"I think she's got that straightened out," Sam said. "I asked her if he was still giving her trouble and she said not for quite a while. Apparently he still texts her or calls her now and then but she has learned she can't even say 'maybe.' I wish he'd come around when I'm home. I think I'd enjoy telling him no."

"You're not a fighter," she said.

"Not at all, but I have perfected that professorial growl. I scare the shit out of some students."

"I'd love to see that," she said. "I think you're a pussycat."

One afternoon in mid-August Marni got a call from Tom, her singular blind date and the cross-dresser of the karaoke girls' night out, which had taken on a whole new meaning in her mind since encountering Tom.

"Marni, I wonder if you'd give me a second chance at a coffee date," he said.

"Oh, my," she said, shocked. "I can't, Tom. And I do mean that I can't, and it has nothing to do with the fact that we don't seem to have very much in common."

"But I'd like to explain about that…"

"But it's not necessary, and it has nothing to do with the fact… It's not about your interest in…other subjects… Oh damn, I'm not finding the right words. Look, I'm on a deadline here. We're busy preparing the late fall and holiday specialties. We work ahead a little. I'm busy with Christmas and winter right now and soon we're going to start on the summer fare, so you see, I'm up to my eyeballs in everything from Bundt cakes to barbeque ribs. I have no time. And I'm about to be a grandmother and whether I like it or not, I am unable to schedule that!"

"Marni, it's just a hobby!"

He couldn't possibly be talking about anything but that stunning pencil skirt and low-cut blouse with blazer he wore on that special night. "You have a great talent there," she said. "I completely enjoyed your performance. And sometime I'd like to hear all about how you make it all look so flawless! Your makeup was incredible!"

"Thank you, but… I wish you'd give me time to explain…"

"First of all, there's no need. You gave a star performance. Second, I'm seeing someone. And third, not to belabor the point, I'm honestly in my busiest time of the year. We film about two months a year and spend the rest of the year preparing and catching up. I'm sorry. Maybe after the baby comes? And, Tom, if that works out, it will only be coffee."

"I'm disappointed. I'm afraid it's all because you saw me dressed up."

"Oh, heavens, I bet you could give me some great pointers!"

"I could come by after work sometime."

"Sorry, Tom. I can't."

After she disconnected and slid the phone back into her pocket, she noticed Ellen and Sophia were staring at her. Ellen lifted a brow. "Seeing someone?" she asked with a twinkle in her eye.

"It's what you say," Marni said. "To be kind."

Sam had to leave town for a couple of days. There was an agricultural retreat in Colorado at the university in Boulder and he was presenting a paper on the sustainability of twelve months of harvest from the hydroponic farming experiment and the effects on the local economy. He would also talk about the changes in the ecosystem if people ate foods grown within a hundred miles of their own homes and the long-term benefits were staggering.

To participate he had to be there in person.

"Would you like me to go with and carry your bags, like your assistant?" Sophia asked.

"I've never had such a gifted assistant," he said. "What will you do while I'm gone?"

"I have work and I'll also read and pick out a movie or two."

"Why don't you call a couple of your friends?" he said. "Have a movie party here?"

"I might just do that," she said. But her closest friends had not only work and school, they also had boyfriends. Both Lia and Clarissa offered to fix her up with one of their guy friends but she wasn't ready. Her experience with Angelo was not something she was ready to risk repeating.

Thank goodness it turned out Ellen was right about him. Not responding at all or issuing a very firm "no thank you" seemed to have finally worked on Angelo. She hadn't heard from him in over a week and by now he had surely found someone more agreeable.

Then she heard Marni speaking with Tom and making it very clear she was too busy to see him; she had other life commitments, including that fictional boyfriend, which really made Sophia chuckle. Marni was so in charge of her intentions. She was going to be like that someday.

But still she was on edge the first night she was alone with her father out of town. He called to check on her and when she told him she was home alone, he said, "I kind of hoped I'd find you were going to spend time with your friends."

"They were busy so I'm staying in tonight," she said. "I found a couple of movies to watch."

She did put the movies on, but she jumped with every sound and the night was passing so slowly. At about ten she went to her bedroom to drag her pillow and favorite quilt to the family room, cozied up on the sofa, turned up the volume on the TV and settled in. She had already checked and double-checked all the locks on the doors and windows. She told herself it didn't matter that she wasn't paying attention to the movie. It's not as if there would be a test. She saw the time on her phone at eleven, twelve, then twelve twenty, then one, then one forty. She wasn't sure when she stopped tossing and turning.

When she heard the chirping of birds, the time on her phone was five fifteen. Morning. And she had made it through the night. She stretched out her arms and legs, made a mewling sound of success and opened her eyes. The curtain on the open slider was blowing in the morning breeze.

And there he was. Sitting in her father's chair. Watching her!

She gasped and sat up, clutching her quilt up to her neck. "Angelo, what are you doing here?"

He lounged in the chair, one leg crossed over the other, leaning back in a comfortable pose. "Just watching you sleep."

"You broke into my house!"

"No, I wouldn't do that. Why would I do something like that when I love you? You called me and I came right away. You let me in. I held you until you fell asleep."

"No. No, you are loco!"

"Little girl, I think you're the one with the mental problem." He pulled his smart phone out of his back pocket and scrolled through the calls. "Here you are, right here." He turned it so she could read the number. "And the text saying you are alone and afraid and please come. And then I find the door open, another foolish thing! Someone could walk right in here and slash your throat!"

"I didn't call you! I didn't send a text to you! Never. I did not let you in! Get out! Get out or I will call the police!"

He leaned toward her. "Would you like me to wait for them with you? So we can show them my phone together. You are one crazy chick, you know that. You should have taken me up on my offer to take care of you and keep you safe because you're running out of options. You're too crazy to get a man now." He went on talking about how happy they had been, how beautiful everything was until she got weird. He told her he should get smart and just walk away because she was turning into a crazy person and didn't deserve all he had to offer.

She was astounded by his vision of their relationship as positive and loving, a completely fictional account. They had done nothing but argue! She worried about setting him off every second. She was always walking on eggshells, afraid of the next tantrum.

Finally she could take no more. "Get out!" She grabbed her phone like it was the only lifeline she had, held it close to her chest and sobbed. It was several minutes before she heard the distant sound of a door closing but she didn't trust it. She cuddled under the quilt, afraid to move. She was afraid to get up and walk to the door or her bedroom. He might jump out at her and scare ten years off her life.

ELEVEN

Wednesday morning in the middle of a hellacious week, Marni woke up sluggishly. She hadn't slept well because she was on the phone with Sam till after midnight. He had gone out for dinner and drinks with some of the conference attendees in Boulder and hadn't called her until after ten. "You know we're too old for this," she had complained.

"Then stop, I dare you," he had said.

So instead of getting some sleep they talked into the night. Rising at six, she was exhausted. And it was going to be a long day. The groceries Ellen had ordered would arrive early and they would be dealing with fish. It was important to deal with the seafood while it was fresh.

By the time Marni had showered, dressed and had coffee, Ellen had arrived. "The seafood is here but Sophia is not," Ellen said.

"I thought we checked the calendar. She doesn't have class today," Marni said.

"I know, I called her and she's not answering. She mentioned that her father was going to be out of town for a couple of days."

"I wonder if she took advantage of his absence and had a late night with friends?"

"Sophia has never been late, not more than a minute or two," Ellen said. "She hasn't been out with girlfriends much lately. If she doesn't answer in the next twenty minutes, I'm going to drive over there. She told me she had an issue with that guy she was dating. The one who was insisting they should date but she wasn't interested."

"Surely not dangerous issues," Marni said.

"I hope not…"

"Okay, we'll go now."

"Should we call her father?" Ellen asked.

"Let's just go see if she's home before we worry him. Right now, I'd be very happy to find she drank a whole bottle of wine and overslept."

"She wouldn't…"

"So we'll go pound on the door. Did you text her?" Marni asked.

"Several times," Ellen said. "Are we overreacting to think something is wrong? She probably just got sidetracked, slept too late…"

But both of them had screaming instincts. Marni drove a little fast and Breckenridge was not a big town. They were pulling into Sophia's drive in ten minutes. They both rushed to the front door and while one pressed the doorbell the other knocked. They gave it a moment, then repeated.

Ellen slid away from the front door and put her cupped

hands against the window to look into the house. Marni rang and pounded. "Can you see anything?"

"Nothing. Do you have a key?"

"Of course not." Marnie lifted the doormat on the off chance there would be a key but there was none. She tilted a flowerpot, also nothing there. Then on a whim she tried the doorknob and voila! It was unlocked!

"Sophia!" she called into the house.

There was no answer and they cautiously moved inside, knowing they were trespassing and invading someone's privacy. The house was dark and stuffy. Tiptoeing like a couple of thieves, they moved into the house and then quickly picked up speed toward the sound of someone crying.

"Oh, God," Ellen said, rushing into the family room toward Sophia. The young woman sat up on the corner of the sectional sofa, her quilt drawn over her, her knees raised, her cheeks wet and pink from crying.

"Oh, my God, are you hurt?" Marni asked.

"He…he broke into the house. He was sitting right there. Is he gone? I couldn't move. I think he might still be in the house! I was afraid to look."

"Well, I'm not afraid to look," Marni said. She marched purposefully to the kitchen, flipping on lights as she went, then opening drawers and cabinets. She came out with a rolling pin.

"What do you propose to do with that?" Ellen asked.

"Beat the tar out of anyone who doesn't belong here. Who broke in, Sophia? Was it that boy you don't want to date?"

She nodded and sniffed. "Angelo. He even made up a story saying I called him and asked him to come, but I didn't. I promise I didn't."

"Did you call the police?"

"I was afraid he was still in the house."

"Did he threaten you?"

She shook her head miserably. "He…he said he loved me but he said by leaving the door unlocked, someone could walk right in and slit my throat." Then she started to cry again. "I don't know how he got inside and I don't know how long he was here."

Ellen opened the blinds and light flooded the room. She took out her phone and called the police. Marni headed down the hall, cautiously opening doors, creeping inside with the rolling pin held up in her right hand, more than willing to pummel some intruder. While she went from room to room, she heard parts of what Ellen was saying to the dispatcher, that she was with a friend who had been the subject of a break-in and held captive by a man making threats. She couldn't hear the other side of the conversation but she did hear Ellen demand a police officer come to the residence and take a report. "Yes, we know who it was! Yes, I can give you a name! Yes, this young woman needs to report a home invasion or something. I found her buried under a quilt and afraid to move; she feared he was still in the house and that he might hurt her. No, I don't know if she was raped."

"He's not in the house," Marni said, returning to the family room. "Sadly."

"I was not raped," Sophia said quietly.

Sophia was so skittish that she was afraid to even go to the bathroom alone. Ellen had to promise to stand outside the bathroom door while she quickly washed up, brushed out her hair and dressed.

"Do the police have to come?" she asked. "He didn't actually do anything. He just scared me."

"Yes, and that's doing something," Marni said. "And he

might do it again or try something even worse. Let's report it, see it through, make sure the police have a record of what's happened. While we wait for them to come, get a suitcase or two—you're going to stay with me."

"Maybe until Papi gets home," she said.

"I'm thinking for a good long while. My house is like a vault."

"You have that security alarm…" Sophia said.

"I have more than that. You'll be fine. You can call your father and tell him what happened and where you're staying. It'll put his mind at ease."

Sophia packed a bag while Marni folded up the blanket and put that with the pillow in Sophia's bedroom. The police arrived much more quickly than Marni expected, and she was able to listen to them talk with Sophia and hear the whole story all over again, from the beginning. Then out came the details Marni hadn't been completely aware of, like the circumstances under which they met. How he had been introduced to her at a bar and then she couldn't drive herself home, so he took her. How she had never gotten so wasted on a couple of glasses of wine before!

"Did it ever occur to you he might have slipped something into your wine? Drugged you?" the police officer asked.

Sophia gasped but said, "No. I never thought that could happen. My friends were all around."

"They might not have been paying close attention to you. And this business of his insisting you called him? Where was your phone while you were sleeping?"

"Right on that table!"

"Can you open it up and show me the call log?"

She did so and there was his number, an outgoing call and

an outgoing text. "Do you suppose he called his phone from mine?"

"How do you unlock your phone? Is it with facial recognition?" She nodded and the officer said, "He could have held it up to your face to open it, keyed in his number or sent himself the text. If you were asleep, you wouldn't know."

"Oh, my God!"

"I think staying with a friend is a good idea. If you'd like to give me the man's name and address, we can check on him, maybe have a little chat with him and advise him to stay away from you. Coming into your house uninvited in the middle of the night is a crime. The next step is to go to the police department and file for a temporary restraining order. Granting one is up to the judge, but I can certainly see why you would feel threatened by his behavior. My guess is that once he realizes the police are involved, he'll decide to leave you alone."

As Marni listened to Sophia's conversation with the police, a strange thing began to happen—she found herself being mentally and emotionally thrust into the past. When Sophia explained how Angelo blamed her for their relationship problems, it was like fighting with Rick all over again. It was so real to revisit that brief but troubled marriage—she was to blame for everything and she was always tiptoeing around, careful to avoid words or comments that might set him off.

But she had let all that go long ago, or at least thought she had. She had buried it deep, never speaking about it. For years people had praised her strength, getting through her young husband's death with such grace, such calm. The truth was she had been set free. She had taken her sweet Bella back to her mother's house where they were safe, and started a new life. She built a wall around her catastrophic memories and enjoyed the bliss of denial. If she didn't think about it, it was as if it had never happened.

But now as she heard Sophia say, "I didn't understand what he was doing," and the police officer telling her, "He was manipulating you, trying to get you to blame yourself," the flood of reality poured down on her for the first time. This secret she had covered up and guarded so well should come out. For girls like Sophia.

"I dated him for only a few weeks," Sophia told the police officer. "Three or four weeks. He had problems with his anger and I broke up with him."

"And that made him angrier?" the police officer asked.

"Yes, and he said it was my fault. He kept saying it over and over, that we were happy until I pushed his buttons. It wasn't like that. I don't know what buttons he was talking about."

"While you were dating him, was he threatening to you in any way?"

"I don't know. I just know he was always picking fights. He was always unhappy about something. Last night was not the first time he came into the house. He did so a couple of weeks ago and he said the door was open and he was worried about me. Last night I know the doors were all locked. I was here alone and checked them many times."

"I believe you," the officer said.

The flashback to the early days with Rick was so real it was almost as if Marni had flown back in time. *We were doing so good until you had to shoot your mouth off and piss me off!* And, *You have everything you need; don't I give you everything you need? But still you complain?* They'd been married almost a year when he hit her the first time. He knocked her to the floor. It was one blow with an open hand, but she could not deny there was escalation. It had been building. Her first response was an overwhelming feeling of shame that she had let it come to this. She made her decision to go home to her mother's house and weather whatever storm would descend on them, but then Rick was called up for active duty. Deployed with the army. And she was free. Bella had barely arrived on this earth when he had his accident—tree versus motorcycle—and he was gone.

While people marveled at her strength, she secretly gave thanks that her marriage was over. She further prayed no one would ever know how terrible it had been. She was happy to have a chance to be seen as a strong and graceful young widow when she saw herself as a stupid punching bag who had made some bad choices for herself and her baby.

"I guess I'm going to be staying with Marni," Sophia said.

"Yes," Marni agreed. "I have a state-of-the-art security system, locks that are impervious to young punks, a gated community with security and cameras with a seven-day loop."

"It would help to give your gate security a picture of the young man in question so they can watch for him," the officer recommended.

"Can you help me with that, Sophia?" Marni asked.

"I think I have a picture on my phone," she said. "But, Marni, are you sure?"

"Absolutely! And I'll talk to your father. We're not taking any chances! And, Officer, when you've had a chance to speak with the young man, will you fill Sophia in on his reaction?"

The young cop directed his gaze to Sophia. "I'll give you a call and let you know when we've made contact. You might want to check into getting some counseling. Go out with groups, stay safe, call us if you have a problem and be vigilant."

"Counseling?" she echoed. "He scared me but he didn't actually do anything to me."

The police officer took a deep breath. "I've worked a lot of these cases. He hadn't hurt you *yet*. He was controlling and manipulative and you have every reason to be suspicious. I hope I'm wrong, but I suspect you were being set up for a long and difficult relationship. I think it would only be a matter of time. It's good this happened. It should put us all on high alert." He gave her his card. "If you're in danger, call 911. If you're worried about something and want to talk about it, that's my cell number. I'll answer or call you back when I'm working."

Marni listened to the two police officers converse with Sophia for about an hour, then it was time to relocate. "When we get home and get you settled, call your dad," Marni said. "And then, a little later I'm going to call him to reassure him and make sure he knows what's going on. When we pass through the security gate, we'll stop and make sure they're aware that you've had a problem with Angelo. They're not armed or anything, but they're very attentive. And my house is very secure. My alarm is hooked into the guard shack and an alarm company that will notify the police."

"Has your alarm ever gone off before?" Sophia asked.

"Only by mistake. When I opened a door without disarming it. It's very loud. But I doubt it's as frightening as waking up to see a man sitting in your living room!"

"I might never get over that."

"I know it feels that way right now."

Unsurprisingly they didn't get a lot done that day. Ellen took it upon herself to make them all dinner. A phone call to Nettie resulted in a visit from her husband, Marvin, who brought an overnight bag and helped himself to one of the guest rooms to spend the night, though Marni had not asked for that.

"I think we're perfectly safe," Marni said.

"Let's give it a day or two, just to be sure," Marvin said.

Marni didn't even bother to try to hide her gratitude. Marvin was a great big firefighter and although she hadn't yet laid eyes on this Angelo, she had no trouble imagining Marvin could take care of him.

It was eight o'clock before she could close her bedroom door and call Sam. "I guess by now you know the story about Sophia's scare."

"I was ready to get an early flight home, but she said she's safe and very well protected. Tell me what's happening."

"When she didn't show up for work, Ellen and I went to your house and found her on the couch, frozen in fear. Apparently Angelo broke into the house. There was no sign of a forced entry and the police suggested he might have picked the lock. Maybe on the slider."

"I'm coming home tomorrow and I'll take over."

"Okay, are you open to some advice?"

"Of course," he said. "You will never know how grateful I am!"

"I think you should come home and apply yourself to beefing up the security at your house. I can recommend a good company. I have an alarm and security cameras you can access on your phone and the company I use will make sure all your doors and windows are secure. And the cameras are so helpful. They even record everything so you have a record of any intruders."

"Do you mind if I ask, what motivated you to get all these bells and whistles?"

"Well, when I built this house it was customized to accommodate my cooking shows. It was my home and my business, which was growing. I was a corporation and the house is in trust to the company, which in the end saved me quite a bit in the divorce settlement. And all the security was meant to keep the property safe and insured. But that's not what you were really asking. I built a smart custom home that I can operate from my phone and it's a vault. I promise you I can keep Sophia safe and secure. In fact, until you tighten up your own home, you're invited to stay here as well."

"That could be dicey," he said. "Though if you don't mind, when I get back to town, I'm coming right over. I want to see Sophia. I want to be sure she's okay. He didn't hurt her, did he?"

"He terrified her by using a soft monotone voice as he explained that they'd always been so happy and she was making a giant mistake in rejecting him and how he couldn't be expected to let her go when she kept calling him back. But, Sam, she never called him back."

"I don't know what to do first," Sam said. "Talk to the police? Talk to this guy and issue a few warnings of my own?"

"Sophia is an adult. I don't know if the police are obligated to talk to you. The officer who interviewed her was very nice. Very understanding. He's a father himself and said he'd be very suspicious of the motives of a guy who said and did the things this… I don't know whether to call him a boy or a man. He's twenty-four years old and not terribly mature in appearance. Sophia showed me a picture."

"I've met him," Sam said. "I thought he looked younger than her. I couldn't imagine what she saw in him."

"He's got some diabolical moves, like insisting that she called him and begged him to come over, even showing her the call log on her own phone. Clearly he found her phone on the coffee table and used it to call his phone, all meant to confuse her or trick her. That's gaslighting at its best."

"How do you know these things?" he asked, sounding shocked.

"I don't know," she hedged. "Probably too much late-night TV. I'm going to find Sophia some counseling. Maybe a support group where she can learn a few things about sexual harassment. And how to protect herself."

"She said it wasn't sexual," he said.

"Everything she described was a power play; he was manipulative, controlling and had some serious boundary issues. Who knows what it would have become if she'd played along. But she knew something wasn't right."

"She should never have gone out with him!" Sam said.

"Hold on now. Who knows what attracted this kid to Sophia; she is beautiful and brilliant. He could have seen her on campus once and fixated on her. You have to remember it is never the victim's fault. Never!" She sighed. "I think we need to broaden your education a bit. I'm not sure what happened here, whether it was coercion or harassment or stalking. But we should figure that out, probably with the help of a professional."

"I don't know where to start," he admitted.

"Don't worry about it, Professor Garner. I know everybody."

Impossibly that made him laugh. "Thanks for helping me with this. I never meant to thrust my family problems on you but I am grateful for your help."

"One of my first resources will be Bella. My daughter being an assistant district attorney will be very useful. She's brilliant." *And,* Marni thought, *someone to whom I owe the truth.*

Ellen had texted Mark that she was working late but would be bringing him dinner. When she texted that she was home he came right over. "Please tell me you haven't eaten!" she said.

"Not yet. What have you got?"

"Cioppino. We've made it a few times and I happen to think it's our best ever. Marni will be using it on her show. It's of no help to you and your food truck—shellfish as a main course is a bad idea for a lot of reasons, not the least of which is it doesn't store well." She reached into the refrigerator and brought out a salad. She pulled a baguette from the oven. She was ready to dish up a generous bowl of the stew but Mark was in her way, already leaning into the pot to study the contents and inhale the aroma. "If you'll sit down, I'll serve you," she said.

"It looks amazing. Why didn't I ever make this at the firehouse?"

"Seafood is iffy; people love it or hate it or sometimes they're sensitive to it. Anaphylaxis at the dinner table is such a buzzkill."

He laughed at that but took his seat at the table and tried to wait patiently. He tore off a hunk of baguette and the moment the bowl was put in front of him, he dipped the bread and savored the taste. He ate very slowly and had a lot of commentary, not to mention all the ecstatic groans and moans. "The fennel and dill—perfect. Hmm, this is so wonderful. The clams have opened so nicely. Ohhh, this is heaven. Garlic, I love garlic. What fish is this? Halibut?"

"That's it," she confirmed.

"And salmon. Both firm and perfect."

"We added some crab, not everyone does. We cracked it first and dropped it in. It's pretty inconvenient to pull it out of a steaming pot and crack it and burn yourself in a sloppy mess. But I love the crab in the stew."

"I love the crab in the stew!" he echoed.

They talked for a while about the meal and a few other

recipes, then she described her workweek schedule, including the fact that they had filmed some four-minute shorts of favorite recipes. "Usually low labor-intensive, quick demonstrations when we'll edit out the cook times and fast forward through the prep."

"What exactly does that mean?" he asked.

"The camera will see small bowls of chopped onion, garlic, vegetables, herbs and so on but we won't film the chopping. We'll film the mixing, sautéing and so on but cut out the cook time. And Marni will do a voice-over. We're using edited versions of older shows as well, making shorter versions available on YouTube and other internet platforms. Marni's subscription list is staggering, growing by the minute. It's hard to keep up with it."

Mark had a second bowl and they talked about his licenses for the RV and trailer, all of which were complete except for a safety inspection. He was talking to someone at the fire department about getting some help in writing grants to provide more capital for his foundation. "And I bought a freezer today. A large chest. I don't know why I didn't think of this in the first place. I need to be prepared by making and freezing so many things from meat loafs to breakfast casseroles to lasagna to pastas."

"I've been looking at recipes that are easy to prepare and go a long way," she said. "I wasn't thinking about freezing but that's so practical. I haven't been thinking about your menus on purpose; it just sort of takes over my brain when I'm supposed to be thinking about other things."

"I appreciate your input more than you'll ever know," he said. "It's almost fire season around here."

"Really, when?" she asked, suddenly surprised. She hadn't given a thought to fire season.

"By next month we'll be in the thick of it," he said. "And we live in the hot zone. California and Nevada are two states with a vast acreage of forests, just waiting for a careless campfire or a lightning strike."

"Are you ready to go?"

"Just after the safety check on all my equipment and I'm told that will be finished this week. I'm going to get a little cooking done in advance. I've met with some grocery managers, looking for a little help and support for the shopping. The second there's a spark, I'm ready to load up."

"When will you cook? Can I help? I'm very fast and very good!"

His smile was so sweet and kind. "I would love that, but I promise not to take advantage of you. I have a few friends who will help if they can. And there are a few local organizations interested in supporting this project but I think once it's proven, there will be more."

"Do you have a name?"

"Mark's Rescue Kitchen. Too dull?"

"No, it's perfect!"

They finished the dishes together, then poured a Courvoisier and retired to the sofa in the living room. They talked about their hopes for the traveling kitchen, their friends, their plans for the rest of the week. Ellen found herself telling him all about Sophia and how she and Marni rescued her and were keeping her safe at Marni's house.

Then Ellen realized that in all her years of close friendship with Marni and her closeness to her sisters, nothing in her life had ever compared to feelings she had when she was with Mark. Not even Ralph. She had deeply loved her dear Ralph and they had had a fun, loving relationship, though cut short by his health problems, but what she was feeling for

Mark was quickly growing strong and deep. Her plan to keep it superficial and manageable was failing because she couldn't wait to see him at the end of the day and thought about him constantly when they were apart.

His hand strayed onto her lap and he took hers, even as he kept talking about anything, mostly his new traveling kitchen. He told her about some of the big wildfires in the area over the past dozen years. She'd lived here all her life and was, of course, aware of the fires as they ate up the hillsides, black smoke filling the sky and choking the valley. She worried about the poor people in the line of the fire as she looked at the bloodred sunsets beyond the mountains. But she'd never really been threatened by one.

She gazed at him and the next thing she knew he had his arms around her and was kissing her. She was amazed that she could still feel that irresistible pull, the almost girlish excitement and anticipation. But Ellen, being practical above all else, stopped and said, "Are we going to regret this?"

"I highly doubt it," he said with a laugh in his voice.

"But we've both been caregivers to terminally ill spouses and I know neither of us want to do that again."

"Ellen," he said tenderly, rubbing a knuckle along her cheek. "In two years or ten years or twenty years when I look back on this time in my life, no matter what condition we're in, I'd rather remember feeling in love than not."

"Love?" she questioned.

"I never thought I'd meet someone like you, someone I'd have so much to talk about with, someone I'd be so anxious to see. If that's not love, it should be," he said.

"And if one of us dies?" she asked.

"You have only two options. To remember feeling the warmth and hopefulness of love or remember feeling nothing much at all. But it's up to you, Ellen. I don't want to trap you. But when you look back at these months and years, will there be a blank space or a feeling of happiness? I promise I'm not looking for a nurse."

"No, you seem to be in perfect health," she said. "But this actually panics me. I'm going to go ahead and say it—I'm terrified."

He smiled. "Here are the options. We can ignore that fearful part and fly by the seat of our pants. Or we can talk it through and make sure we have solutions for what-ifs in place. Or we can just end it now and avoid taking the risk—please don't go with that one. That option is so dreary. Or, we can just go hiking on Saturday."

"Hiking?" she asked.

"I like hiking," he said. "Especially around here. There are some great mountain trails, lake trails. Do you like to hike?"

"I used to but I'll admit they have become shorter hikes lately," she said.

"I'll put some picnic stuff in my backpack. Let's start early. Like six. Can you do that?"

Her smile was wide. She thought about the sun, the summer breeze, the conversation, the rest stops that might include more kissing. She took a deep breath to steady herself. "Yes," she said. "I can do that."

When Sam returned from his conference, he went directly to Marni's house to see Sophia. His first order of business was to be sure she was all right and it was clear that she was. A little shaken and worried, maybe. But she was getting a lot of support and felt strongly about her resolve to stay far away from Angelo.

Then they went together to see Officer Bowen, the police officer who had come to their house. Sophia introduced her father. The police officer shook Sam's hand and smiled broadly at Sophia. "You're looking so much better!" he said.

"I feel better. Did you talk to him?" she asked.

"I did. I took my partner with me and we had a very serious conversation with Angelo. I gave him a very stern warning to leave you alone, to stay away from you. I told him you were entitled to a temporary restraining order if you chose to file a complaint and that I would support such a claim. He was very apologetic, insisted he hadn't done anything wrong and that he was at your house by invitation."

"But I didn't—"

Officer Bowen put up a hand and said, "I told him that story wasn't going to wash with me and that if he bothered you again, I would consider it harassment. He promised to stay away from you. I told him I knew he'd been in trouble before, that there's a record. You should be aware, I think the kid has issues."

"Anger issues for sure, from what Sophia has told me," Sam said.

"He's been in a couple of fights, DUI, vandalism, and battery domestic. He was living with his mother and sister but they had problems with him and said he was abusive. He moved out and no charges were filed. Just be very careful and if you have any issues with him, call me."

After leaving the police station, Sam applied himself to the task of upgrading the security of his home, with a little help from Marni. Breckenridge was not the kind of place where one worried about serious crime. It was a sleepy little agricultural town with a clean and pretty commercial district and several good restaurants. There were many fast-food chains serving everything from pizza to ice cream, hair salons, a hardware store and garden center. There were bigger stores in bigger cities like Reno, not so far away. The police department was small, the crime rate was low, the population was friendly and helpful.

What Sam had to deal with was a domestic situation, even if Sophia had been coupled with Angelo for only a few weeks. He met with the man responsible for the security of Marni's house, but his home was older and much smaller. What he realized was that Marni, being a minor celebrity, not to mention a woman living alone, needed that alarm and other equipment. He opted for a system with motion detectors, security cameras, a very loud alarm and a hookup to a company that would monitor the alarm and if necessary, summon the police. He had all the locks changed and fortified.

Marni wanted him to stay at her house until that work was completed, but he wasn't about to do that. "I'm not sure I wouldn't sneak down the hall and crawl into your bed. And that would be so awkward."

"But what if you find yourself awakened by Angelo in the middle of the night!"

"Nothing could please me more," Sam said.

While the work was going on at the house, Sophia stayed with Marni, even though her father was home. Sam was at Marni's in the evening. He called to check on his daughter a few times a day as well. Then finally the system was fully installed, the gates into the backyard were bolstered, and all the passwords on Sophia's and Sam's devices were changed.

"It's amazing," Sophia said. "But, Marni, can I stay at your house just a little bit longer?"

"Just not ready?" Marni asked.

"I still have the creeps."

"You can stay as long as you want. And your father can come over anytime."

"I'm just a fraidy-cat, I think," Sophia said.

"It's all right, honey. I love having you here."

TWELVE

There was no question that the incident with Sophia got everyone's attention and had them all a little skittish, but it really jolted Marni. She called the college and talked to the head of Sophia's master's program, who was also her intern advisor. She had worked with her to hire Sophia and wrote a monthly report to ensure she would get credit for her work. All Marni wanted right now was a referral to some kind of counselor or support group for students who had been victimized by sexual harassment or assault or stalking. It was clear Sophia really needed the support of others who had gone through a similar experience.

Marni learned there was such a group and that they met on Tuesday evenings so she approached Sophia about attending.

"I don't know if I'm ready to talk about it," Sophia said.

"Then just go and listen to others," Marni said. "The first step is realizing you're not the only one. By far! And I think what you'll learn is that even though Angelo didn't physically harm you, you were assaulted, and there is recovery involved. But you will emerge stronger."

Marni was happy to drive Sophia to the support group meetings and bring her back home, as was Sam. With their support and encouragement, Sophia agreed to attend.

With the end of August, the fall semester classes were beginning. Although Sophia only had a couple of classes a week, she still had reason to be on the campus frequently. She was skittish. She had not heard from Angelo and she was most grateful for that, but she checked her phone constantly and was always looking around to be sure he hadn't followed her.

Marni struggled with what she could do to help. She identified with what Sophia was going through. She spent her free time searching for a plan to do something useful. When she was much younger, she had a mentor she had admired, a TV producer who had guided her in the early years of her cooking show. Her name was Erika and she was twenty years older than Marni. Marni still remembered when Erika advised her, *If you have a problem and can't find a solution, shine a light on it.*

Strangely enough she realized the best person to help her might be Tom, her one-time coffee date. She still had his number, of course, so she called him and asked him if he could meet her for coffee. He agreed so quickly and so eagerly she wondered if she had made a mistake. But Marni was both stubborn and creative so she followed through. Their coffee date and conversation lasted an hour and a half.

She was thinking about that when she planned a special dinner for her girls, the group she relied on, the collection of women who made her feel best. She called Nettie and Bella and talked to Ellen and Sophia, then settled on a Saturday night when they were all available. "I'm cooking for you," she told them.

She decided on crab cakes, seasoned home fries, broiled asparagus, a tomato-and-cucumber salad and for dessert, brownies and vanilla-nut ice cream. That should loosen them up and get them in the mood. Of course they could have any drink of their choice and she had chosen a delightful sauvignon blanc for the dinner.

"What's the treat?" Nettie asked when she arrived.

"I felt like having a girls' night," Marni said. "I'm sorry to be corny, but when it's just us, I feel so strong."

"And you need to feel strong?"

"Let's start with some canapés and a drink or glass of wine. It's deviled eggs on cucumber with caviar."

She made two martinis, two glasses of wine and one sparkling cider for Bella. Everyone wanted to know how Sophia was getting along. They offered her encouragement and support. Marni, knowing she did better at communicating when her hands were busy, began moving food to the table. Sophia offered to help but she waved her off. "I've got this," she said. "Let me serve you."

There was a lot of oohing and ahhing as she brought dish after dish from the warmer to the table.

Once everyone had gathered around the table, Marni took a deep breath and called them all to attention. "I had a reason for asking you all here," she said. "I'm going to tell you my story. Each of you has heard bits and pieces of my life story but I don't think any one of you has heard the whole thing. And I need to share it."

"Are you writing an autobiography?" Bella asked.

"No, darling. But you're my best friends and family and I

want to be sure I haven't held anything back. When I was a little girl, I lived in a very odd but loving family…"

"Are we going all the way back to the day you were born?" Bella asked.

"Hush. Please just let me do this. My little sister was too young for me to confide in. I had two aunts, a mom and dad, and I felt completely secure. I was so confident. Then I met Rick," she said. She looked at Bella. "Your father."

"I know. In high school."

"The end of my junior year. We had a couple of dates. He was one of the most popular guys in school and I never realized, but there's power in that. He was the best dancer, a star football player and he was deadly on the drums. He had that charisma, for a teenage girl it was really something. It gave me power that the most popular, best-looking guy liked me."

"Is this going somewhere? Because you already told me it wasn't exactly the best relationship," Bella said.

Marni was quiet for a moment. She made it a point to make eye contact with Bella when she finally said, "The first time he hit me was after senior prom." Everyone gasped and started to speak but Marni held up her hand to silence them and continued. "We had been dating for a year and I accidentally knocked over my diet Coke in his lap and he slapped me across the face so hard I fell off my chair. He jumped to his feet, yelling that his tux was rented. A girlfriend helped me up, put ice on my cheek. He didn't exactly apologize; he made a lot of excuses. He just reacted from the cold. He was shocked and lashed out. He didn't mean to, it was just spontaneous. His excuses went on and on while I held an ice pack on my eye. I had a black eye so while he was driving me home, we concocted a story about how he accidentally whacked me with his elbow while we were dancing. We both swore to it so no one could trip us up. I agreed to that lie to protect him. And my parents believed me immediately because they liked him."

There was a moment of quiet.

"You told me he never hit you," Bella said.

"I knew you hadn't told me everything," Nettie said.

"I know. I absorbed his abuse because I was ashamed of it. He always told me I brought it on and he wasn't like that, he'd never been like that. That wasn't true at all. His sister told me he was kicked out of preschool for hitting and biting. I disregarded that because he was a child and that had nothing to do with who he was later. But I told myself a lot of stories like that. That hit, that black eye, that wasn't really the beginning. It took me years of looking back at our relationship to try to understand what really happened. Then, right out of high school, he was going to reward me and make everything right by marrying me. And I didn't see how that would play into his hands. He was more in control than ever."

She tried to explain the evolution. Some would call it grooming now but back then neither she nor Rick knew the term or what it meant. He fought dirty, said mean things, blamed her. He was always making excuses and telling her she was the one at fault and he was the victim. He sulked and pouted. It was a good day or night when he stormed out of the house angry because that meant he was going away and she could relax for at least a little while.

"All I learned from all that looking into the past was that anger was always his issue and control was always his purpose. I realized that I should have bailed out of that relationship the first time it felt dangerous, which was long before he hit me, but by the time it was obvious, he was controlling me with his words. He would say he was going to kill me or himself or both of us. I had no trouble believing it. He would tell these elaborate stories of how I had created all our problems. *You were standing right there, wearing that black lace top you know I love, and I was trying to have a conversation with you about where we would go for Thanksgiving and you disrespected me and it turned into a fight and you pushed me and pushed me…* And two things would happen to me—I would make a note that he liked that black lace top and that I had to be more careful and not disrespect him. Of course I hadn't—that was all gaslighting. He was trying to get me to own that I was the problem, not him. Our argument had been so simple—he wanted to go to his mother's house, I wanted to go to my mother's house with my family. The truth was if we disagreed, it was my fault. I couldn't win. But boy I tried. I was always in search of the solution. And there wasn't one.

"Then he joined the Army Reserves and was gone for a few months and I had enough of a reprieve to forget the lessons I learned. I was soon pregnant and more trapped than ever. In fact I was planning to leave him but he was home from the Reserves, out with his friends, got drunk and drove into a tree. I had a brand-new baby and my abusive husband was killed in a car accident."

No one was eating. But only Sophia sat with her mouth open, agog, shocked by this revelation.

"There's a reason I'm telling you this. It's important that women talk, that we share our experiences, that we learn to be candid and open. If someone had told me they'd had a similar experience, it might have saved me a lot of misery and confusion. We have to rely on each other for the truth, the reality. I've since learned that what I went through isn't uncommon. In fact, it's alarmingly frequent." She paused for a moment and smiled at each woman individually.

"I think you know the rest of my story. Bella and I lived with my mother and sister and aunts; I reinvented myself with a cooking show and built a career that was born out of handing out food samples at grocery stores and delis. And it wasn't just my ability to make a living that evolved. Also, my confidence grew and with it, courage. I don't think I would have had that opportunity if Rick had lived."

"Do you ever wonder if you and Rick might have put it back together? Your marriage?"

She took a deep breath. "I have a very clear memory that every time I thought things were going well for us, out of the blue we'd be fighting and I'd be cowering in fear. I think it was Maya Angelou who said, 'when someone shows you who they are, believe them the first time.' Once he revealed himself to me, I had no business in a relationship with him. I thought I was surviving by putting the whole horrible experience behind me and pretending it never happened. I was so young. I told myself I was protecting you, Bella. I didn't mean to mislead you. I also hated that by being honest I'd have to explain that your father was not a nice man."

"I knew," Bella said simply. "Even without all the details, it was obvious to me you had an unhappy marriage. I'm so sorry, Mom. For all you went through."

"Thank you, that means a lot. That brings us to today. A new day."

"Wait," Sophia said. "Is this about me?"

"A bit, yes," Marni said. "I think if you had known from the beginning that I had been the victim of abuse, even though it was a long time ago, you might have come to me for help. At least for advice. We never do that because we think no one else will understand. And when we stay quiet, we keep these abusers safe from being prosecuted."

"Oh, Dios, I could not prosecute anyone…" Sophia groaned.

"We keep them safe from exposure and leave them to hurt the next woman. It's never just one! It's like a damn career path. The best way to stop this insanity is to expose them and to do that, we women have to make it safe for women to tell their truth. To that end, I'm going to take a first step. I'm going to go public with my story and facilitate the opening of a shelter for women and children who are hiding from an abuser. I will invest in a nice large house. I have someone looking right now."

Ellen sat up straight. "Marni, how will you find the time?"

"I'm going to have help from a community foundation. Their biggest challenge is finding donors and my biggest challenge is finding management. We're a marriage made in heaven."

"That's wonderful," Bella said. "I can't think of a more worthwhile way for you to spend your money! I'll help, too."

"You can absolutely count on me," Nettie said. "You should be proud, Marni. When you were going through a bad marriage, having a baby, then suddenly widowed, I was only a kid. You couldn't talk to me about it; I wasn't any help at all. And Mom wasn't much help. To either one of us."

"Well, at that time she was a single mother, living with her sisters, with two daughters to mother alone… Then she lost her sisters one at a time and with the aunties gone, we just limped along as a family. I always felt we were a strange disjointed family, but in all the years since I've come to realize there are lots and lots of families like ours. There are lots of women who have nowhere to turn. I can't change that but if I can provide a solution for just a couple, that could make a difference."

"You've made a very big difference to me, Marni," Sophia said. "I don't know what I would do without you."

"For now, tell me how good those crab cakes are!"

Dinner was devoured, conversation picked up. There were lots of questions about Marni's plans for her shelter plus many suggestions. All of the women showed a great deal of enthusiasm for the project and an unsurprising willingness to help. They lingered over dessert and the evening stretched out late, until one by one they started yawning.

Nettie and Marni did the dishes together with Sophia helping to put clean dishes away, wiping countertops and sweeping the floor.

Nettie, loaded up with leftovers for Marvin, stopped in the doorway to kiss Marni's cheek. "I'm so proud of you," she said. "You've always found a way to make lemonade out of your lemons. It's a gift. Marvin and I will help. In fact, I can tap into the fire department, if necessary. They have a reputation for giving till they drop!"

"Thank you. I'll be sure to let you know what you can do."

It was very late that Saturday night when there was a light tapping at Marni's bedroom door. She was on her phone with Sam and asked him to give her a moment and promised to call him right back. She opened her door and there stood Sophia in her pajamas. There were tear tracks on her cheeks. "Sophia! Is everything all right?"

"I just wanted to say thank you. For the dinner, for the friendship, for everything. I don't know if I've ever had such a good friend."

"Well, I feel the same way," Marni said.

"I'm sorry I'm such a trouble," she said. "I'd like to be more like Bella. Strong and wise and fearless."

Marni gave her head a little tilt and reached out a hand to wipe away Sophia's tears. "None of us is born that way, sweetheart. It's the battles we fight that make us stronger. I'm just happy you're here with me while you find your strength."

"I don't think I could do it without you…"

"You would, but I'm glad we've been together through this. I think you're making me stronger, too. Because of you, I'm finding something inside myself that I needed a little help to give voice to. Thank you for that."

"What you're planning to do is so good. I know you're doing it for me but in the end it will be important to so many women. And I would be so lost if you hadn't stepped up to protect me."

"This is what we have to do for each other," Marni said. "And you will do the same for someone, I'm sure of it."

Sunday morning, bright and early, Ellen and Mark stepped out onto their respective front yards at exactly six o'clock. They were each holding coffee mugs from their own kitchens. "Beautiful morning!" Mark shouted. "Let's take my truck. I put a couple of packs in the back. They are filled with water and snacks."

They were going for a hike in the foothills. Ellen had wanted to go for a hike for ages but hadn't been comfortable going on her own.

Ellen had fallen in love with the Breckenridge valley the moment she saw it. The town, so pristine and well-kept, was tucked neatly between two mountain ranges that were filled with well-traveled trails and national parks. She left it to Mark to make the plans and he did not disappoint. The trail he chose didn't take them straight up the side of a hill but circled it nicely in switchbacks and would open up at the end in a nice little park. They carried backpacks; his held the water and hers, slightly lighter, carried snacks.

The weather was perfect, the sky was relentlessly blue, the temperature moderate and would peak later in the day at seventy degrees. It was an ideal early September day. In less than a month the leaves would begin to change.

"How was dinner with your girlfriends?" he asked as they drove.

She told him about their food and the parts of conversation that didn't include any of Marni's personal business or personal history. Because it was Mark, he was very interested in the food. Then she asked how his prep for his food truck was going and he reported that it was ready to roll. In fact he was spending the afternoon after their hike cooking and freezing. "Let me help with that!" Ellen said.

"I don't want to wear you out," he said.

"Not to worry. If I start to get tired, I'll take a break." She was about to say she'd rather cook than hike, but once she breathed in the clean fall air, she was really hooked on the feeling and couldn't wait to get out on the trail.

There were at least a dozen perhaps twenty hikers slowly making their way up the trail. It was narrow and they walked single file so there wasn't much talking unless they stopped for a break. The air was clean and sharp, no smog up here. In another month things would change dramatically—the leaves on the lush hillsides would resemble a quilt of fall colors and the mountain peaks would be covered with their first, second and maybe third snowfalls. The ski resorts would be open before Thanksgiving.

On one of their rest breaks Mark talked about his son and his family; they were thinking about having Thanksgiving with Mark in Breckenridge and maybe getting a little skiing in. "They know I wouldn't mind doing the cooking. Do you have plans?" he asked Ellen.

"I usually spend it with my sister and her family. That's a lot of people."

"If that changes, you'd be welcome to join us."

"Thank you!" But what she thought was that it would be a bad idea to enmesh their families. She didn't want a perfectly lovely friendship to become too close or too complicated.

They hiked for four hours, then stopped for lunch on their way home. That afternoon they cooked. Mark had everything ready and refrigerated so that all they had to do was mix and package and freeze. They prepared twenty meat loafs, an equal number of pans of scalloped potatoes, some corn casseroles and green bean casseroles. Mark had been shopping and had gallon containers of gravy, dozens of dinner rolls and cases of condiments.

"You act like you expect something to happen any second," Ellen said.

"It's that time of year," he said. "Any minute now there will be word of a fire. The hillsides are kindling."

"We should cook again tomorrow night," she said. "You know what goes a long way and freezes well? Spaghetti casserole with meat sauce. Or lasagna, but spaghetti casserole is easier and faster."

"But you're working all day. I don't want to ask too much of you!"

"I really want to do it, Mark. If it's okay with you. In fact, I would love to go with you to help serve and clean up. If you think it would be helpful."

"But what about work? Your job is so demanding."

"I'll talk to Marni and see how she feels about me taking a few days here and there. I can't abandon her; she's got a grandson on the way. But I should be able to sneak away for a few days here and there."

"It will be a lot of work," he said. "And I've lined up a few volunteers..."

A shiver ran down her spine. "I think this sounds so exciting. I would hate to miss it."

He just grinned at her. "And I would hate to be without you. Whatever you want to do, I would be grateful!" Then he put his arms around her and pulled her close for a kiss that lingered.

"What was that for?" she asked.

"There are certain benefits for being so unselfish," he said.

And she couldn't suppress her own smile. "I'll remember that."

THIRTEEN

Sophia had been nervous at first but she had learned some very transformative things in her support group. One, domestic abuse came in all shapes and sizes and ages. There were a couple of teenage girls and a couple of women with grown children. They must be in their fifties, at least. There were women who were in constant fear of being killed by an abusive partner and women just as afraid and paralyzed by a partner who dominated and manipulated with words alone. There was abuse in same sex unions just as in opposite sex relationships.

And almost all of them, like Sophia herself, were afraid to be alone.

Once her father had finished bolstering the security on their house, and she'd spent a few extra days at Marni's, she went back home, back to her bedroom, back to living with her dad. But she was still skittish and afraid Angelo would sneak up on her. He had not hit her or physically hurt her so she was unsure why she was so afraid. She reasoned it was because she knew, without being told, that he was dangerous and that he wanted her to know she was at his mercy.

But another thing that happened as a result of counseling and her group was that she became fascinated by something other than a future in television. She had begun listening to podcasts and reading every recommended book on the subjects of codependence, domestic abuse, troubled relationships, the psychology of battery and anything related. Her entire world shifted focus.

She'd been in school since she was a little girl and at the age of twenty-two, her brain had never been as busy as it was now.

"You're extra quiet this morning," Marni said. "What's going on in that head of yours?"

Sophia was at the island, chopping vegetables and shredding cheese, working from the list Marni had put out for her. Her hands stopped working and she gazed at her boss. "I am full of ideas," she said.

"You don't sound happy about that," Marni observed.

"I'm not unhappy about it, but it's bringing on ideas of change and I have never been good at that. It's about this idea you have of a safe house."

"Yes? Tell me?"

"I want to be a part of it." There, she'd spit it out, though she'd started at the end and would have to work her way back to the beginning.

"Tell me more," Marni said.

"Okay, let me think." She put down the knife. "I can't think and chop. Here is what occupies my head. From my counseling and my group, I am so interested in therapy, in counseling, in psychology and social work. I have learned so much in such a short period of time and even though it was a frightening experience that drove me this direction, I want to keep going this way. I think I want to make a change. I haven't talked with my father about this yet and I should do that, but I'm afraid he will—"

"Freak out? Blow a gasket?" Marni said.

Sophia nodded. "I have a degree in communication. And I feel driven to learn more about the subject of psychology and mental health. I want to change my direction."

Marni stopped what she was doing and wiped off her hands. "It's only been a short time since a major traumatizing event caused you to consider this. You will recover from the trauma. You can nurture an interest in psychology forever, for as long as it intrigues you, while you build a career somewhere else—"

"I want to switch programs and study psychology and social work. I want to make a big change." She shook her head. "Papi will explode all over me."

"Relax. You're not going to make a decision and change all your plans overnight," Marni said. "You have a lot of people to talk to first, not just your father. There is the counselor, your master's program director, and maybe you should meet with some professionals in that line of work."

"I look forward to that. But I don't want to stop working for you, even if I don't need an intern credit. But, Marni, I want to help you set up that safe house. I think there's a lot to learn there."

"Where did all this come from? I know it's not a matter of your experience and fright driving you to change your career plans."

"It was one voice at a time," she said. "I listened to the stories of the women in my support group, each one having an experience that was similar and yet unique. Each one was in a different stage—a couple had just encountered a dangerous partner, a few had been dealing with it for a long time, some were as close to recovery as one can be. The leader of our group, the counselor, had been an abused wife. She put herself through school after getting free of that terrible time and became a social worker with a master's degree. She works at the college. She teaches also. She is very kind and so smart."

"Sophia, are you still dealing with the fear of Angelo?"

"I might always be afraid of Angelo. And if not him, the idea of someone like him. I wish we could go back to thinking that the right man could be a protector. I might never believe in that again."

Marni smiled sadly. She had had two loves and both had failed her. "I think believing in romantic fairy tales just makes it harder to find the real thing. Instead we should focus on becoming our own hero. There's more security there, I think."

"That's what the counselor says. But she doesn't say how."

"We start by looking inside and being very honest with ourselves. But, Sophia, you must talk with your father and explain to him what you're feeling. It might be a good time to take a leave from your classes. You're not very far into the new semester. You won't get behind. Your credits won't disappear."

"I'm afraid to even tell him. He's so determined about school, about having a plan and staying with it."

"Fine, if that works, but many students change their course of study. Some multiple times. We can't possibly know what will satisfy us for a lifetime when we're very young."

"Did you? Change your mind?"

Marni laughed. "Sophia, I didn't go to college. I was a single mother and had to work. If I was to succeed, it was all on me to make it happen. Every time I saw a path or a break in the clouds, I jumped on it."

"Papi says that's cojones," she said.

"Indeed, it is. What I lacked in formal education I made up for in determination." She grinned. "Or balls."

"I admire you so much. Is it okay that I keep coming to work here? Will you let me help with the safe house?"

"I don't think I could do without you now, not here in the kitchen or later in a safe house. I will welcome your help. But for now, stay the course with your studies, at least until you've talked to some advisors. You can be an advocate for women from anywhere. You might be able to help even more from a position as a broadcast journalist."

Ellen's job wasn't limited to recipe development and food preparation alone. She had several production responsibilities that ranged from scheduling to ordering groceries. She also managed some of the show's financial duties, like keeping the budget and paying the bills. That being the case, she always kept her phone with her, usually in her pocket. She was just finishing up a corned beef hash when her hip began to vibrate.

It was a few days after the women had all had dinner together with Marni, when they had all learned the totality of her history and her plans to provide a safe house for abused women and children. The phone vibrated again.

There was no rush. It could be a sales call that she would then have to block. Perhaps a vendor with a question about her order. Or it could be the production office, asking for something like show dates or schedules. She put out her hash in a fancy dish, took a quick picture of it, then looked at her phone to see who had called.

It was Mark. She went out onto the patio to listen to his

message. "It's happening. It's a small fire just north of Quincy. Cal Fire is there and hotshots are going in; I'm standing by in case they evacuate. It's not far, just an hour and a half. We're not cooking tonight but I'm going to be ready to travel in the morning. I'm checking available shelter areas where we can set up and doing an inventory. Talk soon."

She could hear the excitement in his voice; she could feel her own excitement in her bones. She had put off talking to Marni, trying to figure out what she was going to say. And now it was here.

She went back in the house and found herself face-to-face with Marni. She must have been wearing a startled look because the first words out of Marni's mouth were, "Is everything all right?"

"Yes. I mean, sort of. Um, I've been meaning to talk to you about something and I wish I had. I'm afraid I put this off too long. Can we go to your office?"

"Sure. Lead the way."

Ellen sat on the edge of the chair facing Marni's desk. "Something has come up. I mentioned that Mark has a special project—his food truck. He's been working on it for at least a year and it has quickly become a much larger operation than I realized. No surprise to him! He's always seen the scope of this idea. He plans to offer emergency food service to fire and flood victims in the vicinity of any disaster he can drive to. That would be northern California and Nevada. He was inspired to do this by the size of the fires in the recent past. The Camp Fire displaced fourteen thousand families. Mark is a great admirer of José Andrés. We've been getting ready, cooking and freezing meals for the past week. Once he got the final approval and safety check and licensing, he started preparing food, waiting for the first emergency."

"Ellen! I'm speechless! You mentioned his idea but you didn't go into much detail! I had guessed it was something that would happen in the future."

"I'm sorry," she said. "I should have brought you up to speed. He just left me a message. There's a fire and he's getting everything together so he can go. He has some volunteers from his firefighting days who will help. He seems to have connections everywhere."

"That's wonderful!"

"Marni, I want to help him," Ellen said. "If Cal Fire evacuates people from their homes, he'll find a place to set up his trucks and kitchen. He's fully equipped and I want to go."

Marni's face showed that she was stricken. She stared, open-mouthed. "For how long? When?"

"Tomorrow morning. I don't know for how long. His message said it was a small fire so far but I don't have much information. I can take my own car so if it turns out to be a big fire, I can come back after a couple of days. If you can spare me. Please say you can spare me." She grinned sheepishly. "I haven't been this excited in a very long time!"

"Of course you should go! I don't know how long I can spare you for, but I can get along for now. Ellen, sometimes these fires…"

"I know," Ellen said. "They can go on and on, they're only getting worse, and more and more people are being displaced… After I finish up today's list, would it be all right with you if I quit for the day?"

"Sure. But first you have to tell me all about Mark and this project. You've been pretty quiet about both."

"We've been spending a little time together, but you knew that."

"No, I don't know much. You had dinner together—was that a month ago? Longer?"

"A bit longer, yes. And being next door neighbors, we've had a few dinners together, taking turns cooking."

"You never mentioned…"

"It wasn't that big a deal."

"Well, in this very short period of time, since he took you to get a new battery for your car, you've had a few dinners and gotten involved in a charitable foundation to provide food for displaced wildfire victims. Call me silly, but it feels like there might be one or two pieces missing from this puzzle."

"I don't want you to think I'm foolish…"

"Now why would I think that?"

"Because I am!" Ellen stressed. "We've become very good friends! We've had dinner together almost every night. The times we haven't are those few days he's been out of town, getting his rig ready or visiting his son in Las Vegas, usually both those things at once! And I've been involved in helping to get his traveling kitchen ready for operation. Do you realize how devastating these fires have been the past few years?"

"I do," Marni said. "And I think what you're doing is fantastic! So what in the world is wrong?"

Ellen shifted a bit in her chair and then, remarkably, her cheeks grew rosy. "I really like him," she said in barely a breath.

"Oh? But that's wonderful! He seems to be a very good man."

"He is, I'm convinced of that! He's kind and generous and he has a very sensitive palate."

"Good to know," Marni said with a laugh.

"I'm trying very hard not to make a complete fool of myself," Ellen said. "I'm not looking for romance! My one brush with true love was pretty difficult. When you get down to it, Mark's wasn't much easier. He was married for a long time but in the end, he was a caregiver, taking care of his wife as she slowly died. Neither of us wants to face that sort of thing again."

"Ellen, we've talked about this. You have long-term care insurance, you have your sister, you're well prepared. You're not planning to find some guy to take care of you in your elder years, you have a plan in place."

"Yes," Ellen said.

"And Mark has his family," Marni said. "A son. Grandsons. You don't have to rely on each other for that. Have you talked this through?"

"I've been meaning to," Ellen said. "I don't know where to start!"

"Why don't you start with 'where is this going, Mark?'"

"I was thinking of starting with 'given our ages...'" Ellen said. "I don't want to get more involved before we've hashed it out. Is he looking for a caretaker? Because I'm not! At least I don't think I am!"

"The reality is, when you're twenty years old, it's not unreasonable to think you have forty years ahead. At least! But when you're sixty? I think it's just common sense to work out expectations. Are you sleeping together?"

"Of course not," Ellen shot back. "For anyone to see me naked, I have to be in their will!"

Marni laughed. The most delightful thing about Ellen was how oblivious she was to her own natural beauty. Ellen, tall and lean, had naturally luminescent skin, pink lips, and she still had thick eyelashes. Her teeth were straight and white; not too many sixty-year-olds looked so good. If not for the gray in her hair, she would appear so much younger than her years. "You're so old-fashioned."

"Would you? Sleep with a man you'd only known a few months?"

"If I really liked him and believed he was the real deal," Marni said. "Yeah. I would. If you go with Mark to the fire, where will you sleep?"

"I don't know," she said, just realizing there were some practical details she hadn't thought through. "He has an RV. It can sleep eight. It will be like camping."

"If you're out of town together, maybe you should talk. You know. Ask him what he's looking for. Tell him what you're looking for. Or not looking for."

"What does that mean?" Ellen asked. "I've never been down this road."

"Not even with Ralph?" Marni asked.

"Ralph pretty much took over; he told me what I wanted. And it sounded good." And it was in that moment she realized she really hadn't decided for herself before Ralph came along. That could be a problem. "We had a few good years," she said. And that was all.

"Did you regret it?" Marni asked.

"Not at all," Ellen said very easily. "Ralph was a good man. He was such fun. His life was cut short but the time we had together was good. He was so strong and vital, it was terrible to see him reduced to a mere shadow of his former self. It would be torture to see that in another man."

"Well, I guess you could try to avoid that by never taking a chance. And won't you feel silly if you both live another thirty years. What a waste."

"Of course I'll bring this up, if I can get up the courage."

"Ellen, think of it as something you're doing for him," Marni said. "If it's not about you, you'll get it done."

"Probably true," she admitted.

Marni heard from Sam in the afternoon. He said he would be driving Sophia to her support group meeting that evening, then going back for her two hours later. "I don't have much time but even if it's an hour, can you take some company?"

"Yes!" she nearly shouted into the phone. "Yes, yes!"

She rushed to her room to brush her hair and quickly apply a little fresh makeup. She hadn't been alone with him in a week and before that they'd catch a quick minute here and there, a kiss, an embrace, a whisper or two, just any little romantic contact that would hold them awhile. Their phone calls had become more and more breathy and they were always reluctant to say goodbye.

She put up the garage door so he could pull in and they were caught up once again in the hallway right inside the back door, clinging to each other like a couple of high school kids. Their mouths were stuck together in a series of hot, wet kisses and soft sweet murmurs.

"This can't go on," she whispered. "We're going to break something."

"I'll chance it," he said. "You're delicious."

She felt something on her back, wiggled a little bit and heard the crinkle of cellophane. "Flowers?"

"Someone was selling them on a street corner and since I always come empty-handed, then eat your food, I thought it was the least I could do."

"So sweet," she said, straining to look over his shoulder. "Roses."

"I know they're not your favorite, but it's what they were selling."

"Are you hungry?"

"Only for you," he said, covering her mouth with passionate kisses again.

They bolted apart at the sound of the back door opening.

"Mom? Mom? Do you have company?"

It was Bella, coming in the back door. It was so rare for her to drop by without calling ahead. But then it was also rare for Marni to have plans she hadn't mentioned. She pushed Sam away and brushed down her sweater as if to smooth wrinkles. "In here," she called from the kitchen.

Bella came into the kitchen, her big belly preceding her. "I should have called, I'm sorry."

"Not at all," Marni said. "Have you met Sam? Sophia's father, Sam. He's the guy who brought me the white asparagus bed."

"Yes, I remember," Bella said, rubbing her belly.

"Are you all right, Bella?" Marni asked.

"Yes, I think so. I've just come from the doctor and since I was passing by… I'm having those Braxton-Hicks contractions." She laughed a little nervously. "I thought I might be in labor, but no. Just practice for the real thing. I'm sorry, I didn't mean to interrupt."

"You're fine," Marni said. "Sit down. Tell me what happened."

"Oh, flowers!" she said.

"Bella! What happened?"

"I was in a deposition with a witness and I started having contractions. They got really strong so I phoned the doctor and she said to come in and let her check me out. I was hoping it was the real thing but now I'm afraid I'm not going to know the real thing when it comes!"

"Oh, you'll know," Marni said. "That's a feeling you never forget."

"At least she said it's not too early, but she'd still like me to cook him a while longer, if I can."

"I'd say, get a nap while you can!" Marni advised. "I made a chicken dish today—Maple Dijon. I just put it in the freezer two hours ago. Would you like to take it home for you and Jason?"

"That would be great."

"Are you as good a cook as your mother?" Sam asked.

"No one is as good as my mother, yet she's the one who's skinny!"

"You have a very good excuse to put on weight," Marni said. "I hardly ever sit down to a meal. I taste all day long. I hardly get a chance to work up an appetite. Bella, are you sure you feel okay?"

"I'm fine. By the time I got to the doctor's office, my labor pains had completely disappeared. Sam, Sophia isn't still staying here, is she?"

There were two quick raps at the door from the garage. "Hello?" called the unmistakable news anchor voice of Jeff, Marni's ex. "Hello? Marni? Bella?"

Marni stopped herself from groaning.

He let himself in and came to the kitchen, the focal point and gathering spot of this large and beautiful home. "Am I interrupting?" he asked.

And Marni wondered why people who were clearly interrupting always asked if they were interrupting. "What a surprise," she said in a very cynical tone.

"I'm sorry, I should have called."

And that was the other thing they always said. "That would have at least warned me..."

"Bella, my love, look at you! You have blossomed! Less than a month to go!" Jeff grabbed her arms and planted a tender kiss, European style, on each cheek. "How are you feeling?"

"Like I'm going to pop any second."

"Well, you look absolutely stunning! Never more beautiful."

"Thank you, that's very sweet," Bella said.

Then there was a quick couple of raps on the back door and Nettie called in, "Helloooo. Is someone having a party without me?"

Marni rolled her eyes and thought, *Someone was going to have sex without any of you!* But she said, "So it seems."

"Well, look at this unruly gathering," Nettie said. "We were just on our way to Reno for a dinner at the college and I wanted to drop off your serving dishes. I know how you are about misplacing your dishes." Nettie smiled at Sam and said, "Hello," with a big grin. "Professor Garner?"

He stretched out a hand. "The same. Professor Carlisle?"

"It's a pleasure. We should open a bottle of wine!"

It was fortunate that no one had a lot of time to party, but unfortunate that Sam was going to have to leave in an hour to pick up Sophia. Nettie went out to the drive to fetch Marvin. Wine was opened, club soda with lime was offered to Bella. Nettie and Marvin hadn't seen Jeff in quite a while, there was a lot of chatter about the approach of the new baby, whose name Bella and Jason couldn't agree on, there were questions about the show and whether Marni would be taking any time off.

Snacks were put out, a little gossip and laughter occupied them for about an hour, then the first to leave was Sam. "As much as I've enjoyed this unexpected party, I'm on my way to pick up my daughter. I hope we can do this again sometime," he said.

Greetings were passed on to Sophia, who everyone knew aside from Jeff.

Next Bella grabbed the dinner Marni had offered and hugged her aunt and uncle, her mother and even Jeff and said goodbye.

Finally Nettie and Marvin left. Leaving Jeff and Marni.

"Are you okay if I stay for another glass of wine, or would you prefer I leave?"

"I'm not even sure why you're here," she said. "I thought I had trained you to call ahead."

"I was deliberately defiant," he said with a smile. "I had hoped to have a brief conversation. I have some good news."

She lifted the bottle and poured a bit into their glasses. "Do tell!"

"I found an investor for the restaurant!"

"Congratulations!" she said, giving his glass a clink. "How did that come about?"

"Well, I've been hunting, high and low, and I finally met a wannabe restaurateur who has been looking for just the right business to invest and play in. His money comes from the microchip industry but on the side, he's a foodie. He knows better than to invest everything in restaurants when his talents are elsewhere but he loves food. He loves restaurants. So microchips made him rich and he dabbles in other things. He has invested in a race car, some thoroughbreds, vacation property, and my small but significant family restaurant. He's keeping me afloat. The Basque family who runs the place are happy to have him around; they're so relieved that their jobs are no longer on the chopping block. I'm not going to lose the restaurant, he's invited to use the kitchen as often as he likes, and it's going to make both of us happy!"

"That's wonderful! I almost hate to ask…"

"He bought out Gretchen. He offered her some cash and she took it. I have a contract with my investor and no one else."

Marni chewed on her lip for just a moment, then she smiled and said, "That's probably for the best."

"Gretchen suggested we should consider reconciling," Jeff said. Then he laughed.

"Oh, Jeff! Have you given her another chance?"

"Of course not. I may be stupid but I'm not terminally stupid!"

She felt the instant desire to run him through the events as she remembered them, remind him how he'd been used and abused, mistreated and ultimately robbed. Then he was discarded and abandoned. But she didn't say anything. Clearly he knew the facts.

Then she noticed he had cloudy eyes. He was near tears.

"It's amazing, isn't it? That it can be so difficult to give up someone who isn't good for you?"

"I know," she said. "I know."

FOURTEEN

The first time Sophia had entered this meeting room she'd been terrified and had felt so alone and out of place. There were about a dozen chairs forming a circle. This was her group meeting. She remembered thinking all she wished for in the world was to be like everyone else.

Then she discovered she was.

The women began to pour into the room. It was so interesting that they all claimed the chairs they would keep, returning to that same chair week after week. They were all ages, shapes and colors. Yet their experiences had been so alarmingly alike.

Louise was recently divorced from a man who physically abused her. She was thirty, a single mother of three and a working student. She'd been on her own for less than a year and was trying to put her life back together. She looked very tired most of the time, probably because what she'd taken on was monumental. Her kids ranged in age from four to eleven. She cleaned houses and at night offices so she could also go to school and study. If not for the fact that she lived with her mother, she'd never be able to make it. Although she was awarded full custody and child support, her ex-husband didn't pay any of the money he owed and she was always trying to figure out how to get by. Sometimes she had to decide which bill to pay and which to let lie fallow.

Mary was nineteen and had recently ended a relationship with her boyfriend. They had a fourteen-month-old baby together but hadn't married, which was probably just as well, but of course there was no divorce and therefore no settlement. Mary was staying with her sister's family but there was tension because they were so crowded. She and her sister squabbled. She couldn't figure when or if she should include her ex-boyfriend in her son's life. The ex was an alcoholic and she was worried whenever she let him have their son for a visit.

Claire seemed like someone who shouldn't be in their group—she was over thirty-five, well educated, had a decent job, didn't have money problems, was very put together and seemed confident. Her clothes were nice and her haircut was chic. She had just gotten divorced after twenty years of marriage and her heart was broken. She was trying to figure out what had gone wrong in her marriage. She didn't talk a lot and when she did, she was soft-spoken and articulate.

Stevie was a battered wife, recently escaped from a terrible marriage; Pat was in her sixties and had been verbally and emotionally abused throughout a long marriage.

There were three other women that Sophia had seen a couple of times, but she didn't know much about their history as they weren't present for every meeting.

And there was Laura, the counselor who led their group.

Sophia thought Laura was amazing. She had revealed her own history, her unhappy marriage that led to her studying for a degree and choosing a profession in which she could help other women like herself.

"Tonight I'd like us to talk about a couple of significant things. One, for those of you willing to share, we could learn something from what you thought attracted you to this man who would ultimately hurt you or disappoint you. And two, do you think if the events repeated themselves, would you be drawn to him again? If you met him now, would you want to date him, knowing what you know about relationships?"

"I probably would," Louise said. "He was so handsome and when he was good, he was so wonderful. He's a real sweet talker. He was seductive and sexy. It was a total shock when he first treated me badly. It was like he became another person. Then he begged for another chance and I gave it to him. He started out sweet and complimentary, kind and gentle, then he flipped again. And he was so sorry! He cried and begged me to forgive him. I don't know how you plan for something like that!"

"You get out the second the dark side shows itself," someone said.

"Looking back at my marriage, I can see now that I held the family together and I did way too much forgiving!" Pat said. "I regret that I didn't run like hell the first time he cheated on me. I regret that I didn't leave him but I'd been a stay-at-home mom all those years and couldn't support myself. I waited too long and in the end he left me. For a younger woman! I put up with his abuse when he was just going to leave me with nothing in the end!"

"And would you find yourself attracted to him now?" Laura asked.

"That question comes at a bad time," Pat said. "I don't have a very high opinion of men in general."

A couple of women laughed. They went around the circle talking about their experiences, which led to a discussion on self-esteem and at least three women seemed to think of themselves as confident and sure and yet somehow attached themselves to partners who didn't treat them that way.

Sophia thought her situation was quite different, but when she heard herself describing her relationship with Angelo, she realized it sounded remarkably the same. When she described the night she found him standing in her living room while she slept, waking up to him looking down at her, claiming she had invited him in when she had not, she could see by the reactions of the other women, they found that terrifying.

"My ex hid in my bedroom closet while I was out," Louise said. "One of the neighbors saw him go into the apartment and told me. I didn't go in. I called the police and they arrested him. He admitted he thought he'd kill me in my sleep." Several women gasped. "Then he called me and left me a message, asking me to write a letter to the judge begging for leniency. He wanted me to say I'd forgiven him and that I wasn't afraid of him."

"You didn't, though?" asked one of the women.

She shook her head, then dropped her chin, looking so defeated.

"Louise, we have to be aware of when the situation shifts from abuse to danger. He has threatened your life. Think about a few things, like is there a place you and your children can go that he wouldn't easily find you? Should you talk to someone in social services about finding you a shelter? Do you have relatives in another town that he doesn't know about? Do you have any protection devices like an alarm on a key chain or mace or anything? Do you have an order of protection? That might not keep him away but it will make his punishment worse if he comes near you."

People in the group began offering suggestions that ranged from getting a gun to taking self-defense classes. But Sophia's mind was wandering. How had she not been thinking about how she would defend herself?

"I was thinking about writing a letter for him. I thought if it pleased him, maybe he'd stop being so awful. I thought maybe he'd be grateful," Louise said.

"And you'd be trapped," someone said.

"Forever," someone else said.

"I don't know that for certain," Louise said. "But I know for sure if I don't do what he asks, he'll turn mean again! If I can hold him off…"

"There's nothing you can do to change him," Pat said. "The only thing you can control is yourself. If you want to, you can stay with me for a little while. Until you come up with a better idea."

The group had gone from supportive to critical. Everyone there expressed their fear for Louise and also shared their most terrifying moments in abusive relationships. Although Sophia had only been in the group for a short time, she was already hearing the same things over and over. *If I can't have you, no one can. You'll never get out of this alive. I'll kill myself. If I go to jail, I'll kill myself and you. You're always pushing my buttons! Everything would have been fine if you'd just…*

"I didn't have an abusive husband," Claire said. "I had a coworker who decided we were meant to be together. I did nothing to encourage him. Nothing. But the result of his delusion was that I had a stalker for a long time. Once he caught me alone in a car park and he kidnapped me. I was tied up for a couple of days. That put him in jail for months, and when he got out, he came after me again."

"Oh, my God," came whispers around the room.

"And now?" someone asked.

"I ran away. He hasn't bothered me in a while but I don't think he knows where I am. I left my family, my job, and a dedicated police detective checks on the stalker regularly. He lets me know where he is and what he seems to be doing. He's still in the city I left. I'm getting used to the idea that I'll never go back there. Because, see, he's crazy and the only thing I can do about that is stay out of his reach. He fixated on me. I have no idea why. Maybe I look like his dead wife or ex-girlfriend, I don't know. I've read a lot about delusional people, about people who are fixated for no reason, and unless they seek help, there's not much their victims can do. You must not mention this," she stressed. "Not even a passing remark. You never know when you might be passing on dangerous information."

"Of course not," people said. "Never."

"It's not typical," Claire said. "It's pretty uncommon. It's usually a partner or family member who is abusive and controlling, but it can happen that someone finds you and believes you're his…"

That is Angelo, Sophia thought.

"In the meantime, if any of you need help for PTSD, ask Laura for suggestions, for the names of counselors. I find I still have flashbacks, waking up with a jolt in a cold sweat, afraid. I'm getting better, but it's slow and tedious."

"So unfair!" one of the women said.

"Let's remember everyone, this is not your fault," Laura said. "You absolutely never cause someone to hit you. There are lots of things you can do but the most reliable thing is to get away from the threat and seek safety."

Listening to the stories shared by the women in the group, Sophia always felt her nerves on edge, but there was something about the stories she heard tonight that seemed darker and more frightening than usual. It brought back the helpless feeling of waking up to see someone in the room with her, watching her and knowing if, in that moment, he'd wanted to kill her, she would be dead now.

She had envisioned the support group would make her feel stronger but knowing how pervasive this issue of women as victims was, she was even more afraid. She had talked about this with her counselor. "In time you will feel stronger. For now it's important that you know you're not alone, you're not crazy and it's not your fault. We will work on making sure you trust yourself and can stay safe."

"I want to learn how to not be afraid," someone said.

"Fear is a sign that you must beware. And be alert. We'll work on confidence to go along with it."

When that session of support was over, the women hugged and told each other they would be okay. And somehow, Sophia wasn't sure how, all the nerves of the group session seemed to evaporate and she felt oddly comforted just by the company of like creatures who all walked that frightening path together.

She stepped out of the building. The group had dispersed a little bit early and she didn't see her father's truck so she leaned against the wall and took out her phone. She texted him that she was finished with her group and was waiting for him out front. He was never late, so she knew she had only a few minutes to wait.

She held onto her phone and looked around. Students mingled and walked between buildings. She saw a young couple holding hands and smiling into each other's eyes as they strolled along. She had a sinking feeling and thought, they look so safe and happy. She hoped that's how they would stay.

Then she saw him. *What brutal timing*, she thought. He was a block away, but unmistakably it was Angelo. He leaned against the front of his truck. He was staring at her. He could only know she would be here if he had followed her.

She froze. Her breath caught. She began to look around for her father, feeling frantic. Angelo appeared very calm. A bit of a smile seemed to appear on his lips but she was so far away she wondered if she had imagined it. Then he slowly lifted a hand in an abbreviated wave. She had an unwelcome image appear in her mind—seeing him sitting on the chair across the room, watching her sleep.

Her father pulled up to the curb and she ran to his truck, jumping in and slamming the door. She locked it. "Papi, it's him!"

"Where?" Sam asked, looking a bit startled and confused.

"Over there, leaning on his truck. Right over there."

As Sam looked, Angelo slowly walked around the truck to get in. As Sam and Sophia watched, he started the truck and pulled away from the curb. He drove toward them, passed them and drove away.

"Did he speak to you?" Sam asked.

She shook her head. "He just stared at me."

"He kept his distance, I see," Sam said. "I don't know if that's encouraging or not. He's obviously letting you know he's around. Does he have any reason to be on the campus that you know of?"

She shook her head. "No. Do you think he's following me?"

"Do *you* think he is?" he asked.

"I don't know," she said, her voice wobbly. "He must be."

"Well, let's go get a bite to eat and we'll see if he follows us."

"Can we just go home?" she asked.

"No, we're going to a nice, crowded, brightly lit place. We'll get a little dinner, check our surroundings and then drive home. The long way. We'll see if he is anywhere in sight. Don't be nervous. I promise you, he won't dare even approach you if you're not alone!"

"I'm not very hungry."

"I'm with you. But we have to go on living. If he comes around or does anything threatening, we'll notify the police, but this can't go on forever. When he realizes he's not going to make any progress in this game, he'll move on."

Sophia hoped he was right, but she was a long way from feeling confident.

There was an Olive Garden at the edge of the campus and Sam parked and escorted her in. He asked for a table by the window and they sat down to eat. Sam ordered a beer and got Sophia a glass of wine. She was asked to show her identification and Sam jokingly asked the waiter if he'd like to see his ID.

Sam tried making conversation and it was awkward at first because Sophia was so spooked but after a couple of sips of wine, she began to relax. Sam talked about his day, asked about hers and they ordered dinner. Although she didn't really feel like eating, she took a few bites of her carbonara. It was so rich and delicious that she managed to enjoy it.

"How was your group tonight?" Sam asked.

She shrugged. "It's meant to be encouraging, but... Papi, I want to go home."

"Okay, but eat a little more of your dinner."

"No, I mean home. Argentina. I want to get far away from here."

He put down his fork. "Have you given this a lot of thought? What about school?"

"I can't concentrate on school right now. I haven't been thinking about school for months. Maybe I can pick it up in Argentina. Or maybe I can take some time off and come back to school, but I have no peace! I can't sleep at night, I jerk awake full of fear and worry that someone is in my room, looking at me."

"Do you think running is the answer?" he asked.

"Yes! For now, anyway! I could stay with Aunt Avida for a while."

"And you think that would make you feel safe?"

"Papi, some of the women in the group have talked about the nightmares and the nervous problems. It's not uncommon. I am meeting girls and women who have had abusive boyfriends or stalkers and they feel so frightened and helpless and I'm feeling that way. I want to run away! I wouldn't tell anyone where I am going and if there's one thing I know about Angelo—he doesn't have much money. He can't seem to keep a job and I'm sure he has no savings. At least I have somewhere to go! The women in my group—all they can think about is finding a place where they are safe. It's as if they are all prisoners! Papi, I think it would be best if I went home. At least for a while."

"Alone?"

"I'm not afraid to go alone. I'm more afraid to stay here and be alone for ten minutes!" Tears came to her eyes. "I just want a good night's sleep again."

"Sophia…"

"I don't want to complain, but I don't have any better ideas."

He reached across the table and took her hand. "Finish your dinner. We'll go home and call Aunt Avida. Before we do that, we should talk about a plan. What to do about school, how long you think you need to be in another country, whether I can take you and help you get settled, that sort of thing."

"I don't expect you to take me," she said.

"I want to sleep at night, too," he said, smiling. "We've been together a long time now. I promised your mother I would take good care of you."

It was very convenient for Ellen to live right next door to Mark. Marni not only told her to take at least a few days off but in addition she was very excited to hear every detail about their first food caravan.

At 4:00 a.m., before she got a text from Mark saying they were gathering and getting started, she heard engines, voices and laughter, the occasional shout. It was still dark outside, but she sprang out of bed like a kid! She was ready. She pulled on her jeans and boots and jacket. She brushed her teeth and hair, dabbed a little makeup on her face and lips. No one but her need ever know her jeans, boots and sweater were new. Her bag was packed and she had only to toss in her overnight essentials. It probably took her five minutes.

She peeked out the front door and was amazed to find so many people. It was maybe a dozen. There were vans and trucks and SUVs. The refrigerated trailers were in the street, ready to be hooked up to vehicles.

"Ellen!"

Mark came rushing toward her. He had a leather-bound

notebook in his hand but he reached for her and gave her a light kiss on the cheek.

"You said you had a couple of friends who wanted to volunteer," she said.

"Yes, just about all of them want to be in on this first run. Come on," he said, taking her hand and pulling her toward all the parked cars, trailers and people. "Hey, everyone, this is Ellen. Ellen, here's Eugene, this is Bob, here's Dale. This here is Mike and his wife, Maxi, and their kids, Tim and Shawnee, but they're not all going."

"Nice to meet you, Ellen," Maxi said. "We just got up early so we can send them off, then we'll go home and take a nap. But this is so exciting. I'm a little jealous, this is really a big deal. And these guys who are still working have lots of time off so Mark will be able to keep his caravan staffed with volunteers!"

"I think I'm the only woman on the trip," Ellen said.

Mark pulled her away from Maxi and the kids. "Ellen, this is Paul Manfield, Bob Duncan—we have the two Bobs and call them big Bob and little Bob and I'm sure they hate it but, well, too bad. And here's Art, Julio and Ed. Where's Phil? Oh, there he is. I worked with Phil for thirty years and now our sons work together."

"I had no idea you'd have so many people," she said. "Will I be in the way?"

"Of course not! You're essential crew!"

"Look, I can drive. I can follow you and sleep in my car so the RV has plenty of space…"

A horn tooted, someone arriving and having very little consideration for neighbors who might be sleeping. A big RV drove down the street.

"Okay, looks like we're ready to pull out. You come with

me. You'll stay in my RV and if for any reason you have to get back home, some of these guys will be going back early and you can catch a ride. Get your gear, lock up your house and come with me. You can help me with logistics and any phone calls. We have space in a church parking lot; the church is set up for evacuees and we have a lot of room and with any luck, running water."

"Are you sure?" Ellen asked.

"If you are," he said. "I thought you were excited about this."

"I was. I am! I'll get my things."

"We're going to need your driveway," Mark said. "We're not taking all these vehicles."

"Help yourself," she said on the run.

After making sure everything was turned off in the house and the doors all locked, she stood on the front stoop and watched as these men, she assumed all firefighters or retired firefighters, lined up their trucks and cars, checked the trailers to be sure the hitches were secure and lined up with precision, ready to go. Before she could even walk to the street, Mark came for her. He took her travel bag and carried it to his RV, which led the procession.

"Come up here, Ellen. You're the copilot."

"Are you sure?"

He stopped and just looked at her. "Stop asking that," he said. "I want you with me."

There was something about the way he said it that thrilled her. She grinned hugely. "Yes," she said. "Good."

"It's not a very long drive," he said. "We're lucky that our first trip is a short one. We'll learn from it. If we find we're missing anything, we can send someone back for it. But we're needed there. Some houses have been lost, families displaced and they are close to having the fire under control."

She sat in the cab of the RV in the passenger seat and the feeling it gave her was powerful. It made her feel strong. She felt relevant and important.

Mark took the driver's seat, fastened his seat belt and started the engine. "Here we go!"

Ellen and Mark sat side by side in the cab of the RV and as usual they talked nonstop. He was so proud of his son and two grandsons and couldn't wait for her to meet them when they came for Thanksgiving. He wanted her to tell him how she became a chef.

"But I've told you that story," she said.

"Tell me again," he begged.

The walkie-talkie made a sound, like a blast of air.

"Is that off?" she asked.

He fiddled with the buttons. "Yep. It's off. Tell me."

"Well, I've always loved cooking and learned first from my mother. I wanted to work in a restaurant kitchen, but my first experience with that was brutal. There was so much pressure! It didn't kill my love of cooking but I kept my eyes open for any job in the culinary arts where I could learn and earn at the same time. I took a lot of classes; I did get a degree in nutrition, though it took me years to study while working and the only work I could find with that degree was school or hospital work. But cooking shows or television didn't appeal to me at all. But then along came Marni. I didn't want to be in front of the camera and she needed support for her show.

"That was the heaven I was looking for—a chance to develop recipes and execute them without drawing a lot of attention to myself. I was forty before I found Marni and we've been a team for twenty years."

"I'm glad Marni is okay with you taking time off for this project," he said.

"She's a little excited about it, actually. Her interests are growing as well. Ever since the situation with Sophia and her stalker boyfriend, Marni has turned her attention to creating a safe house for women and children fleeing from abusive relationships. It's changed her, in a way. She seems driven by this project."

"You know what they say. If you feel you're not getting enough, try giving a little more. It comes back at you tenfold."

"You've been in the giving business your whole adult life," Ellen said.

"I feel like I'm just getting started," he said with a laugh. Then he paused. "Look, there's our mark, right out there." He pointed to a plume of smoke. "It's blowing north, northwest. Our address for the St. Elsworth Episcopal Church is just southeast of the fire line. That's where we're going to set up."

"That cloud of smoke—does that look bad?" she asked.

"I've seen worse. Even if it's quickly contained, there could still be a need for housing and food until people get their bearings, find friends or family to stay with, that sort of thing. I wasn't sure we'd be up and running this early but we made it."

"Isn't fire season almost over?"

"Not at all. And even so, there's always something, Ellen. Floods or some other disaster. I was monitoring the emergency radio and caught this one but it's my goal that the Red Cross and other support groups know where to find me." He reached across the cab and grabbed her hand. "It's going to be a long day, Ellen. Please make sure to let me know if you need a break at any time."

"I'm much tougher than I look." She glanced over her

shoulder. "I wasn't paying attention. I didn't realize we were going to be driving alone. No one wanted to ride with us?"

"I think maybe they're letting us be alone. Dale asked me who you were to me and I said we were neighbors and very good friends and that you loved the idea of the food caravan and wanted to help. It was nothing suggestive. But I think some of my friends hope I'll find someone. That's what happens when you're suddenly alone. Everyone wants to pair you up."

"It didn't happen to me," Ellen said.

"You're completely safe," he said with a laugh. "I'm enjoying this."

"You've worked hard to get to this point!"

"Are you talking about the food caravan or being alone with you?" he wondered aloud.

"Both!"

"You couldn't be more right."

"You know, there's something we should talk about. Oh, shit, I don't know if I can do it," she said. She felt her cheeks flame with embarrassment.

"Spit it out, Ellen. It's just me and you, alone in the RV, driving to our first of many adventures. What's on your mind?"

"I think there's something we should clear the air about before we get any more...involved."

"What's that? Come on, I don't bite."

"Well, we both have pretty complicated pasts. We've both been caregivers of terminally ill spouses. I don't know anything about how you feel about the potential for having another one to take care of. I know I have a lot of ambivalence toward the idea."

"Not surprising. But that's something I have taken care

of. For one thing, I have long-term care insurance. It made sense, right. Because my son has two young sons of his own. But he tells me that he will be sure I'm taken care of and have what I need. So you aren't going to stumble into a situation where you'll have to take care of a sick old man. Ellen, I know you're not a professional caregiver. And that's not what I'm looking for."

"What are you looking for?"

"Just something special," he said. "I wasn't really looking, to be honest. I was working on being content to be alone. There are things about living alone that I like. I wake up in the middle of the night and can't get back to sleep and I turn the TV on or read, or if I'm really wide awake, I might go to my computer."

"Sometimes I cook," she said with a laugh.

"I'm not surprised. But even though I should probably just stay alone to keep from being an inconvenience to anyone else, I wouldn't mind having a special person. A person like you. To spend time with."

"We've had dinner together most evenings for months!" she said.

"And I see no reason to stop doing that. If we find more than dinner together to connect us, I vote yes. But you should rest easy that I'm not looking for a nurse."

"And I'm not, either," she said. "I have insurance and family, too, as you know. My sister and her kids will look after Aunt Ellen. Are we clear on that?"

"Sounds like we can relax and enjoy life, doesn't it now?" he asked.

"I must seem so selfish," she said. "Being unwilling to even think about being involved with a man who might need my help."

"Not at all, Ellen. You've already done that. And I don't think you give me enough credit. I'm in pretty good shape. I might outlive you, you know."

"Well, I hope so."

"I think Susan wrote my obituary the first year I was with the fire department. It was updated several times over the years. She told me she had been planning for my death almost since the day we were married. It was her way of dealing with the dangers of my job." He laughed brightly. "Even though I miss her and never deserved her, and wish she hadn't gotten sick, I'm glad that obituary she wrote never got used."

"Well, I'm not writing one for you!" Ellen said.

"If I feel like I'm going down, I'll write my own," he said with a grin.

"You do that. It's just important we're honest with each other. It's all a little scary for me."

"It doesn't scare me," he said. "I am happy to just see where things go. Hanging out with me is not that big of a job."

"Really?" a male voice said over the walkie-talkie. "You got her in the RV helping with the food caravan! You're more trouble than you're worth."

"You're listening, Dale?" Mark shouted. "Shame on you!"

"Tell Ellen not to worry. We'll take care of you!" Dale said, laughing heartily.

Mark flipped the switch to off. "I'm sorry," he said. "Total accident."

She looked at him sternly. "I'm never leaving the RV," she said.

FIFTEEN

Marni was in the kitchen, standing at the island with a cup of coffee, a bowl of fruit and a notepad, paging through a cookbook. This was a typical way she started her day. Ellen was driving with Mark to Quincy, where a wildfire was roaring, so she wouldn't be in today or tomorrow or maybe the next day. She heard the door from the garage open and knew that would be Sophia. "Good morning," she called.

She looked up to see Sophia and Sam coming into the kitchen. They were both wearing expressions that could only be described as contrite. Something was off.

"Well, hello. I wasn't expecting both of you."

"We have something to tell you," Sam said. "I apologize for the suddenness of this. I thought about phoning you last night, but it was late and I didn't want to disturb you. I'm taking Sophia back to Argentina. To her mother's family there."

"Oh? For a visit?" Marni asked hopefully.

"A very long visit. I've taken a leave from my position. Emergency family leave. The university has been very understanding and accommodating. We're going together and I'll stay for as long as it takes to make sure she's settled and comfortable. She has several aunts there. Aunts who are happy to have her for a while."

"How long?" Marni asked, knowing her voice sounded weak.

"I don't know, Marni," Sophia answered. "A couple of nights ago Angelo was watching me when I came out of my group session and it hit me—he is not going away. I think the best thing I can do for myself is find a safe place. I just want to go home."

"Oh, darling, I'm so sorry. And so sorry to lose you! You've been the greatest gift to me!"

"We're going to be flexible about the duration of this visit," Sam said. "It could be a few weeks, it could be a long time. Whatever it takes to give Sophia peace of mind."

"But what if he follows you there?"

"That's very doubtful," Sam said. "Angelo doesn't have much money and seems to have trouble keeping a job. We talked to the police officer who first handled her case and he agreed that without a lot of cash or contacts in another country, it's unlikely he'll manage."

"He doesn't have a passport," Sophia said. "He told me that once and I can't imagine that has changed recently. I'm so sorry I'm not able to give you notice before leaving..."

"I understand. There have been times in my life I wished for a place to run away to. Or run home to."

"I know I'm running away," she said. "I hope you don't think less of me for that."

"I think I might do the same if I were in your circumstances."

"I can't expect you to hold my job for me," Sophia said.

"I also don't expect to be able to fill it in the short term. Let's just see where we are when you feel like coming back."

"I must be truthful, Marni. I might not come back. If I feel safe in Argentina with my family, I might stay."

"The most important thing is that you feel good where you are. I'll manage. I always do."

"You are very kind," Sophia said.

"Will you stay in touch?" she asked.

"Yes, of course. Papi upgraded my phone so I can keep in touch with friends. I'm going to get my things from my desk and work closet."

When Sophia left the room, Marni turned wide eyes to Sam. "I won't lie, this is a blow."

"I'm sorry. I thought about trying to explain over the phone and it didn't seem like the right thing to do. The poor girl is so shaken by this little asshole who stalks and frightens her. I've never felt such rage before. It wouldn't be good for anyone if we ran into each other now. I hate this plan of running away to Argentina but she hasn't seen her family in a few years and that will be good for her. I have to do whatever I can to keep her safe!"

"How long are you staying down there?"

"I don't know. Possibly a long time. I've promised my department I'll do some research and writing and keep them up to date on my plans. I'll call you, a lot. Unless you ask me not to."

"Of course I want to hear from you," she said. "And I want Sophia to feel safe."

"I wanted her to feel safe with me, but I can't be with her

every second. Even driving her everywhere turned out not to be enough. I want her to feel free to enjoy life and this incident has been torture for her," Sam said sadly.

"You're a good father," Marni said. "I don't know that you could possibly do more to guard her. When are you leaving?"

"Tonight. We'll arrive in Argentina tomorrow morning. I'll text you when we're on the ground there."

"Please. I want to know where you are."

"I'll send pictures."

"You can't possibly imagine how much I'll miss you."

"And I'll miss you. I don't know what the future holds. Even if we do come back to the US, we might not come here," Sam said.

"Of course, Sophia could decide she wants to be somewhere else. But we'll stay in touch."

Sophia came back to the kitchen with a cardboard box full of her things. She had tears in her eyes. "I hate to leave you, Marni."

"I will miss you so much. But please stay in touch. Text me, email me, call me. We've become such good friends. We can't let go of that."

"Never. And please say goodbye to Ellen and Bella and Nettie. I will miss our little friendship club and if they want to stay in touch, I'd love that."

"Of course I'll tell them."

Sophia put down her box and embraced Marni. "You have been like a mother to me."

Marni stroked her cheek. "But when you're with your aunts, you will find you have many mothers. And I bet they're bossier than me."

"I'm going to put this in the car," Sophia said.

When she'd gone out the back door, Sam looked over his

shoulder, then he wrapped his arms around Marni and kissed her passionately. He sighed against her lips. "I am falling in love with you," he whispered. "This is agony."

"You are doing the right thing. Just be well and call me."

"You missed your chance to say you love me, too," he said.

"I don't have to say it," she said. "You know it."

When Ellen and Mark drove into Quincy, they immediately found the church that had agreed to be their base. Mark pulled into the parking lot and popped off his seat belt. Ellen didn't move. "You can't stay in here all day," he said. "They'll break down the door, drag you out and tease you relentlessly."

"I'm mortified. That radio was on the whole time!"

"So? We didn't talk about anything embarrassing or too personal."

"Everything we talked about was personal. We talked about our families, about our marriages, about high school!"

"Get over yourself," he said with a laugh. "Come on, we have work to do. No time for foolish pride." And with that he was gone.

For a few minutes she sat in the cab and watched the action in the parking lot. All these big beautiful men began setting up their trailers in the large church parking lot. *Why are firemen so handsome?* she had often wondered. *Is it a job requirement?*

The vehicles were parked on the far side of the lot; the refrigerated trailers were lined up on the point farthest away from the church building and the RVs at the back. Extension cords were brought out and untangled. A large tarp was lifted onto silver poles to provide a covering to shield them from the sun, though the smoke in the air was almost a cloud cover.

She went outside to help. Eugene was the first guy she ran into. "Good, you're going to join us. Don't worry, Ellen.

You're smart not to take on another patient. We'll watch over him if he starts to slide." Ellen groaned. Eugene laughed. They got to work.

It was as if the whole thing had been choreographed. Large folding tables were brought from the church—apparently Mark had arranged to borrow them for his food service. The pastor and church secretary came along, greeting the volunteers and introducing themselves. Mark took Ellen's hand and pulled her over to where they stood talking. The man was introduced to them as Reverend Peter Hollis and the woman was Jan Stanton, the secretary.

"It's so great of you to do this," Peter said. "We've seen some emergency facilities set up in town but other than the Red Cross tent and our sanctuary filled with cots courtesy of the National Guard, we're not well prepared."

"This is our first run, so we're counting on you for feedback," Mark said. "There's no question we're going to make improvements and adjustments. We're going to start with sandwiches and fruit and cookies and as afternoon gets on we'll start some hot meals. Are you sure you don't mind us leeching off your electricity? I can cut you a check for the power usage."

"We have a generator you can use. Maybe we could use a little help with gas but we're prepared to help you with this work."

"I don't see any people," Mark said.

"We have a bunch of people camped out inside and once the word gets out that there's food here, you'll be impressed. There haven't been too many homes lost but there have been a lot of evacuations due to smoke and the risk. Many people have abandoned their homes because they're in the line of fire. Those people are anxious to get back to see what's left.

There are ranches and farms; people are working feverishly to save their stock."

"I hope there's help with that," Ellen said.

"We have rescue efforts from several counties showing up with trucks and trailers. It's not always an organized effort, just neighbors trying to help. You have to be ready to move if the wind shifts or the fire changes course."

"We are ready," Mark said.

Ellen felt such pride when she heard him. They could do this. He knew what to do.

A big stack of heavy-duty table covers was brought out. She noticed that the tables had been set up in an arrangement that left a space for volunteers to move around—several in front, several in back against the RVs. There was a food prep area and a serving area. They began to put out large plastic storage bins, loaves of bread, containers of turkey and salami, huge buckets of mayo, mustard, peanut butter and jelly. There was lettuce, tomatoes, celery and carrot sticks. Apples. Now she knew what to do. This was her wheelhouse. She went directly to the food-prep tables and used hand sanitizer. "I've got this, guys," she said, cleaning her hands and wiping off the excess with a paper towel. She donned latex gloves.

This was where she was comfortable. She put out the condiments, laid out utensils and began slapping sandwiches together. When a sandwich was made, it was wrapped and returned to the plastic bin.

After just a few minutes of this exercise, one of the guys joined her at the work table and began wrapping the sandwiches as she completed them. "Clean hands and gloves, please," she said. Before long another one of the men joined them and got out the apples, putting them in a big bowl. Then someone pulled out the bin of cookies. "I better see if these are okay," he said, eating one.

"Just one," she admonished. "They're not for you." But then she realized the volunteers would be partaking of the food, too, otherwise they might start fainting on the job!

More long folding tables and chairs emerged from the church with some of the men setting them up. A couple of guys carried a picnic table from the far side of the church to the parking lot. Then a second one appeared, the pastor helping to carry that one.

Eventually a couple of women trailing a line of kids came out of the church and wandered sheepishly toward the tables. "Hello!" Ellen said cheerfully. "Feel like something to eat? We don't have breakfast but how about an early lunch?"

"That would be so nice," one of the women said.

"How much is it?" asked the other.

"It's free," Ellen said. "Haven't you heard? We need a sign so people know that!"

"Who's doing this?" asked the first woman.

"These guys are all old friends. Firefighters and retired firefighters and their friends. That's Mark over there. The one carrying the big trash can. It was all his idea. He pulled this together for situations just like this," Ellen said with pride. Mark put the can down at the end of the serving table, pulled a plastic bag out of his back pocket and lined the garbage can. He'd thought of everything. Ellen waved at him and he waved back.

"We have turkey and Swiss with lettuce on whole wheat, PB&J, carrot and celery sticks, chips, apples and cookies."

She visited with the women and got the kids set up with some lunch. The back of Dale's truck was full of bottled water and he brought it out a case at a time. Before long a couple of cars and trucks pulled into the parking lot. Mark hurried to greet the drivers and pointed to the food table. They chatted and laughed a little, then everyone headed for the food table. It wasn't long before there were a couple of dozen people and the sandwiches were disappearing fast.

Ellen noticed that Mark and a couple of others had pulled grills out of the storage space on the underside of the RV. She knew they were already getting ready for the next meal. She wasn't sure what Mark had decided on but knew there were big pans of meat loaf, lasagna, barbeque chicken and turkey breast.

More people arrived, some coming to the church for shelter and some just taking a break to get some lunch. Ellen visited with each one and learned about where their houses were and what condition they were in. Some were just waiting to get more information about possible damages or loss before going to stay with friends or family. A crew of hotshots pulled up in a truck and they all made for the food like they were starving. She learned from these firefighters that they hoped the fire would be contained in another twenty-four hours. It went on like that all afternoon.

The aroma of roasting turkey filled the air and she watched Mark hustling between the RV and the grills, checking on the food. Ellen and the men began to prepare the tables for another meal. This time it was turkey, dressing, potatoes, gravy and green beans. She helped either Mark or Bob in their RV kitchens and was impressed by how much food there was and noted it was perfectly cooked.

By five o'clock there were easily twice as many people hanging around, ready to eat again. The atmosphere was not lighter but there was so much more talking. Everyone had a cell phone out and many were talking and texting, trying to make contact with loved ones. There was a steady hum of conversation because of the number of people, sharing their stories, getting to know each other if they didn't already. They were all ages from children to elderly people. There were even a few pets, but who could even imagine leaving a pet behind.

"Next time I'll remember cat food and some dog kibble," Mark said.

A few ranchers who had been helping neighbors round up stock dropped by and another truck full of hotshots unloaded and grabbed a meal. Some volunteer firefighters pitched a tent on the grassy side of the church and bedded down for the night so they'd be ready to go again first thing in the morning. People tended to stay on, visiting and sharing news, long after their meal was finished. At one point there was a man at least in his fifties with a heavily laden backpack and bedroll who stopped by. It seemed pretty obvious he wasn't a local resident. She turned to Mark who said, "Don't ask. We're here to feed whoever is hungry." As if she could love him more, in that moment she glowed with her pride in him.

By the time the food was stored, all except for the cookies, and cleanup was done, Ellen was exhausted. She asked Mark if it would be okay to take a shower.

"Go right ahead."

"Is there plenty of water?"

"There's an RV park about five miles down the road and I'll take the RV over and refresh everything so there's plenty for cleanup tomorrow. Just remember it's not drinking water. To be safe. And I'll let some of the guys borrow the shower, so close the bedroom door while you're dressing."

Once she was clean and dry, she pulled out a soft and cozy sweat suit. She heard someone come into the bathroom and run the shower so she chose to stay in the bedroom. Where she made her fatal mistake was lying down on the king-size bed. She thought she'd just stay there until whoever was using the shower was done, but that was the last coherent thought she remembered.

She roused again and the RV was dark, but she heard the water running. Either that was the longest shower in history or more than one of the guys had taken their turn. Ellen was no camper and she wasn't sure of the protocol when sharing a small space, and she was the only woman.

Then she realized she was covered with a soft warm blanket. She sighed and cuddled deeper. They hadn't discussed sleeping arrangements but she thought surely she should sleep in the shallow bunk above the cab. Since the RV was outfitted mainly to be a big functional kitchen, there wasn't a couch or living room or pullout bed. But there was that bunk and after the long hours Mark had put in, she thought he should have a decent bed.

The shower stopped. She could hear someone was moving around and she checked the time. It was ten. She wasn't sure what time she had come in for her shower but it wasn't that long ago. Mark cracked the door open quietly and she sat up. "I'll go sleep in the other bed," she said.

"Don't be silly, it's a big bed. We can share if you don't mind."

"You need your rest. Tomorrow will be another busy day."

"So let's get some sleep!" He kicked back and lay down flat on his back beside her. "Lie down, Ellen. You passed out you were so tired. We need our beauty sleep."

Gingerly, slowly, she lay back down. "You covered me up."

"It's cold at night up here in the mountains."

"I was so proud of you today."

"Aww, that's sweet. I was proud of all of us. Tomorrow

will be another long day and then on day three we'll have a little shift change. About five of the guys from the fire department are going to head home and there are replacements ready to relieve them. One of them talked to a crew member from the wildfire detail and it looks like they're a couple of days from letting a few people back into the destroyed area. Just a few at a time, of course."

"To see if there's anything left?" she asked.

"Or to see how bad it is," he answered. "And there's the matter of pets, of friends and neighbors. Thank God for cell phones; at least these people have been in touch with their families. I met a couple whose daughter is at college and they told her not to come home because they're staying with friends. Soon the place is going to be crawling with insurance adjusters. But not everyone will be covered."

"What if we run out of food?" she asked.

"That won't happen. We'll go to the nearest Costco and load up if it comes to that."

"I should call Marni," Ellen said. "She'll want to know what's happening."

"Yes, call her."

"In the morning," Ellen said, rolling on her side.

He immediately curled up against her back, spooning her. "This is nice," he said. "I'm going to sleep like a baby. But I have to warn you, I might snore."

"I might, too," she said happily.

He snored a bit, though it was a mere light rumbling that Ellen immediately found herself attached to and loving the sound. He moved closer in his sleep and she wondered, *Does he remember that it's me? Does he think he's in bed with his late wife?*

She found it was the most natural thing in the world to

press herself closer to him and she fell asleep again. She woke several times but she didn't wrestle around or get out of bed. Then sometime in the wee hours she felt his hands moving, caressing, and she welcomed the sensation. This was not how she thought it would be. In fact she hadn't even allowed herself to imagine it.

He kissed the back of her neck and she turned in his arms.

He kissed her lips. Then he pulled her into his embrace and kissed her more deeply. "Did I wake you with my snoring?" he whispered.

"No, you woke me with your fondling," she said.

"Did you push me away?" he asked.

"No. I liked it," she said.

And then very slowly and a bit awkwardly he began to slide his hands under her sweatshirt and eventually her sweatpants and she moaned. He touched her gently and she pressed closer. There was good deal of mutual touching and exploring along with deeply passionate kissing.

"Is this okay?" he asked.

"Yes, it's very okay," she said. And that motivated him greatly. He was all over her, tugging at her clothes just as she tugged at his. It took a while and it was a little clumsy but they were finally naked and straining together. His fingers slid more deeply into her and he moaned his approval.

Ellen found she had so many simultaneous thoughts; it had been so long since she'd enjoyed this activity; she wasn't sure what to do or what he would like. She could freak out and run except she adored him and wanted this closeness more than just about anything. Finally, clutching each other and rolling around, they were joined. It was a feeling of connection that Ellen hadn't experienced in years.

"Oh, my," she said in a whisper.

"Amazing," he countered.

They rocked together for a while and then, satisfied, they drifted apart. They stayed very close, holding onto each other, sighing in happy sounds. With her head on his shoulder, her face tucked against his neck, she drifted off to sleep once again. In a state of semiconsciousness, she felt him pull the covers over them both.

"Thank you," she said.

"My pleasure," he returned. Then he chuckled.

Marni heard from Sam; he and Sophia made it safely to Argentina. His late wife's family greeted them with a big dinner and family members from near and far gathered to welcome them. He wasn't sure what their plans were going forward but he promised Marni he would call when he could.

She heard from Ellen and the woman whom she'd known and worked with for twenty years had never sounded so alive. She was animated and excited and relayed every detail of the work they'd done from details about the people to stories from the fire. She'd become friends with the firefighters who volunteered with their project and knew all about their families. She was planning to stay with the mission through the weekend and two or three days the following week.

A day passed since Sam, Sophia and Ellen had all left. Then two days, then three days. Marni talked to Bella every day but hadn't seen her in a week as she was getting very close to her due date. She invited Nettie to come by for a glass of wine after work but she was busy with a weekend conference at the college.

Marni's life felt oddly empty. She started wishing she had a dog to walk. She called Bella and asked if they needed food; she'd be happy to take them dinner. Bella and Jason had plans;

Jason predicted it could be their last dinner out before the squalling began.

She decided to talk a walk, to change her mood and scenery. She didn't get far. She was walking down the drive when the sight of a blue truck gave her pause. Leaning against the side of the truck was a handsome young Latino man.

She knew who that must be.

"Angelo?" she asked from her side of the street. "How did you get in here? I didn't tell the security guard to let you in."

He straightened nervously. "I told them I was here to do yard work but I'm here for Sophia," he said. "She called me to come and get her."

Marni actually smiled. "No, she didn't, and you know it. She has a legal order of protection to keep you away. Sophia has gone somewhere where people will keep her safe from you. I don't know the laws outside of the United States but I wouldn't be surprised if they locked you up for harassment and just forgot about you."

"Lies!" he shouted. "She called me to come!"

"Brother, you could use a reality check. I'm going to call the police. Hang around at your own risk."

He stomped across the street toward her. She was unafraid, as remarkable as that seemed. "You dare to call me a liar!" he shouted.

It was said that if you met a bear in the woods, you should stand tall, puff up your chest and growl loudly. You should appear to be a huge threat, never turn tail and run but rather be aggressive and dangerous. She puffed up and screamed, "You're goddamn right I dare!" Then she turned and walked up the drive and back into her house through the garage.

You weren't supposed to turn your back, but she did. She lowered the garage door and locked the inside door. Just then the neighborhood security truck pulled up and the guard jumped out, gestured to Angelo to leave, frantically pointing to the path down the road to the exit. She couldn't help but notice the security guard was rather small. And of course he didn't carry a gun.

But Angelo got into his truck and departed.

Then she began to tremble.

Angelo wasn't a big guy but his shoulders looked muscled and strong. He was taller than her, which wasn't saying much. But she was an older woman and he was decidedly mean. He could take her, no question.

She called the security gate at the entrance to her neighborhood, berated them for letting Angelo in without her clearance and warned them never to admit him. She told them to call the police if he tried to enter again.

Then she called the police. She asked if she could leave a message for Officer Bowen, the same police officer who had given Sophia his business card. Only twenty minutes passed until he returned her call.

"This is regarding my friend and employee, Sophia Garner. The young man who was stalking her and threatening her showed up at my house looking for her. I told him she had gone somewhere safe and he was very angry."

"Good to know," Officer Bowen said. "Did he threaten you?"

"He definitely turned his anger on me, but I turned mine right back on him. He's gone. But I thought you should know."

"Thank you. It might be a good time for me to have another chat with him."

"He claims she called him, which is impossible."

"You're sure of that?" he asked.

"No. I haven't talked to Sophia in a few days, but she fled to Argentina because of him. I can't imagine that she would call him. I think he must be lying again."

"And you're safe behind locked doors?"

She chuckled, remembering when her security system, special locks and cameras were all installed. "He's not going to be able to break in here. I have state-of-the-art security. And I've alerted the neighborhood security staff to watch for him."

"All right, I'll take it from here," he said. "Thank you."

"But what will you say? He hasn't broken any law. I don't have a temporary restraining order preventing him from coming near me. How will you stop him?"

"I don't have a plan beyond listening to him to see what he might be thinking, what he might be up to. After talking to a million or so suspects, one learns what to ask and what to listen for."

"Would you mind letting me know how that goes?"

"I'll give you a call when I know something. Meanwhile, keep the doors locked."

"Of course," she said.

That night, out of sheer boredom, she went to see her sister. Nettie and Marvin had some people over to play cards so she didn't stay long. Just long enough to win twenty dollars. Everyone called her a ringer. The next afternoon she went to see Bella, who was ready to pop. She was reclining on the couch with her feet elevated for her cankles. Fortunately Marni had packed them a low-sodium supper of pepper steak and rice.

Officer Bowen phoned her as she was driving home. "You'll be interested to know Angelo denied ever having visited with you."

"He's lying!" Marni nearly shrieked.

"Of course he is," Officer Bowen said. "Your security patrol verified he was there and was asked to leave. Mind those locks!"

She was at least able to speak with Sam for a few minutes, that night, long enough to tell him of Angelo's appearance and her chat with Officer Bowen. Her follow-up chat with the good police officer had verified that Angelo did not seem to know Sophia had left the country, and he confirmed Angelo did not have a passport so would not be following.

"Does that give you peace of mind?" Sam asked.

"For Sophia, yes," Marni said. "That young twerp doesn't scare me one bit. I've seen his kind before."

What she wouldn't let herself say was, *I want you to come back!*

SIXTEEN

It wasn't so rare that Marni found herself alone. It happened for at least several hours every day. But it was uncommon for her to find herself alone for days on end. In fact, except for occasional weekends, she couldn't remember the last time it had happened. She had always loved that her house, specifically her kitchen, was a gathering place. This was where her friends came. And she fed them.

Ellen had called and said their emergency food service was very successful and she'd be home in a couple of days. Nettie was very busy with school. Bella was constantly in touch to report every twinge and ache. And Marni hadn't slept well. She was having disturbing dreams. Of Rick. She remembered in living color his treatment of her and she wondered if he hadn't died would she be around today. Would Bella?

She hadn't finished her coffee but apparently this was going to be one of those days devoted to deep thinking. She relived the tension of waiting for him to come home, fearing he'd be drunk and mean. She'd woken up after she gasped in her sleep as she recalled the time he'd pushed her so hard she went flying over the coffee table. He'd smacked her in the jaw and left a swollen bruise. "Pregnancy sure has made you clumsy," her mother had said. "Looks like a punch in the face to me," said Aunt Dahlia.

So Marni did what always helped to calm her. She pulled a twelve-inch round carrot cake out of the freezer.

"If you touch me again, I'll call the police," she had told him.

"And we'll see if you live to tell about it," he'd threatened her.

She went back to the freezer and pulled out a ten-inch yellow cake and set them both on the counter to thaw.

She gathered powdered sugar and miniature marshmallows. Next came her packet of food coloring. The bowl of marshmallows went in the microwave for thirty seconds, then she gave them a stir and went for another thirty seconds, back and forth, until they were melted and creamy.

Rick always seemed to hurt her by accident. It was as if he just got so mad and couldn't stop himself. Talk about a serious anger-management issue. Then he would blame her for pushing his buttons. *Why do you push me until I break?* Then he would grovel and be sorry. Sometimes he wouldn't, though. Sometimes he would just leave or go to sleep or stay enraged. Once she hid in a closet, praying he would pass out.

But God bless the army. He would leave again for days or weeks or even months, giving her time to recover.

She mixed blue food coloring into some of the fondant and kneaded it. She rolled it out into a thin but strong sheet and draped it over the twelve inch round cake, smoothing it. There was not so much as a bump or bubble. Next she kneaded and rolled out a sheet of white fondant for the ten-inch.

After Rick's death, she and baby Bella lived with her mother and aunts. Nettie was a young teenager and that was when they really became close. It was the most loving and nurturing time of her life. There was always someone home, always a babysitter, always an open ear. Her mother and aunts even had dates from time to time, though they were dead set against letting a man invade their tight circle. They worked together to keep the baby and the house in order. Marni loved to cook the evening meal and she never had to clean up. Nettie was excelling in school and Marni was able to be a part of that, too, helping her and praising her and eventually helping to pay for college. Marni and the women she lived with had favorite television shows they watched together or sometimes they played cards. It was the calmest, safest time Marni could remember. She even had a couple of significant romances while she lived there, but thanks to Rick she was never tempted to make a long-term commitment.

Dahlia passed away first, then a few years later Ruth followed. Marni's mother, Celeste, lived to be eighty-five and was in assisted living for a couple of years when she quietly passed.

A couple more cakes came out of the freezer and Marni whipped up some buttercream frosting. She didn't have a plan, but the best time for thinking was while creating. Freestyle baking. She divided the frosting, created different colors, got out her piping bags and a variety of tips.

One of the romances she had while living with her mother and aunts was with Jeff. It was not a burning passion but rather a comfortable friendship that brought them together. By that time they were both in television and Bella was in high school; Marni viewed Jeff as warm, dependable and safe.

She'd been wrong, of course. Or maybe she'd been right. But when he succumbed to the charms of Gretchen, he became a different kind of man. The kind who could be unfaithful and abandon her without feeling guilty at all.

She looked at her watch and was astonished to see that hours had passed. She had created a four-tier cake in blue and white and yellow. She had decorated it with stripes, little miniature handprints, balloons, dots and ribbons. It was enormous. And beautiful.

She took just a moment to try to figure out what led to this giant cake. It wasn't just Rick or her mother and aunts. It was bigger than that. It was the pivots in her life that had marked a shift. Major change. From Rick to life with her mother and the start of her baking and television careers. The raising of Bella, mostly alone but with awesome support. Then came Jeff and the relationship with him also marked the biggest growth in her career. Perhaps Jeff was right when he took credit for her success, however a woman wouldn't do that, take credit for her husband's success. No, a wife would just take great pride in her husband and brag about him, boring her women friends to death.

But there was another event that changed everything, more than the presence of Jeff. That was her friendship with Ellen. Twenty years ago Ellen came into her life and that was the pivot that really pushed her over the top. Ellen was not only a brilliant chef, she was an amazing strategist. Her influence was deeply felt on the cooking show. It was undeniable and the numbers proved it. They doubled and tripled their viewing audience in the first five years, then did so again. Marni went from a studio kitchen to her custom home and the numbers skyrocketed again. Ellen and Marni worked closely with their director to plan the filming schedule and it seemed only a minute before the show was syndicated and networks all over the world were picking them up. The internet popularity was soaring as well.

All the major changes in her life had been so challenging, so painful, but the outcomes so plentiful and rewarding. Now another major change was upon her. She was losing Ellen to a new chapter in her friend's life. Sophia was gone. A baby was coming. And the man she longed for was a world away, keeping his daughter safe.

She heard the doorbell chime and the front door open. She hadn't even realized that her cheeks were wet with tears until Ellen entered, walked to the kitchen and showed more shock in her expression when she looked at Marni than when she saw the cake.

"What's wrong?" she asked, aghast.

"What are you doing here?" Marni asked.

"I'm home from the fires so I took a shower, changed and came straight over. And—" She ran gentle fingers over the cake's second tier and said, "Oh, boy. Judging by the size of this cake, you're very upset."

"No, I'm fine," Marni said, wiping the tears from her cheeks.

"Marni, you have been my best friend forever and there are only two ways to get a cake like that out of you. Either the commission was huge for a special program or you're upset about something. And you baked your way out of it."

Marni sank onto one of the stools at the breakfast bar. "When did you get to know me so well?"

Ellen sat on another stool, facing her. "When didn't I? What's got you spinning?"

"I'm headed for a new change, a big one. I don't handle change well."

"You handle change better than anyone I know. What change?"

Marni took a breath. "Sophia is gone. I know I'm losing you to a food truck. I'm going to have to hire new people and I hate hiring people; it's like a rule of the universe that the first three tries don't work out. A baby is almost here and I'm very excited about that but what if Bella doesn't think I'm a good grandmother? And what if I'm not? I still work more than forty hours a week and if my intern and assistant are both missing…" She sniffed loudly. "And I never mentioned this but I secretly fell in love with someone and he's gone, too."

"Ah," Ellen said. "Sam."

"What? What did you say?"

"I thought it was probably Sam," she said again.

Marni turned wide shocked eyes on Ellen. "How could you possibly know that?"

"Oh, I think any observant person could figure it out. They way you looked at him or said his name or got a little girl-ish when you were going to the hydroponics lab. Plus Sophia whispered to me that her father was talking on the phone late at night, saying very sweet things and she hoped it was you on the other end of the line."

"Jeez. We thought we were being so discreet."

"I don't think you've been officially discovered yet. If you want to try to bury it, I'll help if I can. But I think it would make more sense to see if you can find a way to get together, even if it takes some time. Meanwhile, you have the phone…"

"He's staying with his late wife's very large family and we have very little time to talk, but it's better than nothing."

"And you're not exactly losing me to a food truck, though

I hope I'll be free to help when needed. It's exciting," she said with a big grin. "It's rewarding! It's like a dream come true— you work your whole life and want to retire with a flourish! Giving back. Paying forward. Whatever you want to call it. You're doing that with your safe house."

Marni gave a little shrug. "I have an awesome Realtor who knows what I'm looking for and passes a few options by me every week, but we're not there yet. I'm still determined to do this. I want to help women and children in this awful violent bind but, Ellen… I feel terrible saying this… It's not what I do. This," she said, indicating the enormous cake, "is what I do."

"I know, that's okay. We can't all be social workers. But a little help is good, right? That's my plan. I'm not leaving you, Marni. I'd like to go with Mark on another mission or two, but I'm not leaving you."

"You've been thinking about this…"

"I have. Because I'm really fond of Mark and I love helping him with this project. And I love meeting the people we're helping! It can be a little heartbreaking, too—some of these families we're feeding have lost everything. I don't want to give it up for anything and I think you should check it out, too. Maybe do a segment of the show on the volunteers who go to such lengths to feed people who have been through di- sasters like wildfires or hurricanes. But I'm not ready to give up our show, Marni. I feel like we're just getting really good."

"You do?"

"And you need me around when the baby comes," Ellen said. "We'll make a couple of excellent grandmas. We have to shore each other up because little what's his name is going to be around here a lot." She tilted her head toward the cake. "By the size of the cake, you've been thinking about this a lot!"

"I was lonely," she said.

"You were worried," Ellen said. "I thought we were past the point of silently worrying about things. Nothing has changed so much that we'd start not talking about our issues, has it?"

There was a brief knock and the sound of the door connecting to the garage opening. "Hell-ewwww!"

"Nettie?" Marni called.

"It's me," she said, her footsteps echoing as she walked from the back door to the kitchen. "Since you called twice asking me to stop by for a glass of wine I thought that maybe I should check on you— Oh! Holy shit!" she said, eyeing the cake. Nettie stepped closer to the monstrous cake. She reached out a finger and gently touched a blue balloon that seemed to float above red ribbons. "Oh, boy, you must have been really screwed up to make this."

"What are you talking about?"

"You do your best work when you have a big problem to sort out. Remember your divorce?"

"Oh, that," she said.

Marni had cooked nonstop for days when she and Jeff split up. A person could barely walk through the kitchen for the food. The designer cakes and specialty pies were everywhere. There were gourmet meats in special sauces, pastries, fancy veggies, casseroles, shepherd's pie, fried or broiled or grilled meats, gravies and more. She had given away a lot of it but she also rented a freezer for the garage. Some of her best stroganoff, spaghetti sauce with sausage bits, chicken pot pie, broccoli cheese soup and shrimp lo mein went to neighbors, friends and family.

"Did you think no one noticed you were on a tear?" Nettie asked. "It's how you work through things. And the rest of us, the observers, reap the rewards."

"Just be glad I didn't take up knitting to keep my hands and head busy," Marni said. "I know we've joked about it, but I guess I didn't realize everyone noticed."

"Everyone noticed. Should we have a glass of wine while you tell us what's on your mind?"

Marni, as usual, was happy to have something to do with her hands while she talked. She fetched a bottle from the wine cooler and worked on opening it. She put out glasses for Ellen and Nettie. She tried to explain the reality that she was entering a new phase of her life and was anxiety riddled. "Everything is changing, again. Bella's baby is due, Sophia is gone—"

"And took her adorable father with her," Ellen put in.

"Oh, so the father of the intern is meaningful!" Nettie said.

"Very," Ellen confirmed.

"Do you two have secret meetings I should know about?" Marni asked.

She went on about Ellen's new interest, the need to hire some help and admitted that yes, she was missing Sam. She'd grown fond of him and, though they'd kept it on the down-low, he had become an important friend. But during the course of the cake construction, she had visited plenty of important people from her past. Rick, her mother and aunts, young Nettie, all the years of Bella's growing up in a house full of women. But she kept that to herself.

The back door from the garage entry opened and Bella yelled, "Mama?"

"How perfect," Marni said. "Come in, darling!"

"I need a little help," she yelled.

All three women put down their glasses and went to Bella.

She stood in the garage with the back end of her SUV open. It was full of stuff. "I spent a little time at the store."

"I can see that," Nettie said.

"I had three baby showers. The baby shower given to me by my friends and coworkers was just last weekend. It was a couples' shower. It was great and there were a lot of duplicate gifts and rather than return some of them, I'm outfitting your house for when we bring the baby here. What things weren't duplicated by showers, I'm giving to you. The doctor said I should walk so I walked through a few stores."

Marni had hosted a small shower for Bella when she was about seven months along. There had been twenty people present at Marni's house. She cooked, of course. But Bella had one given by her sorority sisters and one by her work mates. They were all fabulous.

"What have you got here?"

"A portable crib, a swing, a baby chair, a bunch of blankets, some soft toys, a mobile, a car seat. Let's bring it in."

"What a fantastic haul," Marni said. "I have some things I've picked up here and there over the past several months, mostly blankets, outfits and disposables like bottles, diapers and wipes." She hefted a car seat out of the SUV. "I never thought of the big stuff. I thought the baby would come with a diaper bag and I'd be good to go. I ordered a crib. It should come in a day or two."

"Should we take all this stuff to a guest room?" Nettie asked.

"No, take it to the great room so we can look it over. I'll find space for it later," Marni said.

In no time at all the place looked like a showroom for baby gear. A glass of juice was fetched for Bella while she made a fuss over the enormous cake. "Let's take some pictures—it looks like it was made for Henry. That's the latest option in our long and tedious discussion of names. I'm hoping there are no more possibles in the next week because I'm ready. If nothing happens in the next week, the doctor is going to induce labor." She grinned at Marni. "You're going to be a grandma very soon!"

It had been quite a while since the women had gathered, and they had a lot to talk about just to catch up. It was like old times but for the mess a day of cake-creating had left in the kitchen. In past times Marni would have prepared fancy snacks but with her kitchen upside down, full of pans, bowls, utensils and general mess, there was no room or time for that. They gossiped over a glass of wine and were just getting around to another when there was a sound at the back door.

"Are you having a party?"

It was Jeff.

"I don't know why he's here," Marni said.

He came into the great room.

"It's just us," Marni said.

He looked at them, smiled, then he saw Bella and his face became so soft and sweet. "Oh, Bella," he said. "Look at you! Ripe as a melon! How are you, sweetheart? Are you just about ready?"

"I think so," she said.

He squeezed in beside her and held her hand. "You look amazing. You have that glow of mothers-to-be."

"It's just heartburn, Jeff."

"Would you like me to find you some ice cream? I know Marni has some around here somewhere."

"No, thanks. I'm fine."

Jeff acknowledged each woman in the room without ever letting go of Bella's hand. He told Ellen she had the blush of sun on her cheeks and asked if she'd been gardening and she said no, but she'd been outdoors much of last weekend. He asked Nettie if she'd been working out and told her she looked fit and fantastic. To Marni he said, "That's quite a cake. It must have taken all day."

"All day," she confirmed. "What brings you to the neighborhood, Jeff?"

"Bragging rights," he said, actually puffing his chest out. "In just a few weeks, the restaurant is running smoothly again. Six weeks maybe and it looks like we're going to turn a profit. I can't take credit for the change, but I can claim to have been a participant in a positive result. We tried out some new hours and it worked. Plus, our take-out menu has expanded and that drove business up. It's such a good feeling."

Then he turned his attention back to Bella and asked about her plans, her health, all the baby gear scattered about the room and in no time at all he had her laughing and her eyes were twinkling.

Marni had the luxury of watching Bella's transformation into a happy young woman who was brightening before her eyes. She remembered, then, her divorce from Jeff had been as hard on Bella as on her; Bella had always loved Jeff and he played a large part in making her teenage years and early college years a positive experience. There was no hope of Jeff ever being more than a friend to Marni but she was so glad they had come to this place.

"Keep me in mind for babysitting, too," Jeff said. "I'm pretty good with kids."

"How do you know?" Bella asked. "And when would you find the time?"

"I will make the time," he said. "What I can't remember from my early uncle days I'll pick up again pretty quick."

They had a pleasant conversation punctuated by laughter. After a while, thoroughly enjoying the magic of being with her people again and not wanting it to end too soon, Marni refilled the wine glasses. This was the best part of her life, having her loved ones in her nest.

Marni was not surprised to realize that she liked her alone time if it wasn't too much, if it was on her terms, and importantly, if people appeared about the time she began to feel lonely. After about thirty delightful minutes of chat and bonding, she noticed that Bella was looking a bit pale. Bella usually had the most charming rosy cheeks but just now she had taken on a grayish pallor. She gently rubbed her round tummy.

"Bella?" she asked.

"Yeah, I'm not feeling great. Could that juice have been a little off?"

"Not if it came from my kitchen," Marni said. "Can I get you something else?"

"No, just give me a moment." Bella stood up, wobbled just slightly, grabbed her belly and groaned. Then, as if on cue, a river of fluid gushed down her legs and pooled on the floor at her feet. Bella groaned again and bent slightly at the waist. Or what used to be a waist.

Jeff was immediately on his feet, helping her to find the sofa behind her.

"Oh, dear," Bella said. "What do you suppose this is?" Then she moaned again, holding onto her tummy.

Everyone's wide round eyes were on her. Waiting.

"I'm going to have to go home and change."

Then she moaned again. It took Marni only a split second to realize it was all happening at once—Bella's water broke and she was in labor. Bella reached for Jeff's waiting hand for an assist in standing but with a moan immediately dropped back down again. She began panting, holding her belly as if she was trying to keep it from flying away. The process repeated for the third time with Bella struggling to stand up. This time she looked behind her and saw the large stain on the cushion and said, "Oh, Mama!"

That galvanized Marni. She moved toward Bella. "That's the least of my worries. Please sit down and concentrate on how frequent those pains are."

"The first one hasn't quite stopped yet! Oh, dear, more stuff is coming." She leaned to one side. "It won't stop. I'm going to need a ride to the hospital."

"Don't even try to stop it, just relax and do your breathing." Marni pulled her phone from her pocket and quickly punched in 911. "If you can, call Jason and tell him to meet us at the hospital." Then into the phone she said, "This is Marni McGuire. My daughter is in labor, first baby, her water broke, it looks bloody and her contractions are fierce and constant. I think we're having an emergency." She held the phone away and stared at it for a second. "No, I don't want to take a minute to assess the contractions!"

Bella let out a wail and grabbed her tummy. "Does that answer your question? We need EMTs and a transport. Fast!" Marni said.

"I want you to stay on the line with me, Mrs. McGuire, so I can talk you through any emergency situation. Emergency vehicles are en route."

"Fine. You're on speaker. Bella, can you call Jason? Jeff, can you make sure emergency vehicles have access to the house."

"Should I call the guard gate?" Jeff asked.

"Don't bother," Nettie said. "The fire department has a gizmo on their truck that opens the gate."

"Are you still there, Mrs. McGuire?"

"I'm here. I'm here."

"Can you please ask the patient to describe her contractions in intensity on a scale of one to ten with ten being the most painful?"

While the emergency operator was talking to Marni, Bella was talking to Jason and telling him to please come to the hospital right away, explaining her mother had called an ambulance.

And then Bella screamed, "Oh, no! Oh, no! Oh, no! He's coming, he's coming, he's coming!"

"No pushing! Pant!" all the women present said in unison.

"I think we're at eleven," Marni said into the phone.

"Can you look and tell me what you can see?"

"I'd have to find a way to lay her down! How far away is that ambulance?"

"I have you at four minutes out. Can you please instruct the patient to pant and not push?"

"Bella, did you hear that?" Marni asked. "Hold my hand, look at my face. We're going to wait for the professionals. Pant like this. Hah-hah-hah-hah! Good, that's very good. Once more. And again. You're doing great."

All Bella could do was moan, then she tried panting again. She turned her face to one side and retched. Ellen and Nettie ran for towels.

"She threw up," Marni told the dispatcher.

"That suggests she's getting close to delivering. I'll be sure the EMT knows. Stand by. Continue panting."

Bella seemed to bravely do her best, but she was reduced to tears of fear. "Oh, Mama, the baby! Is the baby all right?"

"All right?" Marni asked. "Darling, it seems he's ready to get out! Just do your breathing and try to be calm." They heard the sound of a big engine. "Oh, good, the professionals are here. They must have made all the lights! Did you reach Jason?"

"He's coming."

And then suddenly there were a bunch of very large men and a stretcher invading Marni's perfect house, dragging in what dirt they collected at the last emergency.

One man seemed to take charge. "Have you felt like pushing?" he asked Bella.

Instead of answering, she was nearly lifted off the couch and was bearing down.

"Pant!" everyone yelled.

"Let's get her on the gurney and have a look," he said. "Load her. Gently."

Bella was lifted onto the gurney and the EMT draped a sheet over her and deftly cut off her pants. He peeked under the sheet and said, "She's starting to crown. First baby?"

"Yes."

"Then let's go. Always better if we can make it to the hospital. First babies take however much time they need. Who do you want with you in the back?"

"My mother. Please."

"Let's go," he ordered, and two of the men wheeled out the gurney and slid it into the ambulance.

At this point Marni thought everything was going to be all right. That's because she had no medical training and had given birth to one child a very long time ago. They were far from all right. But they loaded into the ambulance, Marni on one side of the gurney bearing her daughter and the EMT on the other. He took Bella's blood pressure, reported it aloud and started an IV. "For drugs and fluids as needed," he explained. Then he threw some small soft baby blankets on

Bella's chest, listened to Bella's big round tummy, confirmed the baby's heart rate, then lifted the sheet for another peek.

"Okay!" he said. "Looks like we're doing it now."

"Doing what?" Marni asked in a near shout.

"Once he starts out, we're guiding him out. Bella, on the next contraction, I need you to push."

"Push?" Marni asked.

"Have him now? In an ambulance? This fifty-thousand dollar baby?" Bella asked.

"Yeah, sorry," said the EMT. "The limo was booked."

SEVENTEEN

The EMT's name was Dan and he was a lovely man. Henry was his seventh baby and he held the record for his company. And all his babies had done well and were very healthy. His firefighting brothers and sisters had nicknamed him Doc.

He had pulled a squalling seven and a half pound Henry from Bella and placed him on her chest. She cradled him and kissed his mucky head and cried and said I love you repeatedly as the ambulance bounced along. When they arrived at the hospital, the emergency OB team was waiting at the curb with an incubator and a bunch of nurses and doctors.

Marni had never been so happy to see this group. She would not have been happier to see Julia Child. They swooped in, but gently, took the baby, took Bella on the gurney and in a parade moved to the birthing unit. They invited Marni to follow. Then it was an hour of examinations and checkups, warming lamps and cleaning up. During this time Jason arrived and after giving Bella a kiss and a cuddle, he watched over his son as he was diapered, warmed up in the incubator and finally placed in Bella's arms again.

Marni's phone was blowing up. Jeff, Ellen and Nettie had followed them to the hospital and were waiting for information about Bella and the baby. Marni texted them that all was well.

When there was a moment, Bella whispered to Marni, "What a wild ride."

"You could sell that delivery on eBay. Thousands of women would bid for only an hour of labor and a slick delivery."

"Forgive me for still shaking from terror," Bella said.

It took hours to make sure everything was fine, to let all the support friends see the baby and Bella and for things to quiet down. Marni was politely waiting for her turn to cuddle Henry and properly bond with him. Her phone kept vibrating so she assumed word had spread and friends wanted to know how everyone was doing.

Bella, Jason and Henry shared a birthing suite. It was such a wonderful way to have a baby. They were brought a lovely dinner and even a split of champagne. There was a rich dessert and a warm shower for Bella. While everyone was getting fed and comfortable, Marni was snuggling the baby. And talking to him.

"You have no idea how dearly you were wanted. How much love and effort brought you to us. Your mama and daddy struggled to bring you into the world and it is no understatement that you will certainly change my life. I'm so looking forward to the years ahead. I will love you every second."

It was nine at night by the time Marni headed home. She had been offered rides by everyone who had been at her house earlier, but she wanted to be alone so she chose to Uber home. Ellen had brought her purse and phone so this was easily done.

While sitting in the back of the car, she noticed that she had messages from Tom, who was now her Realtor, and Sam. She didn't want to listen to either while riding so she waited. In fact once she was home, she put on her pajamas and poured herself a well-deserved glass of wine and took it to her bedroom.

She noticed that her mostly destroyed kitchen and great room had been completely cleaned—it must have been Ellen, Nettie and maybe even Jeff. But the cake stood on the counter like a monument.

She listened to Tom's message first. He had found her a house that could be an excellent safe house if that was still the purpose she had in mind. It was a two-story with five bedrooms, four baths, a large kitchen, huge pantry, enormous great room and finished basement, and it sat on a big lot. It was an older home and could use some upgrading, redecorating and remodeling, but it was big enough.

Then she listened to Sam's voice mail.

"I meant to tell you this when we talked. It isn't my first choice to just leave a message, but since you're busy, this will have to do. In fact, I meant to tell you earlier but I guess it's just as well that it didn't work out. We're fine, so don't be concerned. I made a commitment to my department at UNR. I'm going to conduct some research and write a few papers on establishing a hydroponics lab in Argentina. Since I'm going to be staying here for a few months anyway, it makes sense. Sophia has enrolled in university here, picking up a few classes while she decides her future. If I do some work for the agriculture department, it pays for my time away.

"To that end, I've rented a small bungalow on my brother-in-law's property. I borrowed a truck. Sophia wants to stay with her aunt but I will now have a place to write that isn't crawling with relatives and many small children. And while I'm not happy to be away from you for months longer, at least I have some privacy so that our phone conversations will not be overheard. Because…"

She wondered if the connection had been lost or if the line had gone dead. She even said his name, though it was a voice mail. "Sam?"

"The thought of being away from you for months is terrible. I hate it. But I'm going to do what I can to support Sophia. I can see the difference in her in just days. Not only because she's away from Reno but her aunts and uncles are fussing over her. Her family is so happy to have her home. I forget sometimes, this is her birthplace. This is who she is. Maybe it's where she belongs. That is up to her to decide.

"So, I will stay here with her for a while. I'll call you whenever possible and I'll count the days until I can see you." Again, there was a space of quiet. "I want you to know I love you. Distance can't change that."

Marni felt a warmth spread through her. There was a smile on her lips and her heart thumped. It was so late in Argentina. It was only ten for her but it was two in the morning there.

She found Sam's number in her recent-calls list and tapped it. She felt only a little guilty as it rang and rang and rang. He finally answered. "Marni?" as if a question.

"My grandson was born tonight," she said softly. "He's beautiful. Perfect. I held him for an hour and I can tell he loves me."

There was a deep rumble of laughter. "Tell me everything."

"It's so late there. I'll understand if you want to—"

"Everything," he repeated.

She did. It was nearly midnight for her when they reluc-tantly ended the call. His last words to her were, "We both have important family business to take care of and then, we'll take care of our personal business."

"Yes, we will. I love you, too," she said.

In the morning she awoke feeling as if she was the lucki-est woman alive. And she had a four-layer designer cake to deal with.

So she took some pictures. Then she drove it over to the Breckenridge Fire Department. It was a perfect thank-you gift.

When Ellen got home from the hospital, she saw that the trailers and RV were parked in the driveways and on the street and Mark's house was dark. She wanted to tell him all about her exciting night, but she knew he must be tired from his trip and his long day so she reluctantly just went to her house.

There, on her couch, was Mark. Sound asleep and snoring.

She knelt beside the couch and ran a couple of gentle fin-gers over his brow. His eyes opened and he blinked a couple of times. "Is Marni okay?" he asked.

"Bella had her baby," she said. "He came in a rush and was born in an ambulance. Breckenridge Fire Department did the honors."

He chuckled and sat up. "That must have been quite a show. Mother and baby okay?"

"They appear to be perfect. And the grandmother will re-cover. Did you unload everything?"

"Not all of it, but I'll finish tomorrow. What are your plans?"

"I may not put in a full day, but I'm going to have to see what Marni needs to have done. I think her world is upside down at the moment and it's always been my job to try to set it right." She smiled. "That's actually my favorite part of the job. No, my favorite part is that she needs me."

"You're a good friend." He got up from the couch. "That's such a nice happy ending. Isn't it fitting that the firefighters helped."

"It is." She gave him a little kiss. "And your first effort at the emergency kitchen was highly successful."

"Thanks to you."

"Thanks to all your friends."

"You must be exhausted," he said, giving her a hug.

"I'm pretty tired."

"Are you glad to be home?"

"I am," Ellen said. "I have to admit, I had a good time in the RV. And I loved the work we did. But I like my own bed."

"Of course," he said. Then he gave her a pat on the butt and began to walk to the door.

"Where are you going?" she asked.

"I thought I should get out of your hair. So you can rest."

"Don't you dare," she snapped. "Oh, drat, I'm sorry. Of course if you want to sleep alone… You must be so tired. I'm tired, too, it's just that…"

He grinned and walked toward her. "You want some company, Ellen?"

"I think I got used to sharing that space." Color charged her cheeks. "In less than a week, I seem to have gotten used to it."

"That's fine by me," he said. "So have I."

The birth of Henry was a little like being thrust back in time for Marni. Her cooking show went back to basics. It was reminiscent of the period before Sophia came to work for her. Marni and Ellen struggled to keep up with the schedule and they started doing some filming to get ahead of schedule. This time they were also challenged by Ellen's desire to move into a new schedule, one that allowed for her to spend time with Mark's emergency food delivery.

At the same time, there was a magical quality to her life. She spent an hour or two with Henry every day, more when Bella had something to do like a hair appointment or a trip to the market. Time stood still while Henry was with her. She held him against her and read to him. Sometimes she read him recipes, but he didn't seem to mind. She didn't believe his smile was gas; she had convinced herself it was all for her.

As Marni was bonding with Henry, Bella was blossoming. She'd grown so beautiful in motherhood. The best part for Marni was watching her daughter fall in love with Jason all over again. There was no question that the challenge of getting pregnant and the stress of in vitro had taken its toll. But now that the baby was here and Bella and Jason were able to take some time off, life for their little family had become recharged.

Marni hoped this new energy could last a good long time for them. She knew that marriages and relationships in general were cyclical, had their ups and downs, but still she hoped.

Marni was very busy. She pushed forward with her plans to endow a safe house for abused women and their children. In that effort she became good friends with Tom, the Realtor and sometimes drag performer. Her new foundation was gaining some recognition in the area and Tom was looking for another house to add to it. It was an unlikely but very welcome association. Tom very kindly donated his fees to the foundation so that it could grow. She began to envision that when she retired from cooking, she would be the director of a foundation that helped keep women of all ages safe.

Another person who was emerging as more than a part of her past was Jeff, who had fallen in love with Henry as well. It had taken Bella a very long time to forgive him and reconnect with him, but finally she had. It gave Marni great pleasure to recognize that Jeff was, indeed, a good grandfather. His business was on solid ground, without Gretchen in the picture, and he was very present in little Henry's life. He talked about looking forward to soccer games and school open houses.

She also felt rewarded by the glow in Ellen's eyes. Ellen and Mark were in love and deeply involved in their own special project. Given that it was now late in the year, there hadn't been many fires and she hadn't had to steal away to work in Mark's emergency meal service, which gave her time to enjoy her new relationship that came with a new family.

There had been no stress or trouble from Angelo and Sam reported that he had stopped trying to call Sophia, but the police officer who kept in touch with the case reported that Angelo had gotten himself in trouble again and was in jail. Sam knew exactly how to access public records to follow that young man's movements but it appeared as though Angelo was no longer obsessed with Sophia.

The colorful fall leaves fell away and Marni cooked a spectacular Thanksgiving dinner for her people; their table was full and happy. Henry was a happy baby who was rarely put down; he was passed from person to person, jiggled and snuggled and crooned to.

Her life could not have been richer or more fulfilling. If Bella didn't bring Henry to her, then Marni would go to Bella's. Of course there was one thing missing—Sam. But they talked and texted and emailed all the time. She counted the days and looked forward to his return. And he did promise he would return as soon as he finished his research project and was confident that Sophia was settled. She was very happy in Argentina with her extended family.

It was on a sunny day three days before Christmas when life changed again. Marni was sitting on the floor in the great room, little Henry lying beside her on a quilt when Ellen answered the door. Marni assumed it was a delivery, which happened all the time. But when she looked up, she saw the most wonderful delivery ever. Sam stood over her, a handsome smile on his face.

"Now that's a beautiful sight," he said. He crouched down and sat on the heel of his boot. "Merry Christmas, Grandma."

"It's Mimi, not Grandma, remember that!" she said with a laugh. "What are you doing here?"

"It was Sophia's idea. She's very happy living with her aunts and uncles. They're planning a very big noisy and fattening holiday. She suggested I surprise you with a visit. She didn't have to suggest it twice." He reached out a finger to gently stroke Henry's soft hair. "So this is the new guy. He's very handsome."

Henry looked up at Sam and smiled as big as the sun.

"How long are you staying?" Marni asked.

"I'm going back in about a month for a couple of weeks, mainly to pack up my gear. I have a couple of things to wrap up and then I'll be going back just for brief visits. Sophia plans to complete her masters in Buenos Aires. Then she'll decide where she's settling."

"You're staying?" she asked softly.

He gave a nod. "We started something, you and me. I'm anxious to see how it turns out."

She reached up a hand to his cheek. He leaned toward her for a kiss. It was long and deep and sweet. "I think it will turn out very well," she said.

★ ★ ★ ★ ★

If you loved The Friendship Club, *you'll love the
Sullivan's Crossing series, available at your local bookstore
and airing now on the CW!*

*Read on for a sneak peek at
book one of Sullivan's Crossing*
What We Find

CHAPTER 1

Maggie Sullivan sought refuge in the stairwell between the sixth and seventh floors at the far west end of the hospital, the steps least traveled by interns and residents racing from floor to floor, from emergency to emergency. She sat on the landing between two flights, feet on the stairs, arms crossed on her knees, her face buried in her arms. She didn't understand how her heart could feel as if it was breaking every day. She thought of herself as much stronger.

"Well, now, some things never change," a familiar voice said.

She looked up at her closest friend, Jaycee Kent. They had gone to med school together, though residency had separated them. Jaycee was an OB and Maggie, a neurosurgeon. And...

they had hidden in stairwells to cry all those years ago when med-school life was kicking their asses. Most of their fellow students and instructors were men. They refused to let the men see them cry.

Maggie gave a wet, burbly huff of laughter. "How'd you find me?" Maggie asked.

"How do you know you're not in my spot?"

"Because you're happily married and have a beautiful daughter?"

"And my hours suck, I'm sleep-deprived, have as many bad days as good and..." Jaycee sat down beside Maggie. "And at least my hormones are cooperating at the moment. Maggie, you're just taking call for someone, right? Just to stay ahead of the bills?"

"Since the practice shut down," Maggie said. "And since the lawsuit was filed."

"You need a break. You're recovering from a miscarriage and your hormones are wonky. You need to get away, especially away from the emergency room. Take some time off. Lick your wounds. Heal."

"He dumped me," Maggie said.

Jaycee was clearly shocked. *"What?"*

"He broke up with me. He said he couldn't take it anymore. My emotional behavior, my many troubles. He suggested professional help."

Jaycee was quiet. "I'm speechless," she finally said. "What a huge ass."

"Well, I was crying all the time," she said, sniffing some more. "If I wasn't with him, I cried when I talked to him on the phone. I thought I was okay with the idea of no children. I'm almost thirty-seven, I work long hours, I was with a good man who was just off a bad marriage and already had a child..."

"I'll give you everything but the good man," Jaycee said. "He's a doctor, for God's sake. Doesn't he know that all you've been through can take a toll? Remove all the stress and you still had the miscarriage! People tend to treat a miscarriage like a heavy period but it's a death. You lost your baby. You have to take time to grieve."

"Gospel," Maggie said, rummaging for a tissue and giving her nose a hearty blow. "I really felt it on that level. When I found out I was pregnant, it took me about fifteen minutes to start seeing the baby, loving her. Or him."

"Not to beat a dead horse, but you have some hormone issues playing havoc on your emotions. Listen, shoot out some emails tonight. Tell the ones on the need-to-know list you're taking a week or two off."

"No one knows about the pregnancy but you and Andrew."

"You don't have to explain—everyone knows about your practice, your ex-partners, the lawsuit. Frankly, your colleagues are amazed you're still standing. Get out of town or something. Get some rest."

"You might be right," Maggie said. "These cement stairwells are killing me."

Jaycee put an arm around her. "Just like old times, huh?"

The last seven or eight miles to Sullivan's Crossing was nothing but mud and Maggie's cream-colored Toyota SUV was coated up to the windows. This was not exactly a surprise. It had rained all week in Denver, now that she thought about it. March was typically the most unpredictable and sloppiest month of the year, especially in the mountains. If it wasn't rain it could be snow. But Maggie had had such a lousy year the weather barely crossed her mind.

Last year had produced so many medical, legal and personal complications that her practice had shut down a few months ago. She'd been picking up work from other practices, covering for doctors on call here and there and working ER Level 1 Trauma while she tried to figure out how to untangle the mess her life had become. This, on her best friend and doctor's advice, was a much-needed break. After sending a few emails and making a few phone calls she was driving to her dad's house.

She knew she was probably suffering from depression. Exhaustion and general misery. It would stand to reason. Her schedule could be horrific and the tension had been terrible lately. It was about a year ago that two doctors in her practice had been accused of fraud and malpractice and suspended from seeing patients pending an investigation that would very likely lead to a trial. Even though she had no knowledge of the incidents, there was a scandal and it stank on her. There'd been wild media attention and she was left alone trying to hold a wilting practice together. Then the parents of a boy who died from injuries sustained in a terrible car accident while on her watch filed a wrongful death suit. Against her.

It seemed impossible fate could find one more thing to stack on her already teetering pile of troubles. *Hah. Never challenge fate.* She found out she was pregnant.

It was an accident, of course. She'd been seeing Andrew for a couple of years. She lived in Denver and he in Aurora, since they both had demanding careers, and they saw each other when they could—a night here, a night there. When they could manage a long weekend, it was heaven. She wanted more but Andrew was an ER doctor and also the divorced father of an eight-year-old daughter. But they had constant phone contact. Multiple texts and emails every day. She counted on him; he was her main support.

Maggie wasn't sure she'd ever marry and have a family but she was happy with her surprise. It was the one good thing in a bad year. Andrew, however, was not happy. He was still in divorce recovery, though it had been three years. He and his ex still fought about support and custody and visits. Maggie didn't understand why. Andrew didn't seem to know what to do with his daughter when he had her. He immediately suggested terminating the pregnancy. He said they could revisit the issue in a couple of years if it turned out to be that important to her and if their relationship was thriving.

She couldn't imagine terminating. Just because Andrew was hesitant? She was thirty-six! How much time did she have to *revisit the issue*?

Although she hadn't told Andrew, she decided she was going to keep the baby no matter what that meant for their relationship. Then she had a miscarriage.

Grief-stricken and brokenhearted, she sank lower. Exactly two people knew about the pregnancy and miscarriage—Andrew and Jaycee. Maggie cried gut-wrenching tears every night. Sometimes she couldn't even wait to get home from work and started crying the second she pulled the car door closed. And there were those stairwell visits. She cried on the phone to Andrew; cried in his arms as he tried to comfort her, all the while knowing he was *relieved*.

And then he'd said, "You know what, Maggie? I just can't do it anymore. We need a time-out. I can't prop you up, can't bolster you. You have to get some help, get your emotional life back on track or something. You're sucking the life out of me and I'm not equipped to help you."

"Are you kidding me?" she had demanded. "You're dropping me when I'm down? When I'm only three weeks beyond a miscarriage?"

And in typical Andrew fashion he had said, "That's all I got, baby."

It was really and truly the first moment she had realized it was all about him. And that was pretty much the last straw.

She packed a bunch of suitcases. Once she got packing, she couldn't seem to stop. She drove southwest from Denver to her father's house, south of Leadville and Fairplay, and she hadn't called ahead. She did call her mother, Phoebe, just to say she was going to Sully's and she wasn't sure how long she'd stay. At the moment she had no plan except to escape from that life of persistent strain, anxiety and heartache.

It was early afternoon when she drove up to the country store that had been her great-grandfather's, then her grandfather's, now her father's. Her father, Harry Sullivan, known by one and all as Sully, was a fit and hardy seventy and showed no sign of slowing down and no interest in retiring. She just sat in her car for a while, trying to figure out what she was going to say to him. How could she phrase it so it didn't sound like she'd just lost a baby and had her heart broken?

Beau, her father's four-year-old yellow Lab, came trotting around the store, saw her car, started running in circles barking, then put his front paws up on her door, looking at her imploringly. Frank Masterson, a local who'd been a fixture at the store for as long as Maggie could remember, was sitting on the porch, nursing a cup of coffee with a newspaper on his lap. One glance told her the campground was barely occupied—only a couple of pop-up trailers and tents on campsites down the road toward the lake. She saw a man sitting outside his tent in a canvas camp chair, reading. She had expected the sparse population—it was the middle of the week, middle of the day and the beginning of March, the least busy month of the year.

Frank glanced at her twice but didn't even wave. Beau trotted off, disappointed, when Maggie didn't get out of the car. She still hadn't come up with a good entry line. Five minutes passed before her father walked out of the store, across the porch and down the steps, Beau following. She lowered the window.

"Hi, Maggie," he said, leaning on the car's roof. "Wasn't expecting you."

"It was spur-of-the-moment."

He glanced into her backseat at all the luggage. "How long you planning to stay?"

She shrugged. "Didn't you say I was always welcome? Anytime?"

He smiled at her. "Sometimes I run off at the mouth."

"I need a break from work. From all that crap. From everything."

"Understandable. What can I get you?"

"Is it too much trouble to get two beers and a bed?" she asked, maybe a little sarcastically.

"Coors okay by you?"

"Sure."

"Go on and park by the house. There's beer in the fridge and I haven't sold your bed yet."

"That's gracious of you," she said.

"You want some help to unload your entire wardrobe?" he asked.

"Nope. I don't need much for now. I'll take care of it."

"Then I'll get back to work and we'll meet up later."

"Sounds like a plan," she said.

★ ★ ★

Maggie dragged only one bag into the house, the one with her toothbrush, pajamas and clean jeans. When she was a little girl and both her parents and her grandfather lived on this property, she had been happy most of the time. The general store, the locals and campers, the mountains, lake and valley, wildlife and sunshine kept her constantly cheerful. But the part of her that had a miserable mother, a father who tended to drink a little too much and bickering parents had been forlorn. Then, when she was six, her mother had had enough of hardship, rural living and driving Maggie a long distance to a school that Phoebe found inadequate. Throw in an unsatisfactory husband and that was all she could take. Phoebe took Maggie away to Chicago. Maggie didn't see Sully for several years and her mother married Walter Lancaster, a prominent neurosurgeon with lots of money.

Maggie had hated it all. Chicago, Walter, the big house, the private school, the blistering cold and concrete landscape. She hated the sound of traffic and emergency vehicles. One thing she could recall in retrospect, it brought her mother to life. Phoebe was almost entirely happy, the only smudge on her brightness being her ornery daughter. They had switched roles.

By the time Maggie was eleven she was visiting her dad regularly—first a few weekends, then whole months and some holidays. She lived for it and Phoebe constantly held it over her. *Behave yourself and get good grades and you'll get to spend the summer at that god-awful camp, eating worms, getting filthy and risking your life among bears.*

"Why didn't you fight for me?" she had continually asked her father.

"Aw, honey, Phoebe was right, I wasn't worth a damn as a father and I just wanted what was best for you. It wasn't always easy, neither," he'd explained.

Sometime in junior high Maggie had made her peace with Walter, but she chose to go to college in Denver, near Sully. Phoebe's desire was that she go to a fancy Ivy League college. Med school and residency were a different story—it was tough getting accepted at all and you went to the best career school and residency program that would have you. She ended up in Los Angeles. Then she did a fellowship with Walter, even though she hated going back to Chicago. But Walter was simply one of the best. After that she joined a practice in Denver, close to her dad and the environment she loved. A year later, with Walter finally retired from his practice and enjoying more golf, Phoebe and Walter moved to Golden, Colorado, closer to Maggie. Walter was also seventy, like Sully. Phoebe was a vibrant, social fifty-nine.

Maggie thought she was possibly closer to Walter than to Phoebe, especially as they were both neurosurgeons. She was grateful. After all, he'd sent her to good private schools even when she did every terrible thing she could to show him how unappreciated his efforts were. She had been a completely ungrateful brat about it. But Walter turned out to be a kind, classy guy. He had helped a great many people who proved to be eternally grateful and Maggie had been impressed by his achievements. Plus, he mentored her in medicine. Loving medicine surprised her as much as anyone. Sully had said, "I think it's a great idea. If I was as smart as you and some old coot like Walter was willing to pick up the tab, I'd do it in a New York minute."

Maggie found she loved science but med school was the

hardest thing she'd ever taken on, and most days she wasn't sure she could make it through another week. She could've just quit, done a course correction or flunked out, but no— she got perfect grades along with anxiety attacks. But the second they put a scalpel in her hand, she'd found her calling.

She sat on Sully's couch, drank two beers, then lay down and pulled the throw over her. Beau pushed in through his doggy door and lay down beside the couch. The window was open, letting in the crisp, clean March air, and she dropped off to sleep immediately to the rhythmic sound of Sully raking out a trench behind the house. She started fantasizing about summer at the lake but before she woke she was dreaming of trying to operate in a crowded emergency room where everyone was yelling, bloody rags littered the floor, people hated each other, threw instruments at one another and patients were dying one after another. She woke up panting, her heart hammering. The sun had set and a kitchen light had been turned on, which meant Sully had been to the house to check on her.

There was a sandwich covered in plastic wrap on a plate. A note sat beside it. It was written by Enid, Frank's wife. Enid worked mornings in the store, baking and preparing packaged meals from salads to sandwiches for campers and tourists. *Welcome Home*, the note said.

Maggie ate the sandwich, drank a third beer and went to bed in the room that was hers at her father's house.

She woke to the sound of Sully moving around and saw that it was not quite 5:00 a.m. so she decided to go back to sleep until she didn't have anxiety dreams anymore. She got up at noon, grazed through the refrigerator's bleak contents and went back to sleep. At about two in the afternoon the door to her room opened noisily and Sully said, "All right. Enough is enough."

★ ★ ★

Sully's store had been built in 1906 by Maggie's great-grandfather Nathaniel Greely Sullivan. Nathaniel had a son and a daughter, married off the daughter and gave the son, Horace, the store. Horace had one son, Harry, who really had better things to do than run a country store. He wanted to see the world and have adventures so he joined the Army and went to Vietnam, among other places, but by the age of thirty-three, he finally married and brought his pretty young wife, Phoebe, home to Sullivan's Crossing. They immediately had one child, Maggie, and settled in for the long haul. All of the store owners had been called Sully but Maggie was always called Maggie.

The store had once been the only place to get bread, milk, thread or nails within twenty miles, but things had changed mightily by the time Maggie's father had taken it on. It had become a recreational facility—four one-room cabins, dry campsites, a few RV hookups, a dock on the lake, a boat launch, public bathrooms with showers, coin-operated laundry facilities, picnic tables and grills. Sully had installed a few extra electrical outlets on the porch so people in tents could charge their electronics and now Sully himself had satellite TV and Wi-Fi. Sullivan's Crossing sat in a valley south of Leadville at the base of some stunning mountains and just off the Continental Divide Trail. The camping was cheap and well managed, the grounds were clean, the store large and well stocked. They had a post office; Sully was the postmaster. And now it was the closest place to get supplies, beer and ice for locals and tourists alike.

The people who ventured there ranged from hikers to bikers to cross-country skiers, boating enthusiasts, rock climbers, fishermen, nature lovers and weekend campers. Plenty of hikers went out on the trails for a day, a few days, a week or even longer. Hikers who were taking on the CDT or the Colorado Trail often planned on Sully's as a stopping point to resupply, rest and get cleaned up. Those hearties were called the thru-hikers, as the Continental Divide Trail was 3,100 miles long while the Colorado Trail was almost 500, but the two trails converged for about 200 miles just west of Sully's. Thus Sully's was often referred to as *the crossing*.

People who knew the place referred to it as Sully's. Some of their campers were one-timers, never seen again, many were regulars within an easy drive looking for a weekend or holiday escape. They were all interesting to Maggie—men, women, young, old, athletes, wannabe athletes, scout troops, nature clubs, weirdos, the occasional creep—but the ones who intrigued her the most were the long-distance hikers, the thru-hikers. She couldn't imagine the kind of commitment needed to take on the CDT, not to mention the courage and strength. She loved to hear their stories about everything from wildlife on the trail to how many toenails they'd lost on their journey.

There were tables and chairs on the store's wide front porch and people tended to hang out there whether the store was open or closed. When the weather was warm and fair there were spontaneous gatherings and campfires at the edge of the lake. Long-distance hikers often mailed themselves packages that held dry socks, extra food supplies, a little cash, maybe even a book, first-aid items, a new lighter for their campfires, a fresh shirt or two. Maggie loved to watch them retrieve and open boxes they'd packed themselves—it was like Christmas.

Sully had a great big map of the CDT, Colorado Trail and other trails on the bulletin board in the front of the store; it was surrounded by pictures either left or sent back to him.

He'd put out a journal book where hikers could leave news or messages. The journals, when filled, were kept by Sully, and had become very well-known. People could spend hours reading through them.

Sully's was an escape, a refuge, a gathering place or recreational outpost. Maggie and Andrew liked to come for the occasional weekend to ski—the cross-country trails were safe and well marked. Occupancy was lower during the winter months so they'd take a cabin, and Sully would never comment on the fact that they were sharing not just a room but a bed.

Before the pregnancy and miscarriage, their routine had been rejuvenating—they'd knock themselves out for a week or even a few weeks in their separate cities, then get together for a weekend or few days, eat wonderful food, screw their brains out, get a little exercise in the outdoors, have long and deep conversations, meet up with friends, then go back to their separate worlds. Andrew was shy of marriage, having failed at one and being left a single father. Maggie, too, had had a brief, unsuccessful marriage, but she wasn't afraid of trying again and had always thought Andrew would eventually get over it. She accepted the fact that she might not have children, coupled with a man who, right up front, declared he didn't want more.

"But then there was one on the way and does he step up?" she muttered to herself as she walked into the store through the back door. "He complains that I'm too sad for him to deal with. *The bastard.*"

"Who's the bastard, darling?" Enid asked from the kitchen.

She stuck her head out just as Maggie was climbing onto a stool at the counter, and smiled. "It's so good to see you. It's been a while."

"I know, I'm sorry about that. It's been harrowing in Denver. I'm sure Dad told you about all that mess with my practice."

"He did. Those awful doctors, tricking people into thinking they needed surgery on their backs and everything! Is one of them the bastard?"

"Without a doubt," she answered, though they hadn't been on her mind at all.

"And that lawsuit against you," Enid reminded her, *tsking*.

"That'll probably go away," Maggie said hopefully, though there was absolutely no indication it would. At least it was civil. The DA had found no cause to indict her. *But really, how much is one girl supposed to take?* The event leading to the lawsuit was one of the most horrific nights she'd ever been through in the ER—five teenage boys in a catastrophic car wreck, all critical. She'd spent a lot of time in the stairwell after that one. "I'm not worried," she lied. Then she had to concentrate to keep from shuddering.

"Good for you. I have soup. I made some for your dad and Frank. Mushroom. With cheese toast. There's plenty if you're interested."

"Yes, please," she said.

"I'll get it." Enid went around the corner to dish it up.

The store didn't have a big kitchen, just a little turning around room. It was in the southwest corner of the store; there was a bar and four stools right beside the cash register. On the northwest corner there was a small bar where they served adult beverages, and again, a bar and four stools. No one had ever wanted to attempt a restaurant but it was a good idea to provide food and drink—campers and hikers tended to run out of supplies. Sully sold beer, wine, soft drinks and bottled water in the cooler section of the store, but he didn't sell bottled liquor. For that matter, he wasn't a grocery store but a general store. Along with foodstuffs there were T-shirts, socks and a few other recreational supplies—rope, clamps, batteries, hats, sunscreen, first-aid supplies. For the mother lode you had to go to Timberlake, Leadville or maybe Colorado Springs.

In addition to tables and chairs on the porch, there were a few comfortable chairs just inside the front door where the potbellied stove sat. Maggie remembered when she was a little girl, men sat on beer barrels around the stove. There was a giant ice machine on the back porch. The ice was free.

Enid stuck her head out of the little kitchen. She bleached her hair blond but had always, for as long as Maggie could remember, had black roots. She was plump and nurturing while her husband, Frank, was one of those grizzled, skinny old ranchers. "Is that nice Dr. Mathews coming down on the weekend?" Enid asked.

"I broke up with him. Don't ever call him nice again," Maggie said. "He's a turd."

"Oh, honey! You broke up?"

"He said I was depressing," she said with a pout. "He can kiss my ass."

"Well, I should say so! I never liked him very much, did I mention that?"

"No, you didn't. You said you loved him and thought we'd make handsome children together." She winced as she said it.

"Obviously I wasn't thinking," Enid said, withdrawing back into the kitchen. In a moment she brought out a bowl of soup and a thick slice of cheese toast. Her soup was cream of mushroom and it was made with real cream.

Maggie dipped her spoon into the soup, blew on it, tasted. It was heaven. "Why aren't you my mother?" she asked.

"I just didn't have the chance, that's all. But we'll pretend."

Maggie and Enid had that little exchange all the time, exactly like that. Maggie had always wanted one of those soft, nurturing, homespun types for a mother instead of Phoebe, who was thin, chic, active in society, snobby and prissy. Phoebe was cool while Enid was warm and cuddly. Phoebe could read the hell out of a menu while Enid could cure anything with her chicken soup, her grandmother's recipe. Phoebe rarely cooked and when she did it didn't go well. But lest Maggie completely throw her mother under the bus, she reminded herself that Phoebe had a quick wit, and though she was sarcastic and ironic, she could make Maggie laugh. She was devoted to Maggie and craved her loyalty, especially that Maggie liked her more than she liked Sully. She gave Maggie everything she had to give. It wasn't Phoebe's fault they were not the things Maggie wanted. For example, Phoebe sent Maggie to an extremely good college-prep boarding school that had worked out on many levels, except that Maggie would have traded it all to live with her father. Foolishly, perhaps, but still… And while Phoebe would not visit Sully's campground under pain of death, she had thrown Maggie a fifty-thousand-dollar wedding that Maggie hadn't wanted. And Walter had given her and Sergei a trip to Europe for their honeymoon.

Maggie had appreciated the trip to Europe quite a lot. But she should never have married Sergei. She'd been very busy and distracted and he was handsome, sexy—especially that accent! They'd looked so good together. She took him at face value and failed to look deeper into the man. He was superficial and not trustworthy. Fortunately, or would that be unfortunately, it had been blessedly short. Nine months.

"This is so good," Maggie said. "Your soup always puts me right."

"How long are you staying, honey?"

"I'm not sure. Till I get a better idea. Couple of weeks, maybe?"

Enid shook her head. "You shouldn't come in March. You should know better than to come in March."

"He's going to work me like a pack of mules, isn't he?"

"No question about it. Only person who isn't afraid to come around in March is Frank. Sully won't put Frank to work."

Frank Masterson was one of Sully's cronies. He was about the same age while Enid was just fifty-five. Frank said he had had the foresight to marry a younger woman, thereby assuring himself a good caretaker for his old age. Frank owned a nearby cattle ranch that these days was just about taken over by his two sons, which freed up Frank to hang out around Sully's. Sometimes Sully would ask, "Why don't you just come to work with Enid in the morning and save the gas since all you do is drink my coffee for free and butt into everyone's business?"

When the weather was cold he'd sit inside, near the stove. When the weather was decent he favored the porch. He wandered around, chatted it up with campers or folks who stopped by, occasionally lifted a heavy box for Enid, read the paper a lot. He was a fixture.

Enid had a sweet, heart-shaped face to go with her plump body. It attested to her love of baking. Besides making and wrapping sandwiches to keep in the cooler along with a few other lunchable items, she baked every morning—sweet rolls, buns, cookies, brownies, that sort of thing. Frank ate a lot of that and apparently never gained an ounce.

Maggie could hear Sully scraping out the gutters around the store. Seventy and up on a ladder, still working like a farmhand, cleaning the winter detritus away. That was the problem with March—a lot to clean up for the spring and summer. She escaped out to the porch to visit with Frank before Sully saw her sitting around and put her to work.

"What are you doing here?" Frank asked.

"I'm on vacation," she said.

"Hmm. Damn fool time of year to take a vacation. Ain't nothing to do now. Dr. Mathews comin'?"

"No. We're not seeing each other anymore."

"Hmm. That why you're here during mud season? Lickin' your wounds?"

"Not at all. I'm happy about it."

"Yup. You look happy, all right."

I might be better off cleaning gutters, she thought. So she turned the conversation to politics because she knew Frank had some very strong opinions and she could listen rather than answer questions. She spotted that guy again, the camper, sitting in his canvas camp chair outside his pop-up tent/trailer under a pull-out awning. His legs were stretched out and he was reading again. She noticed he had long legs.

She was just about to ask Frank how long that guy had been camping there when she noticed someone heading up the trail toward the camp. He had a big backpack and walking stick and something strange on his head. Maggie squinted. A bombardier's leather helmet with earflaps? "Frank, look at that," she said, leaning forward to stare.

The man was old, but old wasn't exactly rare. There were a lot of senior citizens out on the trails, hiking, biking, skiing. In fact, if they were fit at retirement, they had the time and means. As the man got closer, age was only part of the issue.

"I best find Sully," Frank said, getting up and going into the store.

As the man drew near it was apparent he wore rolled-up dress slacks, black socks and black shoes that looked like they'd be shiny church or office wear once the mud was cleaned off. And on his head a weird WWII aviator's hat. He wore a ski jacket that looked to be drenched and he was flushed and limping.

Sully appeared on the porch, Beau wagging at his side, Frank following. "What the hell?"

"Yeah, that's just wrong," Maggie said.

"Ya think?" Sully asked. He went down the steps to approach the man, Maggie close on his heels, Frank bringing up the rear and Enid on the porch waiting to see what was up.

"Well, there, buddy," Sully said, his hands in his pockets. "Where you headed?"

"Is this Camp Lejeune?"

Everyone exchanged glances. "Uh, that would be in North Carolina, son," Sully said, though the man was clearly older than Sully. "You're a little off track. Come up on the porch and have a cup of coffee, take off that pack and wet jacket. And that silly hat, for God's sake. We need to make a phone call for you. What are you doing out here, soaking wet in your Sunday shoes?"

"Maybe I should wait awhile, see if they come," the man said, though he let himself be escorted to the porch.

"Who?" Maggie asked.

"My parents and older brother," he said. "I'm to meet them here."

"Bet they have 'em some real funny hats, too," Frank muttered.

"Seems like you got a little confused," Sully said. "What's your name, young man?"

"That's a problem, isn't it? I'll have to think on that for a while."

Maggie noticed the camper had wandered over, curious. Up close he was distracting. He was tall and handsome, though there was a small bump on the bridge of his nose. But his hips were narrow, his shoulders wide and his jeans were torn and frayed exactly right. They met glances. She tore her eyes away.

"Do you know how you got all wet? Did you walk through last night's rain? Sleep in the rain?" Sully asked.

"I fell in a creek," he said. He smiled though he also shivered.

"On account a those shoes," Frank pointed out. "He slipped cause he ain't got no tread."

"Well, there you go," Maggie said. "Professor Frank has it all figured out. Let's get that wet jacket off and get a blanket. Sully, you better call Stan the Man."

"Will do."

"Anyone need a hand here?" Maggie heard the camper ask.

"Can you grab the phone, Cal?" Sully asked. Sully put the man in what had been Maggie's chair and started peeling off his jacket and outer clothes. He leaned the backpack against the porch rail and within just seconds Enid was there with a blanket, cup of coffee and one of her bran muffins. Cal brought the cordless phone to the porch. The gentleman immediately began to devour that muffin as Maggie looked him over.

"Least he'll be reg'lar," Frank said, reclaiming his chair.

Maggie crouched in front of the man and while speaking very softly, she asked if she could remove the hat. Before quite getting permission she pulled it gently off his head to reveal wispy white hair surrounding a bald dome. She gently ran her fingers around his scalp in search of a bump or contusion. Then she pulled him to his feet and ran her hands around his torso and waist. "You must've rolled around in the dirt, sir," she said. "I bet you're ready for a shower." He didn't respond. "Sir? Anything hurt?" she asked him. He just shook his head. "Can you smile for me? Big, wide, smile?" she asked, checking for the kind of paralysis caused by a stroke.

"Where'd you escape from, young man?" Sully asked him. "Where's your home?"

"Wakefield, Illinois," he said. "You know it?"

"Can't say I do," Sully said. "But I bet it's beautiful. More beautiful than Lejeune, for sure."

"Can I have cream?" he asked, holding out his cup.

Enid took it. "Of course you can, sweetheart," she said. "I'll bring it right back."

In a moment the gentleman sat with his coffee with cream, shivering under a blanket while Sully called Stan Bronoski. There were a number of people Sully could have reached out to—a local ranger, state police aka highway patrol, even fire and rescue. But Stan was the son of a local rancher and was the police chief in Timberlake, just twenty miles south and near the interchange. It was a small department with a clever deputy who worked the internet like a pro, Officer Paul Castor.

Beau gave the old man a good sniffing, then moved down the stairs to Cal who automatically began petting him.

Sully handed the phone to Maggie. "Stan wants to talk to you."

"He sounds like someone who wandered off," Stan said to Maggie. "But I don't have any missing persons from nearby. I'll get Castor looking into it. I'm on my way. Does he have any ID on him?"

"We haven't really checked yet," Maggie said into the phone. "Why don't I do that while you drive. Here's Sully."

Maggie handed the phone back to her dad and said, "Pass the time with Stan while I chat with this gentleman."

Maggie asked the man to stand again and deftly slid a thin wallet out of his back pocket. She urged him to sit, and opened it up. "Well, now," she said. "Mr. Gunderson? Roy Gunderson?"

"Hmm?" he said, his eyes lighting up a bit.

Sully repeated the name into the phone to Stan.

"And so, Roy, did you hurt anything when you fell?" Maggie asked.

He shook his head and sipped his coffee. "I fell?" he finally asked.

Maggie looked at Sully, lifting a questioning brow. "A Mr. Gunderson from Park City, Utah," Sully said. "Wandered off from his home a few days ago. On foot."

"He must've gotten a ride or something," Cal said.

"His driver's license, which was supposed to be renewed ten years ago, says his address is in Illinois."

"Stan says he'll probably have more information by the time he gets here, but this must be him. Dementia, he says."

"You can say that again," Maggie observed. "I can't imagine what the last few days have been like for him. He must have been terrified."

"He look terrified to you?" Frank asked. "He might as well be on a cruise ship."

"Tell Stan we'll take care of him till he gets here."

Maggie went about the business of caring for Mr. Gunderson, getting water and a little soup into him while the camper, Cal, chatted with Sully and Frank, apparently well-known to them. When this situation was resolved she meant to find out more about him, like how long he'd been here.

She took off Roy's shoes and socks and looked at his feet— no injuries or frostbite but some serious swelling and bruised toenails. She wondered where he had been and how he'd gotten the backpack. He certainly hadn't brought it from home or packed it himself. That would be too complicated for a man in his condition. It was a miracle he could carry it!

Two hours later, the sun lowering in the sky, an ambulance had arrived for Roy Gunderson. He didn't appear to be seriously injured or ill but he was definitely unstable and Stan wasn't inclined to transport him alone. He could bolt, try to get out of a moving car or interfere with the driver, although Stan had a divider cage in his police car.

What Maggie and Sully had learned, no thanks to Roy himself, was that he'd been cared for at home by his wife, wandered off without his GPS bracelet, walked around a while before coming upon a rather old Chevy sedan with the keys in the ignition, so he must have helped himself. The car was reported stolen from near his house, but had no tracking device installed. And since Mr. Gunderson hadn't driven in years, no one put him with the borrowed motor vehicle for a couple of days. The car was found abandoned near Salt Lake City with Roy's jacket in it. From there the old man had probably hitched a ride. His condition was too good to have walked for days. Roy was likely left near a rest stop or campgrounds where he helped himself to a backpack. Where he'd been, what he'd done, how he'd survived was unknown.

The EMTs were just about to load Mr. Gunderson into the back of the ambulance when Sully sat down on the porch steps with a loud huff.

"Dad?" Maggie asked.

Sully was grabbing the front of his chest. Over his heart. He was pale as snow, sweaty, his eyes glassy, his breathing shallow and ragged.

"Dad!" Maggie shouted.

Don't miss
What We Find
from New York Times *bestselling*
author Robyn Carr,
available wherever
MIRA books are sold!